ROSIE'S UMBRELLA

Praise for Rosie's Umbrella

"A novel with a keen understanding of the complexity of family secrets and the tensions between loving family members."

Kirkus Review
Similar books suggested by Kirkus critics: *Atonement* by Ian McEwan, *Angels And Insects* by A.S. Byatt, and *Last Orders* by Graham Swift

"*Rosie's Umbrella* is a moving meditation as well as a novel, one that crosses continents and time in order to explore the ways in which the ghost of things past, dramatic and disturbing, can go on affecting lives into the future. It is also a mystery – and a real page-turner. Finally and in these difficult times we are living through, with political storm-clouds getting ever closer, it is a tender and affirmative story that reminds the reader of what great consequences our small actions of remembering and affection can have, and how much we can accomplish if we just stick together – across countries, and across the generations. I read it in a single sweep, and recommend you do the same."

Geoff Ward
Principal of Homerton College and Deputy Vice Chancellor at the University of Cambridge, and Chairman of the Fitzwilliam Museum

"*Rosie's Umbrella* is a gripping, page-turning, wild ride, fueled by great passion, deep humanity, and an urgent call for justice."

James Paul Gee
Mary Lou Presidential Professor
Arizona State University

"Wonderful insights into Welsh history and culture. It is easy to forget the struggles of miners."

Yetta M. Goodman
Regents Professor Emerita, University of Arizona

"What an amazing adventure. I've known only Denny Taylor's professional writing, so was thrilled to find that she could keep me spell-bound with this gripping story. To put it mildly, it is a page-turner. If you are searching for a story that will capture all the members of your book club this is it! The discussion following our reading of *Rosie's Umbrella* was lively, informative and sometimes touchingly personal."

Dorothy Watson
Professor Emerita of Education
University of Missouri

"I couldn't put it down in spite of being so busy, a great story and characters AND what a wonderful reflection on memory and history."

Ruth Finnegan, FBA, OBE
Professor, Faculty of Social Sciences
The Open University, UK

"In *Rosie's Umbrella*, Denny Taylor beautifully captures what happens when young adults have opportunities to grapple with injustices that relate to identity, culture, and history. With a bit of support and guidance from adults, like Aunt Sarah and teacher Margaret, all adolescents like Rosie have the potential to find their voices and take action as social agents of change. This novel will inspire young and old to pursue their own social justice investigation."

Monica Taylor
Associate Professor
Montclair University

"Once in a while a novel comes around and not only touches me as a reader but an educator as well. This novel does both. As an educator, I am inspired to be more like Margaret, Rosie's teacher, committed to helping children develop their voice in telling stories. Taylor weaves together a 21st century family complete with secrets of about their history in 19th century Wales. The vivid accounts of both past and present will resonate with all audiences. This is a highly readable, enjoyable book, deserving of wide circulation."

Pat Geyer
Teacher-Educator
Hofstra University

"I LOVED this book!!! It is a powerful and enjoyable read that will leave you wanting more. This novel, although stylistically different from Taylor's other books, is a beautiful integration of story and activism. However, if you're like me, you might need a Kleenex or two at a most unexpected moment! Enjoy!!!"

Kathy Olmstead
Assistant Professor, Brockport College, SUNY

Published by Garn Press, LLC
New York, NY
www.garnpress.com

Garn Press and the Chapwoman logo are registered trademarks of Garn Press, LLC

Book and cover design by Ben James Taylor
Cover image of umbrella from "London Set" by anna42f, used under license from Envato Market.
Umbrella illustration at the beginning of each chapter by Malia Hughes

First Edition, January 2015
Second Edition, January 2017

Library of Congress Control Number: 2017943428

Publisher's Cataloging-in-Publication Data

Names: Taylor, Denny.
Title: Rosie's umbrella / Denny Taylor.
Description: Second edition. | New York : Garn Press, 2017.
Identifiers: LCCN 2017943428 | ISBN 978-1-942146-63-6 (pbk.) | ISBN 978-1-942146-64-3 (hardcover) | ISBN 978-1-942146-65-0 (Kindle ebook)
Subjects: LCSH: Family secrets--Fiction. | Educational change. | Coming of age--Fiction. | Coal mines and mining--Fiction. | Boston (Mass.)--Fiction. | Wales, South--Fiction.| BISAC: YOUNG ADULT FICTION / Mysteries & Detective Stories. | FICTION / Thrillers/Suspense. | YOUNG ADULT FICTION / School & Education / General. | YOUNG ADULT FICTION / Coming of Age. | FICTION/ Cultural Heritage
Classification: LCC PS3620.A941 R67 2014 (print) | LCC PS3620.A941 (ebook) | DDC 813.6--dc23.

LC record available at https://lccn.loc.gov/2017943428

ROSIE'S UMBRELLA

DENNY TAYLOR

GARN PRESS
NEW YORK, NY

In Loving Memory
of
Hetty Coles
Who Took Me to Wales When I was a Little Girl
And Shared Her Stories with Me
And for My Cousins
Barbara Garrad and Sandra Jones
And All Our Children
Grandchildren and Great Grandchildren

All I'm saying is simply this: that all mankind is tied together; all life is interrelated, and we are all caught in an inescapable network of mutuality, tied in a single garment of destiny. Whatever affects one directly, affects all indirectly.

For some strange reason I can never be what I ought to be until you are what you ought to be. And you can never be what you ought to be until I am what I ought to be - this is the interrelated structure of reality.

Martin Luther King
Remaining Awake During the Revolution
Oberlin College, June 1965

Contents

Garn-yr-erw
Wales

July1955

She died within seconds of falling. Just the touch of her fingers was enough to break the board. The ancient wood splintered turning to dust, and the light pressure of her hand became the full weight of her body. The board next to the one that had crumbled did not give way so easily. The impact of her head broke it in two and one jagged edge ripped through her skin and entered her body just below her rib cage. But that is not what killed her. She died when a sliver of bone from one of her ribs, broken by the splintered wood, pierced her heart, and she was dead within seconds.

There were terrified screams up above, but she did not hear them, and there was no time for her to cry out. She fell without spoiling the drop with flailing arms or nightmare noises that would wake those who heard her for as long as they lived. She had just one moment between life and death, a split second before the shard of bone stabbed her heart, when she could see with perfect clarity the colors of the ancient bricks in the light let in when the boards broke. She could see the shadows that went with the echoes of screams from up above, but the patterns of light and the fading sounds were nothing more than that. There was no time to think about them, to name them or to say, "There's lovely", but that is how she felt in those last moments of her life as she fell down the old mine shaft.

Boston
United States

June, 1995

"Rosie!" Tom cried, as he pushed open the door from the stairwell. "Leave it!"

It was the middle of the night and the hospital hallway was dimly lit, but Tom could see her. The doors of the service elevator were wide open and she was on her knees, with her left hand on the crumbling linoleum at the edge of the shaft. In her right hand she was holding an old umbrella.

"I can get it," she said, inching her knees nearer the edge of the gaping black hole that dropped ten floors below. She stretched forward, gripping the black fabric of the umbrella, which seemed to shudder as the crook of the handle disappeared into the darkness.

"Please, Rosie," Tom pleaded, his voice no more than a hoarse whisper.

"Almost."

"Let me get it," he said, as he moved slowly towards her. "You'll fall!"

"I've almost got it," she said, repositioning herself, closer to the edge. The umbrella disappeared as her right arm dropped and then reappeared as she steadied herself and stretched her arm out further.

"Rosie, let me try," Tom said, as if reading the lines of a script. "Please, Rosie," he whispered as he moved closer. "Please."

"I can get it."

"No!" Tom gasped, as he grabbed hold of her and pulled her back. Startled, she let go of the umbrella, which seemed to hover for a moment before falling. The handle splintered as it hit the side of the elevator shaft. The twisted spokes and torn black fabric opened as it fell, and it made only a small dead sound when it hit the top of the elevator at the bottom of the shaft. His arms were tight around her, and Rosie looked at him as if she had never seen him before.

He had become a stranger.

Rosie Llywelyn put her hands under the straps of her backpack and moved the bag away from her shoulders. It didn't help. The backpack was stuck to her T-shirt and she could feel the sweat running down her back. Even though it was early summer, Boston was suffocating, smothered in damp Mississippi heat.

Just a week ago Rosie had worn a sweater and a coat and the wind had still whipped around her. She had walked home quickly then, but now it wasn't the weather that made her drag her feet. Jesse had just said she had found her own truth, but she knew if she was to have a life she still had to find it. She felt vulnerable and afraid. Madness was crowding out the truth, too many thoughts, one on top of another.

She knew she had to go back, begin at the beginning, because she had reached the end. That was the point wasn't it? Go back. Relive it. Begin life again. What other choice was there? That was it wasn't it? Live death or die over and over again.

"Don't count!" she told herself. "You'll reach the beginning when you don't have to count! One – two – oh please don't count!"

In the Public Gardens the city slowed. The sound of the traffic seemed far away, muffled by the hot weather. Rosie found it difficult to breath. Nothing seemed real, not even the park ranger who stood on the stone bridge that crossed over the pond watching the people as they passed him. Someone shouted. It was a distant far off sound. The park ranger glanced over the side of the bridge and Rosie followed his gaze. Two young women were standing in the shade beneath the bridge on the footpath that ran around the pond. One was talking loudly, her whole body in motion, and the other was laughing and shaking her head. Rosie thought they looked like sisters, but they were probably just friends. The park ranger moved on but Rosie stood still, drawn to the two girls standing on the path by the water beneath the bridge. She thought about the elevator shaft, her Dad shouting, and she felt herself falling. Heart pounding she put her left hand out and steadied herself against the wall. Trembling, she closed her eyes.

"Rosie!" she heard her Dad cry. "Leave it!"

Under the bridge a swan boat floated by and the two young women disappeared still laughing. Every day in summer for more than a hundred years, whether it rained or shined, and even in this intense heat, the bicyclists at the back of the swan boats turned the paddles with their feet. When Rosie opened her eyes both the girls and the boat were gone. She had no idea how long she had been standing on the bridge. For a moment she wondered if she had tried to jump. It was a fleeting thought and she dismissed the idea. She would have had to climb up on the wall to jump and then the drop was only about fifteen feet, a sprained ankle perhaps and grazed knees, but not much more than that. Rosie shivered. She suddenly felt cold on this very hot day. She could smell the dank air of the old shaft. Feel it. Taste it. *See it.*

"You all right?" a man asked her, in an English voice like her Grandfather's. The man, who was wearing blue check shorts, was with a woman with red lipstick and big gold hoop earrings. They had stopped beside her and were leaning over the wall throwing peanuts into the water for the real swans that had been circling the swan boat. Rosie watched for a moment. She was having difficulty separating the past from the present.

"Heat got you?" the woman with hoop earrings looked concerned. "Want some water?" she said, offering Rosie her water bottle.

Rosie managed to smile. She shook her head, and without speaking she walked on. Someone screamed. She could hear her Dad yelling, "Rosie!" She felt a jolt as her heart started racing and skipping beats. Unable to stop herself she started counting. "One-two-" And again she heard her father's anguished shout, "Rosie!"

"Smile!" a red-faced man in a Red-Sox baseball cap shouted from somewhere behind her as he stepped backwards, moving further and further away from a tiny woman who was standing with a small boy in front of the statue of George Washington. His "smile" had brought Rosie back into the moment and her heart slowed. She looked over her shoulder at the man, and then she moved to the edge of the path so she wouldn't be in the photograph. The woman, who was not much bigger than the boy, draped her arm around the boy's shoulders as they posed for the camera. Rosie glanced behind her again. The man was still moving backwards to get a better shot of George on his horse. She looked at the boy. His eyes were crossed and his tongue was out but she was sure the man wouldn't notice.

"Take the picture!" the woman shouted, looking hot and bothered. "Or we're leaving!"

"Yes," Rosie muttered under her breath, "take the picture," feeling relieved that she could no longer hear her Dad shouting at her.

The woman glanced at Rosie and her look of total exasperation changed to a sticky sweet smile, but when the boy, who must have been nine or ten, looked at Rosie he screwed up his face and poked his tongue out even further.

Rosie was sure they had heard what she'd said. She smiled at the woman joining in the conspiracy and then stuck her tongue out at the boy. The woman started to laugh and so did the boy, and Rosie smiled, wanting to laugh, but there was no laughter left in her.

"Got it!" the man yelled, from somewhere off in the distance.

Rosie waved at the woman and the boy and walked on. Ahead of her she could see great jets of cold water shooting onto the grass and masses of ducks swimming in a giant puddle that had spilled over on to the path. People had gathered to watch them. A tourist in a yellow T-shirt and brown shorts, carrying bargains from Filene's Basement, stopped to rest. Some college students, who had been lazing the afternoon away before the sprinklers came on scrambled to their feet, grabbing their notebooks. Making sounds close to shrieks, they laughed at each other as they pulled at their wet shirts, which were stuck to their bodies, and wiped off the covers of the textbooks that they had dropped on the grass, not wanting to read in the stifling heat. One of the young men grabbed a young woman who was soaking wet and kissed her. Unclothed by the water, her T-shirt transparent, she laughed, pushing him away, and then, as if realizing he was covering up her nakedness, she grabbed his wet shirt and pulled him back, kissing him the way he had kissed her.

Rosie was used to seeing people kissing in the park. All sorts of things went on there, but this was a scene. Only a short time ago she would have stood there and watched, looking at the young woman's body, thinking about her own, wondering if she had been grabbed like that would she have grabbed the guy back? She would have imagined what it would be like to be kissed like that, slurped up, wet with longing, but not today.

The puddle was getting bigger. Rosie thought it must be more than twenty feet across.

Two men in starched white shirts, carrying suit jackets, stopped and stared at the wet girl. One of them said something that she could not hear and the other laughed. They both had amused looks on their faces, but walked on, glancing for a moment at the ducks swimming around in the water, as if they had not seen the girl.

The one loosened his tie.

"I'll tell you my real challenge," the other man said, as if he was still in his office, his voice fading as Rosie walked by them quickly, not wanting them to look at her.

The man, the more serious one, who was still talking as if he was in his office, reminded Rosie of her father. She did not want to think about her Dad. She tried to remember if she had ever seen him kiss her mother, but she had not. For a moment she could think of nothing else. She could see her Dad coming home from the office, worn out, bent over, saying hello to her mother, touching her on the shoulder, asking about her day, telling her something about his, but no kiss.

She turned the thought around. Tried to remember her mother

kissing her father. If he had tried to kiss her mother when he came home she was sure her mother would have silently walked away. It was not that her mother didn't care for him. Rosie was sure that she did. She took his jacket and listened to what he had to say. They talked a lot about their work, about politics, dinner, Rosie, but not about themselves. No, Rosie was convinced that even when they were alone in their bedroom, late at night, even if they had sex, if they ever did, they did not kiss.

Sarah kissed them all, on the forehead, on their cheeks, arms around them. She could see her mother when Sarah kissed her, lightly patting Sarah's back, and her father smiling at Sarah, but never losing the sadness in his eyes. Rosie reached the conclusion that there were no mouth kisses in her house. No tongues that touched. No licks. She was grateful for the warmth she felt thinking about the way Sarah's love was full of hugs, but her thoughts quickly turned and stabbed her heart as she longed for Sarah.

A little boy was running into the puddle. "Matt! Where are you going?" his father yelled at him, and then after a moment's hesitation he took off his sneakers and waded into the water after the boy. "You've gotta wait for me pal!" he said, grinning.

Rosie slid her backpack off, and looping one strap over her right shoulder, continued walking. She felt lonely. Her eyes filled with tears and for one frantic moment she thought she was going to start crying. A mother duck with a line of baby ducks behind her had left the pond with the swan boats and was crossing the path right in front of her. Before she could stop herself she started counting them. She thought this was a different kind of counting, not the dark, hopeless, desperate "one – two – three – ", but counting that was part of a different memory and childhood joy smashed into her grief. Her heart was beating faster. Walking slowly, it was as if she was speeding up. There were eight ducks. The mother duck waddled into the puddle of fresh water and the ducklings swam in after her. Rosie pretended that the tears running down her face were beads of perspiration, and she used her hand to brush them away as she began to count the ducks again.

"Eight," she said to herself as the last duckling swam by. Grabbing at other thoughts, she tried to remember who wrote *Make Way For Ducklings*. Aunt Sarah used to read it to her. "Don't think of Sarah," she told herself. "Think of the book. You know who wrote it". When she got to the bronze statues of the ducks she remembered, "Robert McCloskey! Don't count them!"

"One – two" her thoughts were racing as she tried not to cry. She forced herself to smile, and then made a sound that began as a giggle but ended as a sob.

"You've got to stop counting," she told herself. "Stop counting the ducks!" She counted eight, "Eight – eight – eight – stop it! There are eight! Eight – nine – NINE! Stop it!" Her voice was screaming inside her.

"Don't count! Don't say it!" Her backpack slid off her shoulder and she dropped it on the ground, fished in her pocket for a hair band, and tried to gather-up her damp frizzy curls in a ponytail. Her heart was pounding. She tried to watch the tiny children who were sitting on the backs of the bronze ducks with their mothers and fathers bending down to take photographs of them, but this time there was no stopping the hot tears that filled her eyes and splashed down her face.

"Ten – ten!" Rosie sobbed out loud. "TEN!" The jagged sound of the word was filled with sorrow that softened to an asphyxiating "ten".

The cries of a small child drowned out the sound of Rosie's sobs. The little girl had fallen off the bronze mother duck and everyone was watching as her mother bent and picked her up.

Rosie stood still, staring at the mother and the way she held the little girl.

There was a photograph of a very young Rosie with her arms around the neck of one of the ducklings on her father's desk in his law office on School Street. Rosie couldn't remember if it was still there. She didn't go to her father's office very often. She tried to remember when the picture had been taken. She was a little kid and her mother had been the one bending, holding on to her while she wrapped her arms around the duckling's neck. She could not have been more than three, maybe younger, two?

"Rosie. Rosie," her Dad had called to get her attention. Now she did not want to hear her Dad call her by her name ever again.

Rosie pressed her lips together. She noticed a woman with a small boy watching her, and she pretended she was having trouble getting her hair up, and the woman, knowing about bad hair days, decided Rosie was just exasperated, and she picked up the small boy who was with her and put him on the mother duck's back.

"Hold on tight," she said, and then to the man who was watching them through the lens of his camera, "There, get another one," and then to the little boy, in a sing-song voice, "Look at Daddy and smile."

A golden retriever ran by and licked the back of Rosie's hand. Slimed, she wiped it off on her skirt, picked up her backpack and walked on along the path. On another day, in a previous life, she would have laughed and stroked the dog on the head, but not today. She made her way between the stone pillars of the park gate, and even though the stifling heat made it difficult to breath, she ran across Beacon Street as the signal changed to red. On Charles, she crossed over to the Starbucks side of the road. Rosie could smell the coffee as she made her way between a spaniel and two black labs tied to a lamppost outside DeLuca's grocery store. She thought to herself that the dogs were only a lick away from the crates of fruits and vegetables on display outside the store. Random thoughts, dogs, ducks, trivial, silly, all she wanted was to fill her head with nothing that made her remember. She wished there was such a thing as a memory eraser, but there was not.

Weaving her way through a group of French tourists who had stopped to admire the architecture, Rosie crossed the bottom of Chestnut Street and continued along Charles. She smiled at the homeless man who was sitting on the step outside the laundromat. Sometimes her mother gave him money. He recognized Rosie and nodded at her, then held out his hand to some tourists. The tourists looked the other way and sped up. Rosie dug in her pocket for the change from her lunch money and she gave it to the man. She turned left and crossed Louisburg Square where Louisa May Alcott once lived.

She'd read *Little Women* with Sarah last winter. Lying back on pillows on Sarah's bed, they had each read a page, back and forth, one page then another. Oh why did she have to think of Sarah? Away from the park and the people she gave way to her tears.

"*Poor Jo! These were dark days to her, for something like despair came over her,*" Sarah had read.

Rosie had read, not knowing how much like Jo's her own grief would become. "*'Oh, Beth! come back! come back!' she did not stretch out her yearning arms in vain; for, as quick to hear her sobbing as she had been to hear her sister's faint whisper, her mother came to comfort her.*"

Rosie and Sarah had marveled at Louisa and gossiped about her family, who would have been destitute if Louisa hadn't written about Meg, Jo, Beth and Amy. Sarah told Rosie that Louisa had bought the house on Louisburg Square with the money she earned from *Little Women*. Rosie told herself not to think about Sarah! No! "One- think of something, anything, *two*, dogs, ducks, *three*, please stop!"

In the shade of a maple, behind the locked gate hidden in the railings of the very private garden at the center of Louisburg Square, a woman was sitting on a rug holding the hands of a baby who tee-tered on chubby legs, bouncing up and down. Rosie thought again about her own mother. It was hard to be mad at her. She wanted to think about the fun times they'd had together, but instead all she could think about was what her mother had done to Sarah. "Don't," Rosie said, not worrying if anyone could hear her. Every time she thought about the hospital, her heart started pounding. She wanted to understand what had happened. Over and over she thought back to the day she had come home and found Sarah so distraught it had frightened her.

"She can't stay with us!" Mary Llywelyn, Rosie's Mom, had said, as she reached out to hold Rosie's hand. "You have to see that. Please understand. We can't take care of her."

"No!" Rosie had shouted, pulling her hand away. "I don't understand. How can you send her away! *I'll* take care of her."

"And who'll take care of her while you're at school?"

"She'll be alright!"

"No she won't. One of us would have to stay home to take care of her."

"*You* stay home, then!"

"You know I can't do that."

"*Won't! You mean!*" Rosie had yelled, shocking herself as well as her mother.

A maid, neat and tidy in a blue uniform with a white apron, opened a basement door and carried out two green plastic sacks of garbage, which she dropped on the edge of the sidewalk before she retreated rapidly down the steps to the basement and disappeared behind the door.

"Why won't you?" Rosie whispered to herself, as she walked on up the hill. "Why won't you stay home and take care of her?" The primly starched maid reminded Rosie of Sarah and her perfectly proper appearance–the way she used to be. Grey straight skirt, cream cotton blouse and pale blue cardigan, hair pulled back, neatly, primly, no wisps around her face, no make-up, plain and simple, no fuss.

"Why didn't she remember what had happened to her?" Rosie asked herself, as she stood by the railing watching the baby chuckling and drooling. She thought about the way in which Sarah had become so disheveled, so dirty, so strange. She had been so strong, so resolute. She had an I-can-cope-with-anything attitude towards life. She had to have that because she was a nurse, and she worked the night shift in the emergency room at Massachusetts General Hospital, just around the corner from Charles. Since Rosie was a baby, Sarah had taken care of her while her mother taught at Boston University. They had always had a good time together. Even though Sarah looked prim and proper she was great fun, and she and Rosie were more than good friends. They were best friends. Rosie knew that Sarah loved her more than anyone else in the world. They high-fived victories, danced tangos when good things happened, and chased each other around the supermarket, shouting, "I love you!" when they were really silly.

"I love you more than all the tea in China," Sarah used to say, sounding very English, in a very proper sort of way.

"How much is that?" Rosie used to ask, with her head on one

side.

"I don't know!" Sarah would say, pulling a face. "A lot! Heaps and heaps! More than all the grains of sand in the Sahara Desert!"

"How much is that?"

"I don't know!" Sarah would laugh. "Sometimes I think I love you much too much!"

Then, laughing with her, Rosie would ask again, "How much is *too* much?"

"Rosie!"

She loved laughing with Sarah. They laughed at little things, silly things, sometimes at things that no one else thought were funny. Rosie's Dad would just stare at them with a look of total bewilderment, wishing they would stop.

"Come on Tom Llywelyn! Giggle a little!" Sarah would tease her older brother. "Live a little!" as if she did not know that he could not.

Then the thought of Rosie's Dad giggling would make them both laugh even more. Just laugh. Rosie used to think he was just preoccupied with his work, but now she knew why he never laughed, she realized she had not seen the sadness etched into the lines on his face or the sorrow in his eyes. Neither it seemed had Sarah. They would laugh together, laugh at his not laughing 'till Sarah had her legs crossed, and Rosie had to run to the bathroom before she wet herself, and Tom, not knowing what else to do, would make a wan smile, and shake his head, and go back to reading in the newspaper, leaving Rosie and Sarah giggling hysterically at the joke, at Tom, but mostly at themselves, because they both just loved having fun together.

The mother of the baby in the garden waved and Rosie gave

a little wave back. She continued walking up the hill, still thinking about Sarah. She thought over and over about the day when Sarah had stopped laughing, trying to make sense of what had happened to her, trying to understand why her parents had sent Sarah away.

It was late March when Sarah had come home from the hospital at 9:00 a.m. after the night shift, and she'd gone straight upstairs to her room. When Rosie got home from school Sarah was not there to greet her and so she thought she must still be sleeping. She had made a cup of tea for Sarah and she had taken it upstairs to her room. She'd found Sarah lying on top of the bed still in her scrubs. Immediately Rosie knew something was wrong. Sarah always showered as soon as she got home from the hospital. Sometimes, if they were shorthanded in the emergency room, or if a doctor was in the middle of some procedure, or she was comforting a patient, Sarah would stay, but not more than an hour or two. When she got home she always showered, made some toast, had some tea, and then went to bed so she could get up early in the afternoon before Rosie arrived home. But there she was still in her uniform, just staring at the ceiling, her face pink and blotchy and her eyes red and swollen, as if she had been crying uncontrollably, inconsolably, all day.

It had been cold with a few snowflakes falling as Rosie had walked home from school and found Sarah. At first she'd been disappointed, even a little annoyed that Sarah hadn't made tea, but she'd quickly realized something was terribly wrong.

"Are you sick?" Rosie had asked, alarmed to see her Aunt so distressed. Sarah cried at old movies, like *Gone with the Wind* and *Casablanca*, and at good stories like *Little Women*. She'd laughed through her tears when she took Rosie to see the movie of *Little*

Women. Sarah had squeezed Rosie's hand and whispered, "Now I can cry at the movie as well as the book!" Rosie understood Sarah's *Little Women* tears, but these tears were different. The look on Sarah's face had troubled Rosie. She didn't understand it, and couldn't figure out what was going on.

When Rosie had asked Sarah if she was sick, she had turned her head and looked at Rosie with a blank stare. Rosie was convinced that her Aunt didn't know who she was.

"Are you sick?" Rosie had asked again.

"No, no, luvy," Sarah had said, speaking in a small soft voice that Rosie had never heard before. "I've got a bit of a headache, that's all."

"I've brought you a cup of tea."

"There's lovely," Sarah had said, sitting up and trying to smile. "How did you know I wanted a cup of tea?"

Sarah had taken the tea from Rosie, but her hands had trembled so much the tea spilled into the saucer. She had tried to steady the tremors that were shaking her body, but it was no use. The tea slopped over the edge of the saucer making her nurses uniform wet, then the cup left the saucer completely and landed upside down on the bed.

"I'll get a towel," Rosie had said as she rushed into the bathroom. "Are you sure, you're okay?" she had asked again as she started mopping up.

"Well, no," Sarah had said, her voice trembling as she ignored the wet tea stains and sank down in the bed. "I don't think I am."

"Did something happen?"

"I don't know." Sarah had said in a whisper, as tears started rolling down her face, slowly at first, and then Sarah began to sob.

"I'll call Mom," Rosie had said, trying to sound calm as she ran out of the room in alarm and rushed up the stairs to the privacy of her mother's office where she telephoned her at the university to tell her that she'd got to come home quick.

"I'll be home in a couple of hours," Mary had told her daughter. "Sarah can't be *that* sick."

"You've got to come *now!*" Rosie had told her mother, as she started to cry. "*Now!*"

They'd learned later that nothing unusual had happened to Sarah except that she'd got stuck in an elevator with a patient who she was accompanying to surgery. A minor op, a small incision, a quick snip, a few stitches, nothing serious, nothing life-threatening. The elevator had shuddered and stopped between floors for no more than thirty seconds, but Sarah had become ashen and fainted. Then there had been a small jolt and the elevator had started to move again. When the doors opened at the next floor, two doctors found the patient, who had got off the gurney, holding Sarah's hand, while the two men from transport were trying to revive her.

When Sarah had regained consciousness she'd thought she must have fainted because she hadn't had time to eat. She'd reassured everyone that she was okay, and as her shift was nearly over she insisted on staying to finish her paperwork. The nurses said she was quiet and had a "faraway" look on her face. They'd joked that the piles of paperwork they had to fill out made them all want to get away. But Sarah was not okay.

After that Sarah stopped taking care of herself. She would not shower. She dressed in old clothes that she bought in the thrift shop on Charles, where they used whatever money they made for nursing scholarships. Sarah had taken clothes there for years, now she was buying the oldest, ready-for-the-dumpster, skirts and blouses that she could find in the store.

When Mary or Tom spoke to Sarah she just looked at them as if they weren't there. She did talk to Rosie, but nothing that she said made any sense. She spoke quickly, babbling, her vowels changed, she used words that Rosie had never heard her use before and she punctuated everything she said with, "*There's lovely!*" "*Fancy that!*" and "*Never!*"

When Rosie didn't understand what she was saying, Sarah would get frustrated and start crying like a child. Then her eyes would grow wide and a look of sheer terror would pass over her face and she'd ask over and over again, "Where's Rosie's umbrella? What have you done with our Rosie's umbrella?"

The first time this happened Rosie had got her red umbrella out of the hall closet and tried to give it to Sarah, but Sarah didn't want it and she'd pushed Rosie away so hard that she fell back against the wall with such a thump that it knocked the wind right out of her.

"*That's not our Rosie's umbrella!*" Sarah had screamed hysterically.

Hearing the noise Mary had run out of the kitchen where she was getting supper. Gasping for breath, Rosie had turned to her mother and shouted, "I don't know what to do!" She'd expected her mother to take charge of the situation, to comfort her and say soothing things to calm Sarah. But Mary had just stared at Sarah as if she'd just had a terrible shock. Her eyes were luminous and glazed over, and she looked at Sarah as if she could see something that Rosie could not. It was at that moment that Rosie became convinced that her Mom knew what had happened to Sarah.

"Tell me what to do!" Rosie had yelled as Sarah's screams had turned into grief stricken sobs. *"I don't know what to do!"*

"There's nothing you can do," her Mom had said, sobbing now almost as loudly as Sarah.

"What's wrong with her? What's wrong with Sarah? You know don't you? Why won't you help her? What's wrong with you?"

"For God's sake Rosie, stop asking questions!" Mary had shouted, so angry that Rosie felt she had been slapped.

Sarah had stopped crying the moment that Mary shouted at Rosie. She had stood as if struck dumb, silently rocking back and forth looking down. Mary had stood across the hall from Sarah, staring at her, through her, making noises that sounded like deep sighs or soft moans. Sarah looked up at Mary and they stared at each other, as if … as if what? Rosie thought. Rosie had stood there silent and still, watching them, knowing that whatever was happening, she wasn't a part of it. For the first time in her life Rosie had felt totally and utterly alone.

"There's nothing that any of us can do," Mary had said in a flat, empty voice, no longer looking at Sarah. She had detached herself from the situation, and had gone back into the kitchen, leaving Rosie to help Sarah climb the stairs up to her room. Sarah had lain down on her bed exhausted by her grief. Rosie had sat with her, holding her hand, and eventually Sarah had fallen asleep.

On Pinckney Street, which runs up the hill along the edge of Louisburg Square, trucks belonging to carpenters and painters blocked the road. The houses were old and always in need of repair. She could see inside one of the houses that had been left to decay and was now totally gutted. Men were shouting and joking with one another. They had taken off their shirts and one man was using his shirt to mop up the sweat that ran down his face and neck.

"She even talks like someone else," Rosie muttered to herself, losing the voices of the construction workers as her thoughts turned inwards. "How could she have changed so completely?"

Two months after Sarah had got stuck in the elevator her condition had not improved. Mary and Tom had taken her to their family doctor who had recommended a specialist. The "specialist" was a psychiatrist, and he'd wanted to meet the whole family. Rosie had said she didn't want to go, but quickly changed her mind when

Sarah had said she wasn't going either.

"Oh, I'll come," Rosie had said, "Let's go together."

The psychiatrist was a big man with large pink hands and thinning grey hair. He'd invited Sarah into his office and she'd followed him in without speaking, and he'd closed the door. So they'd sat in the waiting room, which was painted grey with uncomfortable blue chairs. Rosie's father had brought the newspaper and he sat and read. Her mother had brought a folder of students' essays and she'd got a pen out of her bag and wrote as she read. Rosie wished she had brought a book, but before she could ask her father, he pulled out the Arts section of the paper and gave it to her. She took it without saying thank you. No one was speaking and she didn't want to break the silence.

After about half an hour the psychiatrist had opened the door and invited them in. Sarah had been standing with her back to them staring out the window. The room was bare, with the same grey paint and more blue chairs, but there was a scroll of Chinese calligraphy on the wall. The psychiatrist took off his glasses and used them to gesture that they should sit down.

Her father had said, "Well?" as if he expected a report, and the psychiatrist had looked at her Dad.

"It's complicated," he'd said, followed after a few seconds by "interesting." Nothing more. He'd asked Tom about what had happened to Sarah when she'd got stuck in the elevator, even though Tom only knew what Mary and Rosie had told him.

Rosie remembered thinking that her mother had not liked being left out of the conversation, and she knew that in other circumstances Mary would have made sure the psychiatrist addressed her as well as Tom, but her mother had said nothing.

Rosie had thought she had more in common with Sarah than her parents or the psychiatrist. The three of them behaved as if neither she nor Sarah was in the room. Then abruptly, as if he knew what she was thinking, the psychiatrist had turned and smiled at Rosie.

"When I spoke with your mother on the telephone," he'd begun, glancing at Mary, as if to acknowledge that he knew she'd also felt left out, "she said your Aunt Sarah has always taken care of you when you come home from school. I understand you like to hang out together. Can you tell me what happened when you came home on the day that the elevator malfunctioned?"

"I made Aunt Sarah some tea," Rosie had said. "She didn't feel well so I telephoned my mother." She'd said nothing more. She'd looked at Sarah, who didn't seem to be there at all. Her mother had already told the psychiatrist on the phone about Sarah fainting in the elevator at the hospital and about what had happened in the hall when Sarah had pushed Rosie against the wall, but she'd recounted the events again, leaving out that she had become hysterical and shouted at Rosie. Mary had glanced at Rosie, and Rosie was sure the psychiatrist had seen the "say nothing" look her mother had given her. It was the look her mother used to give her when friends or graduate students came to dinner, and Mary thought Rosie was talking too much, or being silly, or difficult.

For a while no one spoke. Breaking the silence, the psychiatrist had looked kindly at Rosie and he'd asked her if she would like to share anything else. Rosie had shaken her head. She wanted to tell him she loved her Aunt Sarah that she didn't know what was going on, but both her parents were looking at her, so she'd said nothing. Instead she'd stood up and walked over to the window where Sarah was standing. She'd caught hold of Sarah's hand as if it was a lifeline, not for Sarah but for herself. Sarah had given her hand a squeeze. Engulfed in her own grief, Rosie had tried to imagine what had happened to Sarah for her to be so grief stricken.

The psychiatrist had watched in silence.

He'd said he wanted to meet with Sarah twice a week, but Sarah had refused to go and would not leave her room. Mary canceled two doctoral seminars at the university and she'd talked with her students on the phone. There were hall scenes, night scenes, but it was her mother and father who were fighting. Not Sarah. Rosie had never heard them yell at each other before. Somehow they had got through life without connecting, but Rosie had become acutely aware that they were connected, tied together, bound in a silence that now made her think of the school project she'd done on Munch's Scream. It was as if something dreadful was repeatedly occurring and they were perpetually screaming, but making no sounds.

"She's your sister! You stay home!" Mary had shouted.

"Next week. I'll stay home next week!" Tom had yelled back.

"No! She's your sister!"

"I know she's my sister! I understand you're upset, but –"

"Don't tell me you understand! What *I* don't understand is why *you're* not upset. You were there! *You should have stopped her!*"

"Stop it! You think I don't know that?"

"Stop it? Stop it! I'll stop it!"

"You can't stop it. You know that. We did it for Sarah. And now there's Rosie!

"Don't!"

"I can't stay home this week." Tom had said, no longer shouting, holding his head. "I have to be in court."

"I told you this would happen," Mary's voice was barely audible. "I should never have listened to you. We were insane. Totally delusional."

Rosie had been sitting on her bed listening intently as her mother's voice had trailed away, "Sarah," she'd whispered, knowing that Sarah could hear them too. Tears were running down her face and she didn't know what to do. She wanted Max, but she hoped that the cat was in with Sarah. Max loved Sarah. Then Mary screamed. *"I should never have listened to you!"*

The front door slammed.

Rosie had known it was her mother who had left the house and that her father was left standing in the hall staring at the front door. It was what he did when he was upset. Stand. Not move. Stuck. A few minutes went by before Rosie heard him climbing the stairs. By then she had torn a page from her notebook and written "KEEP OUT!" with a black marker, going over each letter making jagged lines back and forth, so the sign looked as if it was screaming like her mother, shouting like her father, and angry, confused, and hurt, like she felt.

Her father reached the second floor as she came out of her room and taped the sign on the door. He watched her without speaking and she did not look at him. When she was sure the tape had stuck she went back in her room and slammed the door. Tom had stood staring at the sign, holding on to the banister, wanting to tell Rosie that he loved her, but knowing he could not.

Walking home in the suffocating heat, Rosie thought about the fight. She thought about it every day. At first it made her cry. Thinking about it was worse than counting. Counting. Try not to count. She kept hearing her father say, *"We did it for Sarah. And now there's Rosie!"* It didn't matter that she now understood what they had been fighting about, she would remember for the rest of her life her Dad saying, *"And now there's Rosie"*.

As the days and then the weeks went by, Rosie had been more worried about her mother than she had been about Sarah. Her mother had lost weight and there were dark circles beneath her eyes, but Sarah seemed much better. Each day when Rosie had come home from school she'd boiled the kettle and made tea, and spread thick marmalade on toast for Sarah. She'd knock at the door and Sarah always opened it. "There's lovely", she'd say, taking the tray and going back into the room and closing the door.

On the day Sarah had let Rosie come in and sit with her, Tom had come home and told them that the psychiatrist had recommended that Sarah be admitted to a psychiatric unit in a hospital on the outskirts of Boston, and despite Rosie's protests, Mary had quickly agreed.

Both Tom and Mary had looked relieved.

"How could they send her away?" Rosie asked, reliving the moment as she walked on up Pinckney in the heat, remembering the psychiatrist who was washed so clean he smelled contaminated. "What was wrong with him? Why did he send her away? Couldn't he see that it was her parents who needed locking up, not Sarah?"

Rosie had spent most of the weekend going from her room to Sarah's and avoiding being in any room with either her mother or her father. Neither of them seemed to notice. On the Monday afternoon when Tom drove Sarah away she had stood in the hall and said goodbye to Rosie. Her hair, usually so neat and tidy, was uncombed and unwashed, and stuck to her head. She had looked forlorn in an old blue skirt that almost reached her ankles. She had a flowered apron that she called a "pinny" tied around her waist, and Rosie's mother had tried to get her to take it off, but Sarah ignored her. Rosie had helped Sarah dress, and she had watched as Sarah put on her stockings and tied them up with bandages just above her knees. Downstairs in the hall Sarah had been calm and she'd smiled at Rosie. Mary had started crying. She'd kissed Sarah and gone upstairs to her office. Rosie suddenly realized that was the only time she had ever, *ever*, seen her Mom kiss anyone.

"I won't be long," Sarah had told Rosie, her voice rising and falling as if she was singing. "I'm only going to the Co-op to fetch a loaf of bread."

Rosie had no idea what Sarah had meant by the "Co-op".

"I'll be back as soon as I can," Sarah had said, as she clutched the handle of her old thrift shop umbrella, but Rosie could tell by her eyes that Sarah had known how long she'd be gone. She was convinced that Sarah had understood that she wasn't coming back, that the papers her father had got her to sign would be used to keep her in the hospital, and that she was going to stay locked up, at least for a while.

Just before she had walked out of the house Sarah had kissed Rosie's cheek. "There, there, my lovely," she had said with a sad smile, "Now don't you cry, there's a good girl."

But Rosie had cried, and she could not stop crying. She had never been this unhappy. Her family had never been this messed up. She had never been separated from anyone she loved as much as Sarah, and she'd *never* been separated from Sarah.

Rosie had watched as Sarah got into the back of her father's car, and she could still see the frightened look on Sarah's face as she knelt on the back seat and waved at Rosie as the car moved slowly down Pinckney Street. Rosie had waved back, frantically at first, and then slowly, her arm barely moving as she stood on the pavement long after the car had disappeared. She'd stood for the first time in her life feeling totally alone.

Rosie lived at the top of Pinckney on the flat of the hill, in a tall narrow red brick townhouse with freshly painted black shutters and window boxes filled with red and white ivy geraniums. For a moment Rosie banished her memory of the car and Sarah leaving, and she took the key from her pocket and focused on unlocking the front door. Inside it was hot and stuffy and the stale smell hit her as she stepped inside the house.

In her head she could hear Sarah as she used to speak. "Is that you Rosie? I'm in the kitchen. I'll put the kettle on. Come and have tea." "Tea" to Sarah was a meal of bread and butter or scones with lemon curd and raspberry jam, fruit salad, and cake.

Rosie didn't bother to call out. Before Sarah had got stuck in the elevator she would make a pot of tea when Rosie arrived home and drink it black with lots of honey while Rosie sipped a cup of hot chocolate. Even when it was hot like today Sarah used to still drink tea, but she would make lemon barley water for Rosie.

"An English custom," Sarah used to say. "Barley water is so good for you when it's hot." Then she'd ask, "How about some chocolate cake?"

But Rosie now knew that Sarah wasn't English. She was Welsh. The lilt in her voice, the way she spoke now, was how she spoke as a child, kept hidden somehow from memory, to protect her from remembering what had happened to her.

When she came home just after her father had taken Sarah to the hospital, Rosie would still stand for a moment in the hall imagining that her Aunt was in the kitchen brewing tea. Remembering made Rosie feel dizzy, and she felt as if she couldn't breathe. It was as if she was perpetually coming home from school, with one "is that you Rosie?" bumping into another. She pressed the buttons on the thermostat in the hall and reprogrammed it to a frigid sixty-five degrees.

She went into the kitchen, dropped her backpack on the table and opened the refrigerator, but she couldn't find anything that she wanted to eat.

The day after Sarah had been taken away Mary had canceled her doctoral class and stayed home, because she didn't want Rosie to come home to an empty house. She'd spent the afternoon making lasagna, because Rosie loved lasagna, especially when her Mom made it with lots of creamy ricotta and her thick, home made garlicky pasta sauce, but Rosie had refused to eat it. She'd pushed her plate away, and made a peanut butter and jelly sandwich, which she took up to her room.

"I wish Dad had sent *you* away and left Sarah here!" she had shouted at her mother as she stamped up the stairs. "*I hate it here without Sarah!"*

White faced and trembling, Mary had thrown Rosie's lasagna in the garbage, plate and all. She'd got the aluminum foil out of the drawer and covered the top of the leftover lasagna, and when it was cool she had put it in the refrigerator. But by then Rosie had long since locked herself in her room. For the rest of the evening Rosie had refused to speak to her mother, and because Mary didn't know what to say to her daughter, she'd left her alone.

To take her mind off what was happening Mary had sat in her office reading student papers, but most of the time she'd stared at the typing on the page thinking about Rosie. She'd refused to let herself think about Sarah, and even Rosie shouting at her was less painful than thinking about Sarah. Unable to concentrate, she'd sat back in her chair and closed her eyes.

Sarah. How could she *not* think about her?

She could still see the look on Sarah's face when she'd arrived home after Rosie had telephoned her at the university. She could hear Rosie shouting, both angry and afraid, *"I don't know what to do"*. In her mind she could see Tom looking at her. She could not separate him from her own pain. He looked so lost. She'd been so angry with him. She'd winced when she thought about what she'd said to him. How could she have said that he should have stopped her? It was cruel. She could hear him shouting, *"You think I don't know that?"* and she'd imagined what it must be like for him remembering day in, day out, every day. It was bad enough when *she* remembered. But Tom? How could he remember and still exist?

Memories from long ago had filled her mind. Enormous shadowy people towered over her, wringing their hands and crying like Sarah was crying now, crying so much that their sobbing overwhelmed her, and for one terrifying moment, Mary thought she would end up like Sarah and lose herself in grief. But she didn't. She remembered, which was worse.

The next morning Rosie had been alarmed by how sick Mary looked. She'd apologized to her Mom before she'd gone to school. She'd promised that she would eat the lasagna that night for supper, and she'd eaten it, some of it, just a little, to show that there were no hard feelings, that she'd not meant what she said, that she loved her Mom just as much as she loved Sarah, just differently.

Rosie remembered that when she'd arrived home two days after she had shouted at Mary she'd found her mother had inexplicably left her some more of the lasagna on a plate covered with tin foil in the refrigerator. The creamy garlic sauce was cracked and dry and the pasta looked like thick flaps of clammy cold skin. Rosie had stared at the plate.

"What was she thinking?" she'd asked herself at the time.

She remembered in vivid detail. She'd shuddered as she'd taken the tin foil off the plate. She'd got a fork out of the cutlery drawer and pushed the lasagna into the garbage disposer. She'd run the water and flipped the switch. Inexplicably the angry sound had made her smile, just for a second as she absorbed the noise, imagining that she had made it, that it had come from deep inside her. She'd watched, mute, as the bloody glop of the sauce was washed away down the sink. She'd found half a bottle of coke at the back of the refrigerator, but like the lasagna, it was past its best, and when she opened it there was no fizz. She'd emptied the remains of the bottle into a glass and took a long drink, and was surprised when the flat sugary liquid bubbled up suddenly as she drank.

Inexplicably the memory of the lasagna steadied Rosie. She

remembered she'd put the coke bottle on the counter by the kitchen sink, picked up her backpack and glass, and gone out into the hall and slowly climbed the stairs. She'd hesitated when she reached the second floor. She could see the angry KEEP OUT! on her door. Without thinking about it she'd climbed on up to the third floor. There was no "keep out" sign, but she rarely went up and she could not remember Sarah ever going up there.

Still standing in the kitchen, Rosie remembered opening the door to her parents' bedroom. The only difference between now and then was that it had still been cold outside and the heat had been set at seventy-two degrees. Mary had left in a hurry and the ceiling fan was still turning. Rosie had switched it off and looked around. The room filled the front of the house. On the dressing table were lots of pictures of Rosie when she was a baby with red corkscrew curls, when she was six without her front teeth, and more recently, tall and thin with masses of red-brown hair, laughing, frowning, and just fooling around, at Disney with Mickey Mouse, jumping waves with her Mom and Dad at Cape Cod, horse riding with school friends in New Hampshire, sitting on her English Grandfather's knee when she was a baby, and hugging her dear, sweet, and now totally batty Aunt Sarah. There were no clues to dark secrets in the photographs. They looked like a normal family. No, not normal, perfect. Perfect. "We look awesome," Rosie had thought, "but we're not."

Rosie had looked more closely at the photographs. There were no photographs of her mother and father on their wedding day. She'd never thought about it before. Instead of looking at the photos that were there she'd started to look for the photos that were not. What photos were missing? Her father had often told her that she looked just like her mother, but there were no photos of her mother when she was a child. She'd imagined her father playing with Sarah when they were children, but there were no photographs of them when they were little. There were no photos of Sarah, except the ones with Rosie. There were no pictures of her Grandfather when he was a young man, and she had not seen him since she was six.

Rosie had bitten her bottom lip and then touched it with her finger to see if she had made it bleed. It was as if her family did not exist before they had her, except, of course, they did, or she thought they did, even if they kept their memories hid. She'd turned and walked out closing the door.

On the third floor at the back of the house, next to her parents' bedroom, was her mother's study. Rosie had stood in the doorway and looked around. Three walls were filled with books from floor to ceiling. A huge window made up of small panes of hand made glass took up the fourth wall. Rosie had walked into the room and for a few moments she'd stood looking out at the back yards of the red-brick houses on Mount Vernon Street that were filled with flowers.

Mary had a big old mahogany desk in front of the window but the chair was on the window-side and Mary sat and looked in at the bookshelves and at the door so no one could come in and surprise her.

Rosie remembered thinking that her Mom did not like surprises, which made sense to her now but had not then.

The desk had been thrown out when Tom's law offices had modernized and Mary had reused it. On the day Rosie had gone up to the third floor the desk was covered with student papers that spilled over the edges onto the floor. Ancient academic journals and dusty books were stacked in precarious piles on the Oriental rug, ready to topple if touched, but there were no old photographs of her family in Mary's office.

"No photos at all," she remembered thinking. "Why was that?"

Squeezed into a corner of the room was a big comfortable old leather chair, on which Max their fat alley cat had been sleeping. Max had large double paws and he was a longhaired tabby. When Sarah had first brought Max home he'd been more dead than alive. He was totally emaciated, he had lost most of his fur, and he was covered with large open sores. Mary had looked at the oozing cat and she'd told Sarah to get rid of it, but Sarah, knowing that Mary loved cats as much as she did, persuaded her to let the cat stay.

Sarah had kept Max in her room and Rosie had helped her bathe his sores, which had quickly crusted over. Within a month the scabs had almost disappeared and his fur, which was quickly growing back, hid the scabs that were left.

Sarah had said it was the poached salmon which Mary fed him that helped him get well, but Rosie had said no, she thought it was the cold cuts her Mom bought for Max at DeLuca's.

Mary had laughed at them as she fed Max tasty morsels with her fingers. She had told them she didn't know why she'd let them keep such a mangy old cat, but she enjoyed taking care of him as much as they did, and she loved it when he finished eating the food she had brought him and purred at her as he licked her fingers. Even Tom Llewellyn had grown fond of the cat. When he was working late at night and went downstairs to get a glass of milk he would pour some into a saucer for Max to drink.

When Max got better he'd turned into a magnificently fat, tiger-striped cat, and was devoted to Sarah, absolutely loved Rosie, and was so fond of Mary he spent every afternoon in her study curled up in the sunbeams from the fractured light of the old glass that on sunny days landed on the big old easy chair. Now Max was Rosie's only after-school companion. She picked him up and buried her face in the fur of his neck and pretended to purr. Max reciprocated. He purred loudly as Rosie sat down, knocking the books off one of the arms of the chair. She put her glass of soda in between some student papers on the table by the chair and dropped her backpack on the floor.

Rosie felt agitated and exhausted at the same time. She remembered small inconsequential details with clarity, while larger painful memories flashed through her mind so fast she was hardly aware of them.

It seemed such a long time ago that she had come home to the vomitous lasagna.

"Where's Aunt Sarah?" Rosie had asked Max. "I know you miss Sarah," she'd said, stroking him. "I miss her too."

Max had jumped off her lap and padded softly out of the room and down the stairs.

"Max! Come back! She's not there!" Rosie had called after him as she'd got up, toppling the books balanced on the other arm of the chair. She'd finished her soda and left the glass on her mother's desk. She knew it would irritate Mary, but more than make her cross it would upset her. The wet stain left on the wood would remind her once again that Rosie was home alone now Sarah was gone. It would nag at her when she was stuck in yet another meeting at the university, and she would be angry with Rosie's father, because after taking Sarah to the psychiatric unit at the hospital, he'd gone straight to Logan Airport and flown to New York to attend another deposition.

Since Sarah had been hospitalized Tom had hardly been

home, and he'd rationalized his absence with excuses about urgent meetings in the New York law office, which he'd insisted he had no alternative other than to attend.

She remembered the day after her Dad had signed Sarah into the psychiatric hospital, he'd come home from the hospital and he'd packed his briefcase and an overnight bag, and he'd left at 6:00 a.m. the next morning in a taxi for Logan Airport to catch the Delta shuttle to New York. Mary had watched him go, not saying a word. She put her arms around Rosie and kissed her on the forehead before telling her to get ready for school.

"A kiss," Rosie thought now. She remembered she'd been surprised by the kiss and not knowing what else to do, she'd put on clean clothes, gathered her books, and left the house without saying goodbye to Mary, and walked to school. It was actually where she'd wanted to be. She'd needed the normalcy and her friends were good company.

Now, back in the house, she longed to be at school.

She remembered Max had come back upstairs and he'd rubbed against Rosie's legs as if to tell her that he couldn't find Sarah. Rosie had picked him up and tucked him under her left arm. She'd caught hold of one of the straps of her backpack and dragged the bag across the floor so that it knocked over several stacks of books and more student papers. She'd done it deliberately to make sure her mother would know she'd been in her office and she'd wanted Sarah to come home.

"Now I know everything," Rosie thought, "and nothing at all."
She was still trying to expel the recurring memory of the lasagna
and almost gagged at the thought of food.

"Without a past how can I have a future?" she asked herself
as she climbed the stairs.

"One – two -" she said out loud. "No! Not now!"

"Find your own truth!" she said, blocking the count by thinking about Margaret and Jesse.

Rosie's bedroom was on the second floor. Her room was bright
and inviting. She'd chosen the colors when she was much younger.
The walls were a deep pink. The patchwork quilt was a mixture of
bright oranges, pinks and yellows, and the rug was several shades
of blue. Her mother had said she would get tired of it.

"We can always get more paint," Sarah had said with a laugh.

Max arrived and rubbed against Rosie's legs. She picked him

up. Once in her room, Max jumped from her arms and landed on the patchwork quilt that lay in a heap on the unmade bed.

Rosie stood still. Her mind returned to the photos in her Mom and Dad's room, or more accurately, the photos that were not there. She remembered the first time she realized it was not just that people were absent, but places were missing as well, there were no old photos of houses with her Mom or Dad playing outside, no landscapes, no walks in the country, no beach scenes with children playing.

Now she knew why.

She thought back. She remembered her Dad saying, "We did it for Sarah," and trying to figure out what they did. He'd also said, "And now there's Rosie", and she'd wondered, "Why is that? Why am I here?"

She knew what had happened but the questions remained. Rosie felt trapped. It was an overwhelming feeling that made her nervous about being in the house on her own. There were robberies all the time on Beacon Hill. She'd read about them in the newspapers. What if someone broke in? A truck slowly rumbled by the parked cars on her narrow street. A dog barked. Rosie heard a front door slam and she wondered if it was the door to her house, but it sounded far off and she was sure it was further down the road.

"I'm not nervous," she said, trying to convince herself that she was not. "After all," she reasoned, "I've been here for months on my own every afternoon after school. It's no good worrying about someone breaking in."

Suddenly she felt nothing mattered.

"Without Sarah I'd be better off dead," she said to herself. Then, feeling her skin crawl, she whispered, "Maybe I'm already dead.

Maybe we all are. Maybe we don't exist. We only think we do."

She sat on her bed and cuddled Max, trying to push the thoughts she was having about dying out of her head. It was as if today was yesterday, or the day before, last week, a month ago, 1995, *or* 1955.

"You can live your whole life thinking that you know who you are," she thought, "and then find out that you do not."

"Find your own truth," she whispered, reaching back into her memories of Sarah and what happened after she got stuck in the elevator.

Suddenly she could smell the dank air of the disused shaft and she could hear her father shouting "Rosie! No!" and once again she was crying, counting. She hated the empty house, hated the emptiness she felt inside her, the loneliness, the feeling of not belonging anywhere. Not here, not there, not now, not then.

She wanted her father to come home. She wanted her mother to be there. The way it was before Sarah got stuck in the elevator, when they read *Little Women* together, and cried and laughed at nothing more than an old story that was so much less fraught with perils than the one they were in.

She imagined that they were in a play and at the end they all came out on the stage, held hands and raised their arms and bowed while the audience clapped, before they all left the theatre and went home.

Even though she was angry with her Dad, and when he was home he didn't have much to say to her, just the sound of his voice talking to clients in his office, which filled the whole fourth floor of the house, would make her feel better.

He often talked on the telephone, and although Rosie couldn't hear what he was saying, she always knew when he was talking to a client. Then he sounded confident and unhurried. He used a different voice when he talked to other lawyers. On those calls his voice was authoritative, commanding, and sometimes demanding. But when he talked to his secretary his voice was tense and he often sounded irritable, at her, at his clients, other lawyers, life in general, late flights, missed connections. Rosie wondered if his secretary got fed-up of listening to him, if she knew he complained to her because he could not talk like that to her mother. When he spoke to Mary he was always matter-of-fact, "this is the way it is", "no good complaining about it". There were no ups and downs in their relationship. It was flat, except for the fight when her Dad had said he could not stay home to take care of Sarah.

Rosie wondered if her Dad was all right. It was different now. She was angry with him and worried about him at the same time. Last night she'd found out how much he loved Sarah, that's why he kept going to the New York office. She'd thought again about her Dad packing his bag after he'd taken Sarah to the hospital and running out of the house to catch the shuttle to New York. In her mind it became a scene, like in a movie, that you play over and over again.

"Frankly, my dear, I don't give a damn," were the last words Rhett Butler had spoken to Scarlett O'Hara in *Gone with the Wind*. Sarah often watched it on her VCR, and Rosie used to watch it with her curled up on Sarah's bed with Max.

She thought for a moment that her mother looked a bit like Clark Gable, and then the image came to her of Mary saying good-bye to Tom the morning after he'd taken Sarah to the hospital. She imagined hearing her Dad, who did not look a bit like Clark Gable, saying to her mother, "Frankly, my dear, I *do* give a damn, and so I *must* leave," as he picked up his briefcase and overnight bag and left.

Rosie shook her head as if to expel the foolishness of the image, and she thought about her Aunt Sarah. Since she was a small child Sarah had carried all the grief, bottled it up, held on to it, but now she had given it to her Dad and he could no longer hide from what had happened when he was a child.

It occurred to Rosie that she couldn't hide either, even though the truth had been hidden from her. Now she was out from the shadows, out in the open for the first time in her life, standing in the harsh light.

Rosie had known at the time that there was more to it. She'd hardly seen her Dad for weeks and she'd thought he'd forgotten all about her, but that wasn't it. She knew that now. *Knowing* what she knew now made her even more angry with her parents, but also sad for them. They should have told her. It wasn't right that she did not know. Her life was so complicated, but she knew nothing about it. She thought again that the only way she could put into words how she felt was that she had grown up hidden from herself.

Sometimes Rosie could hear her mother talking to a student on the telephone in her office on the third floor and her father talking to a client on the fourth floor at the same time. Once she'd shouted up, "Why don't you shut your office doors when you're on the phone!" But what she'd liked best were the breaks in the silence, when everyone was talking at the same time, including Sarah, who would call to her from her room.

"Rosie! Come and look at this!" Sarah would shout, sticking her head out the door, waving a newspaper or a magazine that she'd been reading. Sarah had liked to share odd stories especially about women who had done interesting things and had died.

"No obituaries!" Rosie would shout back as she got up from her desk where she'd been doing her homework.

Sarah would tell Rosie about some ancient old woman's youthful adventures, and then nodding her head and smiling at Rosie she'd say, "I'm sure you will do something just as brave!"

"Before I die," Rosie would say.

"Oh, long before that, just after you finish college, I expect," Sarah would say, giving her a teasing look, and they would both laugh.

Rosie was sure anyone listening would have found their conversations inexplicable, but to her they were magical. She walked along the hallway on the second floor and stood outside Sarah's room.

"Rosie! Come and talk to me while I get ready for work," Sarah would call to her, and even though Sarah was not there, Rosie could still hear her. "Come on! Before I have to go and fix all those in-growing toe-nails!"

Of course, there were no in-growing toe-nails, just heart attacks, car accidents, and people who'd had been shot, heavy duty stuff that Sarah didn't talk about. Once while she'd been getting ready for work Rosie had picked up the little book of *Hospital Sketches* by Louisa May Alcott that was on Sarah's bedside table and flipped through the pages.

"He died then," Rosie read, "*for, though the heavy breaths still tore their way up for a little longer, they were but the waves of an ebbing tide that beat unfelt against the wreck, which an immortal voyager had deserted with a smile. He never spoke again, but to the end held my hand close, so close that when he was asleep at last, I could not draw it away.*"

"Have you ever held someone's hand as they died?" Rosie had asked Sarah.

"More times than I care to remember," Sarah had replied, taking the book away from Rosie and putting it back on her bedside table. "Sometimes it happens peacefully. Just sleeping and waking without gasping for breath. Then there are long pauses and quick breathing, before the breathing becomes rhythmic, slows, with long gaps in between, and just gently stops."

"It's not always like that," Rosie had said.

"No, not always, but dying is a part of living," Sarah had said, matter of fact. Her voice had then trembled when she added, "I just can't stand it when a child dies."

Sometimes Sarah would tell Rosie when it was a child who had been badly hurt, but only if the child survived. If the child died she would say nothing. Instead, when Rosie came home from school, Sarah would ask her if she wanted to go down to Rebecca's Café for an ice cream, and they would chat about silly things and Rosie would never let on that she knew that some little kid had died. She would make Sarah laugh with tales from school and ask her personal questions like: When did she first wear lipstick? Had she ever worn lipstick? Could she remember her first kiss? What was it like making love for the first time? Had she ever made love? She had made love, hadn't she?

"Jesse kissed me once," Rosie had said, "no tongue, just lips."

"Rosie!" Sarah had said, pretending to be shocked and changing the subject. "Let's take some sorbet home for your mother," she'd said, "and some rum raisin for your Dad."

"I want vanilla!" Rosie had pretended to wail, making Sarah laugh. The sorbet-rum-raisin-vanilla joke went back to when Rosie had been three or four years old, and neither of them quite remembered what had happened except that Rosie wanted some vanilla ice cream and was inconsolable because they didn't have any.

After Sarah got stuck in the elevator she would talk to herself in a way that Rosie had never heard her talk before. She would have entire conversations the way young children do who have imaginary friends. Sometimes she spoke as if reciting an epic poem that could go on for hours. Other times it was as if someone was talking to her and she was responding.

"There's lovely!" she would say, her voice rising and falling, "Never! Well! Who would have thought it?"

Sometimes Rosie would hear her say, "Poor Grethel" and "Our Rosie," as if she was in the room with her Aunt taking part in the conversation.

"Where's our Rosie's umbrella?" Sarah had kept asking. And Rosie, cautious after the first time, but anxious to understand what Sarah was talking about, would go into her Aunt's room, and sit on her bed and ask, "What umbrella?" and Sarah would say, "Why, our Rosie's, of course luvy," as if she wasn't Rosie.

"Why do you want an umbrella?" Rosie would ask.

"For when we go for our walk," Sarah would say, looking confused, in her pink floral pinny and yellow dress. "For our walk my darling girl."

Then Sarah's eyes would fill with tears, and she would start sobbing, and her sobs would quickly become loud cries and then screams, as if something terrible was happening, and Mary would come, running up the stairs, yelling "Rosie! Go back to your room!" before she even knew if Rosie was in with Sarah, and Rosie would storm out of Sarah's bedroom, pushing past her mother in the hallway, go into her own room, and slam the door.

For a moment she would just stand there trying not to cry, but the tears would come and she would run over to her bed, and bury her head in her pillows. She'd cry because her Mom had never shouted at her before Sarah got sick, because she felt her mother did not love her, because she'd become cruel instead of kind. Mostly, Rosie had cried because she did not know what was happening to Sarah, and her mother did, but she would not tell her. She'd cried because she felt as if Sarah had died and she was mourning for her.

"It's as if I died too," she'd whispered to herself, "as if I was born dead."

Ironically, it was true. Emotionally *she knew* what her mind did not, beyond logic, beyond reason, as if somehow deep inside *she felt* what Sarah knew.

Rosie tried to stop breathing. No sound came from the house. Max had stretched himself out and gone to sleep and was no longer purring. Rosie breathed slowly, trying to stay calm, not count, not cry. What she wanted most was to stop the rapid thoughts that were bumping into each other as they filled her head. She'd thought about a conversation that had taken place at school, about not being afraid of finding your own truth. For a moment she felt peaceful, as if she was floating. Then the phone rang and made her jump and she knew the thoughts would come back, racing through her mind and causing her to feel fearful. Quickly, Rosie searched for her phone, which she found tangled up in the quilt on her bed. It was her Mom.

"Are you okay?" Mary asked her voice strained.

"I'm fine," Rosie said, the peaceful moment over. "Couldn't find the phone. How's Sarah?"

"Honestly?" Mary said. "I don't know. She's heavily sedated. I sat with her for as long as they would let me this morning, but I don't think she knew I was there."

"Is Dad with her?" Rosie asked.

"Yes," Mary said, sounding guilty as well as worried. "I'll be home soon. I didn't want you to come into an empty house today, but one of my students collapsed in class and had to be taken to hospital. I had to contact his parents. Not easy. They live in France."

Mary knew this was too much information, but she wanted Rosie to understand that she would be there if she could, and that she was not just in another meeting. "I should have stayed home today," she said. "Let's go to Figs."

"You've got to be kidding!" Rosie said, the words slapping Mary. "After what happened at the hospital last night you want to go out to dinner?"

"No, no, of course not," Mary quickly said. "I just want to make sure you eat."

Rosie's mind speeded up as she remembered the last time they'd gone to Figs together just after her Dad had taken Sarah to the hospital. Her thoughts became muddled again. Figs, her Mom's student collapsing, last night at the hospital, her Dad, Sarah, were mixed up. Mary was asking her something, telling her something, but Rosie couldn't make out what she was saying. Her mother's voice sounded like an echo.

"Rosie? Rosie?"

"I'm fine," Rosie said, without a hint of emotion in her voice. "Bye."

The last time they had gone to Figs had begun in exactly the same way. Rosie had arrived home on the Thursday after Sarah was hospitalized and Mary had phoned warm and friendly, talking as if nothing had happened, as if Sarah were okay, and as if she had never stopped caring. "I'm sorry I'm late," she had said, sounding apologetic, in an I-love-you voice that was unable to just come out and say it. "The Dean called a meeting. He's such a turd. I won't bore you with the details." Mary had changed the subject, "How was school?"

"Okay." Rosie had replied.

"Why don't you get your homework done and we'll go to Figs when I get home," Mary had laughed, nervously, trying to make light of the situation. "I could eat a whole pizza!" She had not waited for Rosie to reply. "Do you have homework?"

"Yes."

Mary had been bright and breezy, even though she knew Rosie could have ended the conversation in a second by simply hanging up. She'd hoped that Rosie would at least fill in the yes-no gaps, so she had rushed on, "Do you have a lot? What have you got to do?"

"I have to find out something about the origin of my name."

"Rosie?"

"No, Llywelyn."

"Why?" Mary had asked after a moment of silence.

"Why not?" Rosie had responded, irritated with her mother, and becoming more interested in the project. "The semester is almost over and we've finished all the requirements so Margaret suggested we find out something about our own histories, our 'family heritage' Margaret called it." Again, silence.

"Mom?"

"Sorry," Mary had said quickly and then, after another hesitation, she'd tried to sound enthusiastic. "What a great project," she'd said, but Rosie had known she didn't mean it.

"I didn't know our name was Welsh," Rosie had said.

Again she'd waited for her mother to respond.

Silence.

"Anyway, I'm going to study Wales." Rosie had said. "Of course, we all know Jesse O'Malley's name is Irish. But he has a postcard that one of his Uncles just sent him from Harlech Castle, which is in Wales, and he's going to give it to me."

Rosie had continued, even though she never liked to talk about school or her homework, and she wasn't interested in Jesse's postcard, just Jesse. She'd kept talking because she was trying to figure out why her mother had sounded like someone who'd just been told something bad was about to happen. But maybe that wasn't it, Rosie had thought. It was more like her Mom had sounded as if she'd been found out, as if she'd done something bad.

Unaware of Rosie's thoughts, Mary had suddenly laughed and said she was sure Jesse would find a battle to write about, and Rosie had laughed too.

Rosie had dismissed her earlier suspicions. To her surprise she'd found she was relieved to have this opportunity to talk to her Mom about something other than her Aunt Sarah.

"Rachel Gordon already knew her family came from St. Petersburg," Rosie had said. "Her mother's always talking about Rachel's Great Grandparents leaving Russia."

"I'm glad you're friends with Rachel," Mary had said.

"Do you know she speaks seven languages? Her Mom I mean, not Rachel," Rosie rattled on, "if you include Latin and Greek". She'd suddenly wanted to say, "I love you," but unable to bring herself to say it. She'd said, "I'd love to learn Welsh" instead. And then, after a pause, she'd said, "Why didn't you tell me our family's name was Welsh, or didn't you know?"

"Yes, I knew," Mary had said, still taken aback that in the middle of this family crisis Rosie was going to study her family history and Wales. "It never seemed important I suppose."

"You'd rather I study South Africa," Rosie had said, because that was the last major research project she had done, "write some more about the history of apartheid, and Nelson Mandela." Mary had chuckled, grateful for this turn in the conversation so they shared common ground. Rosie had received an award for the report on Nelson Mandela that she'd written the year before in 1994 when he had become South Africa's first Black President.

"Too bad!" Rosie had laughed. I'm going to trace our family history back to Wales! Will you help me?"

"Yes, yes, of course I will," Mary had said, trying to sound enthusiastic. "Goodness is that the time? Rosie, I've got to go. I've made myself late."

Rosie took this to mean that *she* had made her mother late. "Okay. I'll see you later. I think I'll call Dad and ask him to help me."

"No!" Mary had said, too quickly and with too much anxiety.

"I won't talk to him about Sarah," Rosie had tried to calm her mother, not understanding why she sounded so concerned.

"Oh. Why not!" Mary had laughed at the terrible absurdity of the situation. "Call him. He probably knows a lot about Wales." Then in the hurried voice that she used when she was thinking about her next appointment, "His New York telephone number is at the top of the list of numbers I put in the drawer of your desk. Gotta go! Get your homework done then we can go to Figs and have a pizza when I get home."

"Okay."

"Never trust a round pizza!" Mary had recited the slogan of Figs where the pizzas were rectangular and not round.

"No more lasagna!" Rosie had said.

"Rosie! I've gotta go. Love you!"

"I love you too," Rosie had finally said it, but her mother had already ended the call. "Even if I am angry with you about Sarah I still love you," Rosie had said listening to the dial tone as she spoke.

She'd taken the list which was headed "Emergency Telephone Numbers" out of the drawer. There were two numbers for her Dad, one in Boston and the other in New York. She sat back down on her bed with Max and punched the New York number, two-one-two.

The receptionist had picked up on the first ring.

"Llywelyn, Lewis, and O'Malley."

"I'd like to speak to Mr. Llywelyn" Rosie had said, trying to sound grown up and business-like.

"I'm sorry. He's in a meeting."

"This is Rosie Llywelyn."

"Oh! His daughter! Hi! Let me put you through to his secretary."

"Mr. Llywelyn's office."

"This is Rosie. I'd like to speak to my Dad."

"Oh, hello Rosie. How are you?" The secretary had been familiar even though they had never met. "Do you miss your Dad? I think he's coming home tomorrow. Can I give him a message?"

"I'd like to speak to him."

"I'm sorry dear. Unless it's urgent he's given strict instructions that he is not to be disturbed." The secretary had hesitated. "Is it urgent?"

"No." Rosie had sighed. "Just tell him I wanted to ask him if he knows anything about Wales."

"Oh, homework!" The secretary had laughed. "I'll tell him when he comes out of the meeting. I went to Wales years ago. The weather was awful. I went to Carmarthen Castle when it was blowing a gale."

"I'm not interested in castles," Rosie had said, knowing that she must have sounded rude.

"Well the only other things you'll find in Wales are the choirs and sheep."

"Thanks. But I'm not interested in choirs or sheep." Rosie had rushed on to cut the secretary off before she could say anything else. "Just tell my Dad I called. Thanks. Bye."

Rosie wasn't sure if was the Wednesday or Thursday after Sarah was hospitalized that Mary had come home and they had pizza at Figs, but she did remember that she'd sat down at her computer to do a search for information on Wales while she'd waited for her mother to come home to go to Figs. She'd checked her email first and found two messages. There'd been one from Jesse:

> hey welsh woman! found out in 1404 owain glyndwr, the leader of the great welsh uprising, captured har-lech castle. owain was crowned prince of wales but the english bombarded harlech in 1408 with stone cannon balls. owain glyndwr must have been like william wal-lace. did you see braveheart? i think u r stupid if u don't study wales. Jesse

Rosie had smiled. She knew Jesse liked her. She had been friends with him since they were in kindergarten, but recently he had been spending a lot of time just looking at her. Maybe Jesse was right. Maybe she was stupid about a lot of things.

She thought about what Jesse had said in class about finding her own truth and it steadied her, made her feel less of an after-thought. She imagined telling Jesse she would like to go out with him. Or just asking him if he wanted to come over and hang out after school. No one would know. She thought about the young woman in the park pulling the young man towards her and kissing him.

"Find your own truth!" she said to herself as she returned to what had happened to Sarah. "It's a quest," she said. "Think of it as a quest."

The second email was from <nightwatch> whoever that was. Rosie had clicked the mouse:

> **Hiya my lovely. This is the first email I've ever sent! Or will send when I am finished writing it!**
>
> **One of the nurses let me use her computer and I've now got my own email address! I don't think she is supposed to let me do that, but I told her how much I miss you and I think she felt sorry for me. She even showed me how to send a message!**
>
> **I'm writing you a story. I'll send it as soon as I finish it. I love you. Be a good girl for your Mom and Dad.**
>
> **Love Aunt Sarah**

Rosie had been laughing and crying all at once. She'd written quickly:

> **Aunt Sarah! I miss you! Are you okay??? I hate it here without you. Send me the story soon! I love you 2! Rosie**

She'd pressed send and waited. Sarah had written back:

Don't worry about me my lovely girl. The doctors and nurses are nice. They have me taking lots of medicine and I sleep a lot. There it is, Luvy.

Rosie had written:

I wish you could come home Aunt Sarah.

Sarah had written:

Sorry luvy. No such luck. Never mind my darling

Rosie had always talked with Sarah about her homework and she did so now without having any idea of the impact it would have on Sarah:

I'm studying Wales. Jesse thinks I should study Welsh castles.

Rosie had waited staring at the monitor. It took a while and Sarah's response had surprised her:

It's funny you should be studying Wales at school when I've just remembered that I am Welsh, which makes you Welsh too my luvy.

I had a think about castles. What about Tretower? Must date back a thousand years. I found a picture of it in a book just before they admitted me to this hospital.

It's strange what you remember and what you forget. When I was a little girl we visited the court and the castle. One of my Uncles used to tell us that's where they learned to rustle sheep.

You never know, the story I am writing might help you with your report! Hope so. Wouldn't that be funny! I'll send it to you when it is finished. Be a good girl for your Mom and Dad. Don't worry about me. I'll be alright. Love Sarah.

Rosie had written back blurting out on the screen all the questions she wanted to ask Sarah:

Why didn't you tell me our family is Welsh? Why didn't Dad tell me? Or Mom?

She had pressed send and regretted it immediately. It was the kind of question she would mutter to herself as her mother left the room and shut the door. She waited. No response. Annoyed with herself she'd tried to focus on her math homework. When Sarah's next email had arrived it took her a moment to pick up the thread:

I forgot Luvy. I can't explain it. Sorry. I'd like to help you with your homework. You might find coal miners and riots more interesting than castles or sheep. There were riots in Blaina in the 1930's. You could write about the terrible conditions in which the coal miners and their families lived. Did you know the Llywelyns were miners?

Why don't you see what kind of information you can find about Big Pit? I've been searching myself. I have been trying to locate myself, if you understand what I mean. I think one of my Great Uncles (he would be your Great, Great Uncle) dug coal there. Many of the miners and their families lived in Blaenavon. You might do a search for that.

Your Great Nana was born in Blaenavon. The iron works was there from the nineteenth century. I've been reading about it. The miners who still live there are trying to make it into a living museum because it was part of the industrial revolution. It would make a good school report if you wanted to write it.

I have to go. I'll try and send you the story tomorrow night. I hope I can come home soon. Love Aunt Sarah.

Rosie had quickly sent another email:

I hope you do too. I miss you so much. Love Rosie.

Rosie sat for a long time thinking about Sarah's first emails, while she waited for Mary to come home. She thought going to Figs again was a bad idea. Maybe, she thought, her Mom wanted to get through the meal without an argument.

Everything was muddled. It was like rehearsing for a school play. She'd learned her lines, but each time she spoke them they came out different. There was no sound in the house except for Max who was doing his ablutions, his rough tongue worked on cleaning his double paws.

Rosie stared at Max, not really seeing him. It was momentary. In less than no time she was back remembering the first emails from Sarah just after her parents had put her in the hospital, her Dad in New York, and her Mom inexplicably deciding she wanted to go to Figs for dinner. Rosie clearly remembered she had yelled at Max.

"Shut up Max!" Rosie had shouted angrily, startling Max. "Sorry," she'd said, getting up from her desk and going over to the bed and stroking his head. Max had looked at her as if insulted. Then he'd stretched and to show there were no hard feelings he started to purr.

Rosie had gone back to her computer and had searched for information about "Big Pit". To her surprise there was a lot. She'd skimmed, reading quickly:

Sunk in 1880 and incorporating much earlier coal and ironstone workings ...It produced coal on a large scale until it closed in 1980.

She'd searched for Blaenavon:

Blaenavon was a major producer of the world's iron and coal in the 19th century. The coal and ore mines can still be seen as well as the homes of the workers and their families. ...

She'd typed "Blaina":

Following fifteen years of deepening depression and hardship there was an uprising organized by the people of the coal mining towns of South Wales. ... The Blaina riots in 1935 stand as a testimony to the courage and determination of the coal miners and their families to change the policies of the English Government at Westminster.

She'd followed links away from Blaina, chasing threads about coalminers, before returning to the website that had the most information on the 1935 riots. She'd stopped to check if Jesse had sent her another email and found another from Sarah.

Hiya my darling girl! Just remembered! My Grandfather, your Great Grandfather, played the tuba in Blaina brass band. He told me when I was a little girl that the band went to London and played at the Crystal Palace before it burned down! All of a sudden I remembered he used to tell me he had six "b's" after his name! He was the Best Blinkin' Blower in Blaina Brass Band! I am so glad I remembered! Have to go! I'm supposed to be sleeping!

Quickly, knowing her Mom would be home any minute Rosie had written back:

Hiya Aunt Sarah, I am so glad you remembered that too! Mom is on her way home. Please write again tomorrow. She is taking me to Figs. I hope you sleep well! Love Rosie.

Rosie remembered she had just pressed "send" when the front door slammed and her Mom had arrived home.

"Rosie! The meeting was canceled!" Mary had called up the stairs. Not true of course, but she didn't want Rosie to know she had skipped it to have dinner with her. "Do you still want to go to Figs? You can finish your homework when we get back."

"Sure!" Rosie had yelled, shutting down her computer. "Coming!"

Mary had dropped a bag of books on the floor in the hall. She was tall and slim with short red curls, an older version of Rosie right down to her brown and gold freckles and hazel-green eyes. Jesse had once asked Rosie if her Mom was Irish and Rosie had just said "no", and Jesse had said, "She looks like a Celt, you do too", and Rosie had shrugged. It didn't seem important back then.

"Rosie! Come on! I'm hungry! Let's go to Figs." Mary had called up again, shifting her weight from one leg to another because she had been sitting in meetings all day.

Rosie had run downstairs catching hold of the banister as she missed one step. She'd felt off kilter, as if she might cry, but she tried to hide it from her mother.

"Don't fall!" Mary had shouted, a bit too loud, sounding alarmed. Then seeing Rosie had regained her balance she laughed. "Come on! Let's go!"

When Rosie had been a little girl she had an imaginary friend called Lilly, and her mother still liked to tell her friends about Lilly when they had a party, and sometimes they actually asked Rosie about Lilly. Tales of Lilly ended any possibility there was of Rosie telling Mary any of her secrets. She'd told Sarah instead, knowing that Sarah would never tell. So she'd decided not to say anything about the emails she'd been writing back and forth to Sarah.

"There are stories you never tell," Sarah used to say, and Rosie thought it was strange that Sarah used to say that, given the stories she was now writing about when she was a child.

Rosie wondered if things would have turned out differently if she'd told her Mom when they went to Figs that she and Sarah had been writing to each other. Would that have made things better or worse? Rosie shuddered. If –

She closed her eyes tight and blocked the thought.

She thought about going to Figs with her Mom after her Dad had taken Sarah to the hospital. They'd shared a salad and waited for their spicy shrimp pizza. Rosie had told her mother about Big Pit and about the Blaina riots. Her mother had looked surprised and had been strangely quiet. Usually she helped Rosie organize her reports but on this occasion she'd just said, "I'm sure you'll write a good report."

"Do you know anything about Big Pit?"

"No." Mary had responded, too sharp, too quickly.

"What about the Blaina riots?"

"No." Mary had responded looking worried. "Did you ask your Dad?"

"No. He was in a meeting." Rosie had pulled a face, pretending she didn't notice the anxious look on her mother's face, "too busy to talk to me."

"Rosie," Mary had said, disapproving.

"Have you ever been to Wales?" Rosie had asked before she could stop herself.

"No," Mary had said, softly this time, her eyes dropping down to the red check tablecloth and then up at her daughter. "Let's talk about something else."

"What about Dad? Has he been to Wales?"

"Ask him."

"He's too busy to talk to me."

"That's not fair!"

"Yes it is! I called his office. His secretary said I could only speak to him if it was an emergency!" Rosie had leaned forward. "It is an emergency! Sarah wants to come home! Ask her!"

"Sarah's not well," Mary had said.

"Yes she is!" Rosie had said. "It's *you* that's not!"

"*Stop!*" Mary had said in a frantic whisper.

"Sarah says we're Welsh not English," Rosie had said, speaking quietly, her green eyes flashing at her mother.

"When did she say that?" Mary had asked, leaning forward across the table, the color draining from her face.

"On the phone," Rosie had said, regretting it immediately. "She called."

"On the phone," Mary had repeated. "She called?" Looking intently at Rosie she had picked up her glass of water and drank slowly. Then she'd put the glass down and smiled at Rosie as if nothing had happened, but Rosie was not about to let it go.

"We're not English are we?" Rosie had said, knowing her mother thought she was lying about the phone call.

Mary had sat, looking down at the red check tablecloth.

"Dad comes from Wales and so does Aunt Sarah. Why don't we have any photos of you and Dad when you were children? Why are there no photos of Aunt Sarah?"

"I don't know!" Mary had said, her eyes flashing now.

"Are you Welsh?"

"Stop interrogating me!" Mary had responded, smiling, eyes wide, telling Rosie to stop with a look that stretched back to when she was a little girl.

"Where were you born?" Rosie had asked loudly, standing up so quickly her chair had tipped backwards hitting the chair of the man was at the next table sitting behind her. "I don't even know where my mother comes from!"

Mary had stood up quickly and apologized to the man, who had turned around with an angry look on his face until he saw Mary, and then he'd smiled and said something about the impetuousness of youth, and they'd both laughed.

"Let's pay the bill and get some ice cream at the 7-Eleven," Mary had said, searching for her wallet. "Maybe I'll get some sorbet. I have stacks of student papers to read."

Rosie remembered walking home with her mother after the scene she'd made in Figs. Inexplicably they had held hands. She was not sure why. Perhaps they'd reached out and held hands because they'd been so angry at each other they'd both needed comforting. Rosie didn't know. She told herself not to over think it. This part of the story wasn't important, or at least, she didn't think it was at the time.

When they'd got home she'd run straight up the stairs. What Sarah had written to her had changed her life forever. At school Margaret Dorsey had told them to write their family story, but she didn't have one. She knew nothing about her "heritage", as Margaret called it. She knew she was first generation American and that her mother and father were "immigrants", but until now the word "immigrant" had not seemed to apply to them. Even her name seemed to have changed. She'd thought it would be like Jesse suddenly finding out that there was no "O" before "Malley". The spelling of Llywelyn hadn't changed, but her name was not the same. Even being "Rosie" was different, although she didn't know how different.

"Rosie!" her mother had called up the stairs. "Want some ice cream?"

"I'll have some tomorrow when I get home from school," Rosie had shouted back, getting up from her computer to close her bedroom door.

Remembering that her Mom had asked her if she wanted any ice cream when she'd got back from Figs just after Sarah had been hospitalized upset her.

"Ice cream?" she said out loud.

Rosie's cheeks were flushed. She felt confused. When did she go to Figs with her mother? Was it today that the golden retriever had slimed her in the park? Was it yesterday that her father had driven Sarah away in her old blue skirt and pinny? So much had happened, how did everything get so mixed–up?

"I won't be long," she heard her Aunt saying. "I'll come back soon."

"Rosie!" She heard her Dad shout. "No!"

"One–two–three!" Rosie was crying. "No! Four–five! No! No!"

When was today? Yesterday? She didn't know. How long was it since she had read the first story that Sarah had written? She sat down on the bed whispering "no" as images of the gaping black elevator shaft filled her head. She started sobbing, unable to cope with the rapid thoughts that came and went so fast she was not sure she was thinking them.

She lay down and pulled Max towards her and cuddled him.

Max got comfortable and started purring.

"Night Rosie," Mary had said, coming into Rosie's room after a gently knock. She'd wanted to say sorry to Rosie for what had happened at Figs but couldn't find the words. She did not want to speak and so she'd bent down and kissed Rosie on the forehead. "Try to sleep. I'm here if you need me."

"Thanks. I'm okay," Rosie had said to the empty space where her mother had stood, after Mary had left and shut the door.

"It's as if no one has died, or tried to commit suicide," she whispered, wide awake and in the present, "and everyone in our family is still alive".

Rosie's room was still filled with sun light in the late afternoon. She got off the bed and went over to her computer. She moved the mouse to get rid of the screen saver and logged on.

She'd saved Sarah's first story and she'd read it over and over, but she wanted to read it again, impulsively, compulsively, seeking comfort in the familiar that had once been so strange. She opened the folder that she had called "Umbrella". She closed her eyes thinking of Sarah in the hospital after all the terrible things that had happened. She desperately wanted Sarah to come home.

Each time she'd read the exchanges between them she'd learned something new. The first time she read the emails in Sarah's English voice, but after she'd read the first story it was Sarah's Welsh lilt that she could hear. Now, after that terrible night, she wanted to read what Sarah had written and hold on to her. Rosie clicked on the folder and then the email:

Hiya my lovely. I've written you a story. When I was at school I loved to write, but it's a long time since I've tried to put my thoughts on paper and I've never tried to write a story on a computer! I've called my story "Rosie's Umbrella."

The first time Rosie had read the words "Rosie's Umbrella" she had just stared at the screen and for a very long time she'd remained perfectly still. She could hear her Aunt Sarah talking to herself. "There's lovely!" "Never!" "Where's our Rosie's umbrella?" Rosie thought Sarah had written a story about her. In her mind Sarah's voice was so real to her that without thinking, she had turned and looked behind her as if Sarah might be standing there, talking instead of writing. Then she had gone back to the screen and typed:

I love you Aunt Sarah. Just tell me what's wrong!

Rosie had watched the screen and when no email had arrived she'd got out her chemistry homework. She had to write a research paper on one of the elements in the periodic tables and she worked on that while she waited. Somehow the analytic task so devoid of emotion held her attention and made it easier for her to wait for Sarah. Even so she checked her email every few minutes and was relieved when Sarah wrote back:

I can't tell you luvy. Each time I try to talk about it no words come out. Writing helps. I keep typing and then pressing delete. There isn't a single story there are many. I keep revising what I am writing. I am not sure what might have happened and what actually happened. I am trying to remember and all of a sudden something will come to me, a memory, like the cuckoo clock and I write it down. Sometimes my thoughts are too terrible to remember and so my mind hides what happened in the stories I am trying to write, like the one I am sending

you. When you read it you will learn a lot about your own history, your family. Please read it.

At the time Rosie had been sure it didn't have to be that complicated. Looking back she knew that it did. Now she felt as muddled as Sarah. She didn't know what she was imagining and what was real. For the first time she'd begun to understand why Sarah's memories had stayed hidden from her for so many years. When she'd first read the email in which Sarah had tried to explain how she'd felt, Rosie had written back:

> Sorry Aunt Sarah if I am impatient. I love you very much and I want to know what happened to you. I want you to come home. It's no fun here without you. Maybe if I read the story I will begin to understand.

Sarah wrote back quickly:

> I've written three stories Luvy. I keep adding to them. This is the first one. It was difficult to write. I found myself writing as if it had just happened but of course it was a long time ago. I was just a little girl. I've been trying to figure out how old I was when the story takes place. It must have been 1955, forty years ago, but I am not certain. It might have been a year earlier or a year later but no more than that. When I was at school I always found it hard when someone read a story I'd written. At least on a computer you can check your spelling. This is the story of Rosie's umbrella. But before you read it is important that you know that even though the story of Rosie's umbrella is very short it will change your life forever. I worry that your Dad will be cross that I have sent it to you. He could have told you himself and he didn't. I hope he won't be too angry with me for sharing my stories with you. After all, they are your stories too.

Rosie felt shivers down her spine as she opened up the attached file and printed the story. The first time she'd read the story on the computer screen, but since then she had always printed it. She didn't know why she always printed another copy. The first time made sense, then it had become part of the ritual of reading, now it was the counting, the compulsive reliving of a terrible moment.

"One – two –" Her heart was racing "– three – four–five –" She grabbed the back of the chair as she began to fall. "Rosie no!" she heard her Dad shouting. "Leave it!" Breath. Hold on. Keep your eyes closed. Breathe, breathe slowly, take a breath, and breathe. Shaken to her core, Rosie took the paper copy of the story from the printer and climbed on the bed with Max and pulled the comforter over her legs.

Rosie's Umbrella

"I need to go badly," Sarah whispered. Her legs were crossed and she had her I-can't-wait look on her face.

"But they're still there!" Rosie said as she took another look around the gate of our Nan's back yard. Gritting her teeth Rosie turned to face Sarah, "We'll have to go past them," she told her.

"No!" cried Sarah, both frightened and fierce at the same time.

"But you said you can't wait."

"I can't!"

"I have the umbrella," Rosie told her, "if we go quietly they may not see us."

"Do you think we could creep by?" Sarah asked hopefully.

"Yes," Rosie said, and then to encourage her a little more she added, "why don't we leave the bucket of water here, then if we have to run at least we won't get wet."

Sarah agreed.

"You go in front of me," Rosie told her, "and then if they come at us I can hold the umbrella behind us."

Sarah crept out and stood flat against the wall while Rosie slipped quietly through and lifted the latch to shut the gate. Sarah clutched the iron key and Rosie held tight to the old umbrella. They crossed the coal dust road that ran down the back of the houses and tried to look as if nothing was happening in case someone came out of a back gate. Then, as Sarah reached the old stone steps that led up the grassy bank, she stopped dead making clouds of coal dust as she dug her feet into the grit.

"They're watching us," Sarah said, too loud to go unnoticed.

"I know," Rosie whispered sharply, looking at the fat white geese that stood on the grass near the top of the steps looking harmless with their sideways glances and innocent stares.

Rosie slowly pushed in the metal catch that held the umbrella shut and gently opened it up.

"Go on," she urged.

Sarah slowly climbed the three stone steps and the geese turned their heads. One of them made a sound low in its throat and Sarah froze. Rosie climbed the steps behind her and gave her a push towards the row of lavatories that stood together just a few yards away from them. It was the push that did it. Instantly, the geese erupted with gaggling cries. They stretched their long necks and hissed as they ran at Rosie and Sarah's legs and pecked at their feet. Sarah made a run for it and Rosie followed holding the umbrella behind Sarah to stop them pecking her. Sarah took the big iron key, pushed it in the keyhole, and turned it in the lock. Then quickly lifting the latch, she pushed open the door and almost fell inside. Rosie turned to face the geese, and slowly closing the umbrella, she stepped back inside the lavatory and bolted the door.

They stood for a minute getting used to the darkness until the big white toilet with its smooth wooden seat was caught in a shaft of sunny light that slipped through a crack at the top of the door.

Sarah looked at the big white bowl and rolled her eyes, "I don't want to go now," she said.

Rosie groaned.

"I'm sorry," Sarah said.

"If we wait a minute you'll probably want to" Rosie said, and then in exasperation she pulled down her pants and sat down. "If you won't, I will," she told Sarah as she peed in the hole.

Sarah grinned and pulled down her pants, waiting her turn. Then as Rosie got off she got on, and she sat swinging her feet way up from the floor.

"Well," Rosie said, "you're up there on the throne, now do something quick."

"I want you to wait outside," Sarah said.

"Sarah! Hurry up! I went with you in here!"

Rosie turned her back and hummed a tune.

"Finished," Sarah said, jumping down.

"Now let's get out of here," Rosie said, "We still have to bring the bucket of water."

As Sarah pulled up her pants, Rosie slid the bolt back quietly and opened the door. Then she closed it quickly.

"They're still there?" Sarah asked in disbelief.

"Right outside the door."

"I'm not going out!"

"Alright! We'll stay here!"

And there they stayed feeling foolish and unhappy. They stood in silence hoping the geese would waddle off but they stood guard outside the door waiting for it to open and for them to come out.

Rosie and Sarah watched the coal dust floating in the shaft of light. They talked about nice things, like going on the bus to Abergavenny market with their Mam, and climbing the Coity Mountain with their Dad when he came home to Wales.

Then old Florrie Lewis unlocked the toilet next to their Nan's, and they listened to her as she coughed and peed and poured a bucket of water down the hole. But when she left and Rosie and Sarah looked outside, the geese were still there all fat, innocent, and clean.

"Why didn't they chase Florrie Lewis?" Sarah asked.

"They're waiting for us," Rosie replied.

"That's not fair!"

"I don't think Florrie Lewis is afraid of them," Rosie told Sarah.

"But she's not afraid of anything!" Sarah replied, not understanding what Rosie was saying.

"That's not it" Rosie said, "The geese don't chase Florrie Lewis because *they know* she's not afraid."

Sarah paused, "I think they chase us because we only come here in the summer."

"Maybe."

"They think we're not Welsh," Sarah added gloomily.

"That's silly Sarah. Those geese don't know anything about us except that we're afraid of them."

Sarah turned away and looked through a crack in the door. Then she shifted her position to look down the row to their Nan's back gate.

"It's Gwenny," Sarah told Rosie, "She's coming out of our Nan's. She's looking over here."

"Don't call her!" Rosie said in acute embarrassment. "I don't want her to know we're frightened of the geese."

"I can't see her," Sarah continued with her running commentary. "She must be coming up the steps."

"Shoo! Go on! Shoo!" Gwenny shouted, clapping her hands as she ran at the geese.

"Rosie Llywelyn? Are you in there?" Gwenny asked, the lilt in her voice making her question sound like a melody.

"Is that you Gwenny?" Rosie called, casual like, with a bit of a lilt. "Just a minute. Sarah's stuck on the toilet."

"Rosie!" Sarah squealed indignantly.

Rosie put her hand over Sarah's mouth and called, "We're just coming." And then she opened the door and we stepped out squinting at the bright sunlight.

Gwenny saw their squints and smiled."You must have been in there a long time," she said, as she looked up the back at the waddling geese. But then she looked at us with a puzzled look.

"What are you doing with that old umbrella?" she asked.

"Keeping out of the sun," Rosie said, putting up the umbrella and standing in the shade.

When Rosie had read Sarah's story the first time she'd smiled when she read the first sentence. Sarah often used to laugh so much she had to rush to the bathroom. But the second sentence had taken her smile away. For a moment Rosie had thought she was the "Rosie" in the story, but she quickly realized that she was not. On the screen in front of her was another Rosie, but their first name and last name were the same. Suddenly finding out that there was another Rosie Llywelyn had been difficult for Rosie to take in.

Each time she'd read the story she had more questions to ask, but the first time she'd read it she immediately focused on Rosie's umbrella, not her own umbrella, but on the umbrella that belonged to the other Rosie. She had thought about Sarah screaming hysterically "that's not our Rosie's umbrella" and knocking the wind out of her when she pushed her against the wall in the hallway down stairs. She'd read the last two sentences over and over.

"What are you doing with that old umbrella?"

"Keeping out of the sun."

When Rosie had read the story for the first time she had suddenly understood why Sarah had got so upset, and why she'd never go anywhere without the old black umbrella with the curved wooden handle that she'd bought at the thrift store on Charles.

"Where's our Rosie's umbrella?" Sarah had kept asking, even when the sun was shining. "What umbrella?" Rosie had asked. Sarah had never really answered and, except for that time in the hall, all she ever said was, "For our walk, of course, my lovely, for our walk."

A few days after Sarah had got stuck in the elevator Rosie had asked her mother if she could take Sarah for a walk.

"Make sure you hold her hand," Mary had whispered to Rosie. "Don't let her wander off." Then Mary had turned to Sarah, "Now Sarah, hold Rosie's hand," she said. "I don't want you to lose her."

Sarah had laughed, but there were tears in her eyes. "Never!" she'd said. "I'd never lose our lovely girl."

And Mary had suddenly looked flustered as if she'd said something inappropriate, but she'd laughed too and Rosie, not knowing why they had suddenly seemed distressed, had laughed with them.

Together they'd walked down Pinckney Street, Rosie holding her Aunt Sarah's hand and Sarah holding her old umbrella. On Louisburg Square Rosie had shown Sarah the hidden gate into the private garden that just looked like part of the railings. Sarah had admired the gate as if she'd never seen it before, and she had held Rosie's hand tight and told her not to go inside.

"Keep away from the edge," she'd said. "Don't get too close."

They'd cut across to Mount Vernon Street and walked down

onto Charles Street and waited at the light before going across the road to Rebecca's Bakery. Sarah did not want to sit inside and so they'd sat with their coats wrapped around them outside on a bench shivering as they ate chocolate and vanilla ice cream. Then they'd walked along Charles towards the Public Gardens.

Sarah had looked in the windows of antique stores at old china dogs and porcelain statues. "There's lovely," Sarah had said, over and over again, and then to Rosie, "don't you think they're beautiful!"

But when they'd reached the Public Gardens and walked through the big iron gates, Sarah had become upset and she'd clutched Rosie's hand tight.

"They're watching us!" she'd said in a fierce whisper.

Sarah had let go of Rosie's hand and frantically tried to put up the umbrella.

"Who's watching us?" Rosie had asked, grabbing her Aunt's hand.

"The geese, the geese!"Sarah had said, over and over, in a whisper that grew louder until it became a screech then a scream.

Ahead of them children were playing around the bronze statues of the ducklings in Robert McCloskey's famous story. As they'd walked along the path Rosie tried to sooth Sarah.

"They're statues Aunt Sarah, they won't hurt you," she'd said.

"I don't like them!" Sarah had shouted, waving her umbrella. "I want to go home!" Then Sarah had started sobbing, "I don't want to go! I don't want to go!" A baby started to cry as Sarah had begun to scream, and mothers picked up their small children and moved away from her.

An older woman had been walking towards them along the path she'd smiled kindly at Rosie and touched her arm. "Can I help?"

"No" Rosie had said to the woman, adding a distracted "thank you" as Sarah's screams subsided into grief stricken moans. "It's okay Aunt Sarah," Rosie had said, "It's okay." She'd turned and walked back towards the entrance of the Public Gardens, pulling Sarah who had seemed to have trouble walking away from the statues of the ducks, and away from the mothers clutching their children,

"It's okay, it's okay, let's go home. It's okay," Rosie had said, over and over, "It's okay."

"Yes," Sarah had said sweetly, closing the umbrella as if nothing had happened. "Maybe we'll see Gwenny Morgan on our way home."

"Gwenny Morgan," Rosie had whispered to herself, the first time she reached the end of the story. After the connection she'd made between the other Rosie and the umbrella, Gwenny had been the next connection that Rosie had made between what was happening now and what had happened in Wales so long ago. Perhaps she was able to make the connection because Gwenny did not seem to be so painfully linked to her own life.

Back then Gwenny meant nothing to her, except that her Aunt had mentioned her on that day when she had been so frightened when she saw the ducks in the Public Gardens. For Rosie this connection helped her find her way into the story. Once that happened her head was filled with questions that she wanted to ask her Aunt Sarah. She'd jumped off her bed and sat down at her computer, opened up her email, and pressed reply to the email that Sarah had sent with the story attached, and began to type:

> If Rosie Llywelyn is your sister Aunt Sarah then she must be my Aunt. Why haven't I met her? Why didn't you tell me about her? Why didn't Dad tell me? She's his sister too! Why doesn't she come and visit us? She's never even sent me a birthday card? Why hasn't my father ever mentioned her? She must have done something terrible. Is that why Mom and Dad don't talk about her?

When she'd first asked all these questions Rosie had pressed send and waited for Sarah's response, but in the late afternoon as she sat waiting for her mother she continued reading, searching for any nuance in the small and seemingly insignificant threads of the story about the lives of her two Aunts that were woven together creating the pattern for her own life, which she did not get to choose.

She wanted to know what had happened to them, but she also wanted to know what was happening to her, as their story became a part of her own story.

"Find your own truth," she whispered, again thinking of Jesse and Margaret, *and* Rachel she thought to herself. "Don't forget Rachel." After a moment she re-read Sarah's response to her questions:

> I'm sorry, Luvy. My memory isn't working well. It's like Swiss cheese, full of holes. Some things I had completely forgotten I am suddenly remembering. The doctor said I've suppressed memories that are too painful to remember. All I can do is ask you not to jump to conclusions. Go slowly. You've lived with me all these years you have to trust me. Give me time to work it out. I can't suddenly be expected to remember everything that happened when I didn't remember anything, not a thing, for so many years.

When she'd first read what her Aunt had written Rosie knew

she was asking too many questions and that Sarah was upset.

> **I know our Rosie would want me to tell you about her, that's partly why I am writing these stories. Mostly, I am trying to understand what happened myself. I have to go. It's late. I'm sure your mother will be up soon to make sure you are in bed going to sleep and not at your computer. One last memory before I go. I keep remembering that our Nan, your Great Nana's belly wobbled when she laughed. She would laugh and I would laugh at her wobbling then we would both laugh and laugh. Sweet dreams my darling girl. I'll write again tomorrow. Love you lots, Aunt Sarah**

Rosie imagined her Great Grandmother laughing. She felt a tremendous sense of longing to have known her, and to have laughed at her laughing, just like Sarah and her sister, Rosie. She tried to focus on the questions she had asked Sarah. Rosie realized now that her questions must have been very upsetting when Sarah had first read them. She wondered if the doctors had known Sarah was sending her the stories she was writing. "Probably not," she thought. When she'd received the first story she'd decided not to share it with her parents.

Sarah's emails had made her realize that something terrible had happened to Rosie. In a way Sarah had answered her questions early on by the things she did not write, and after reading "Rosie's Umbrella" she'd known deep inside that the real Rosie Llywelyn was dead.

"Can I come in?" Mary had asked, as she'd opened the door an hour or two after the disastrous dinner in Figs. "Are you still working?" Rosie's mother had pretended to be surprised. "I just talked to your Dad, he said he'll be home tomorrow. Come on, get into bed or you'll never get up in the morning."

Rosie had just read Sarah's story for the first time and remembering now she smiled when she re-read Sarah's "your mother will be up soon to make sure you are in bed" at the exact moment that Mary had walked into the room.

Rosie had quickly closed her email and got up and walked over to the bed and gathered up the pages of the story of "Rosie's Umbrella" that were scattered on the bed after Max had been lying on them.

"Goodness," Mary had said as she saw the typed pages in Rosie's hand. "You've written a lot. Can I read it?"

"Not yet," Rosie had replied, putting the story in a folder, which she shoved into her backpack. "I haven't written much. All I have so far is some stuff I got off the Internet." She had dropped her backpack on the floor and walked into the bathroom to brush her teeth.

"Did you find a lot about Wales?"

"More than I expected," Rosie had said, splashing warm water on her face.

"What's wrong with the soap?"

"Bad for my skin. Can I have some Apricot Scrub? Rachel uses it, and she say's it's great." And then, as casually as she could, Rosie had asked, "Do you know why Aunt Sarah keeps looking for my umbrella?"

"No," Mary had responded, too quickly again and sounding a bit irritated, but trying not to repeat the scene in Figs. She had picked Max up off the bed and put him on the blue rug, folded the comforter and put it on a chair. She smoothed the wrinkles out of Rosie's bottom sheet and she was just plumping the pillows when Rosie had run across the room and jumped on the bed.

"I just wondered," Rosie had said, trying to sound nonchalant, "about the umbrella, I mean."

"It's one of Sarah's eccentricities, I suppose," Mary had said, smiling at Rosie as she covered her with a sheet. She went into the bathroom and came back with the light cotton blanket from the linen cupboard. "Your comforter is much too hot," she'd said, "you'll never sleep." She'd unfolded the blanket and Rosie watched as it floated down onto her bed. She'd smiled at her mother, and Mary had kissed her on the cheek and softly tiptoed out of the room as if Rosie were already asleep.

"I know," Rosie had whispered to Max, as he jumped back on the bed and padded about until he made himself comfortable. "Don't jump to conclusions." Max had curled up at Rosie's feet. "But if Sarah was frightened of geese when she was a little girl, doesn't that explain what happened when we went to the Public Gardens?" Rosie had lain very still, then she'd quickly sat up and said to Max, "It also explains why she kept asking for Rosie's umbrella." Max had looked at her as if he'd understood, but she'd not lost touch with reality enough to believe that he did.

Rosie had shivered. She could feel the blood beating silently in her wrists and temples. For a moment she'd felt unable to move. She'd looked around as if she might find the other Rosie Llywelyn hidden somewhere in her room, but every shadow was familiar. Nothing was strange. She'd reached over to turn on the bedside light, and even though it was hot she got out of bed and took her comforter off the chair. Shivering she shook it out and wrapped it around herself. She thought of her mother and the cotton blanket floating down on top of her and the one night merged with the other, past and present, wrapped up together, indistinguishable in her head.

Rosie had curled up on top of the bed safe inside her comforter and Max had rearranged himself, cuddling up beside her, purring. She thought of Sarah in the psychiatric unit at the hospital and the other Rosie Llywelyn. Her life would never be the same again.

Sarah had been right. Reading the story of Rosie's umbrella had changed her life, but she didn't understand how knowing about the past would change what happened in the future. All she wanted was for Sarah to come home. How could a story make that happen? "Be patient," she'd said to herself, as she drifted off to sleep. Then, in a faraway voice that seemed to bounce around in her head, she'd heard herself saying, "But what happened to Rosie Llywelyn? How did she die? Is she really dead?"

At school, Rosie's class had met in groups to share their research. In the last few weeks Rosie had realized how much she enjoyed the ordinariness of school, even if her parents did pay a lot of money to send her there. She was in eighth grade, but she had been at the school since kindergarten and it was familiar and safe. She had known some of the students since she was in first grade and she had some friends, including Jesse O'Malley who had been in kindergarten with her. His father was a partner in the same law firm as Rosie's father. Jesse said he was studying Irish legends and myths. He had talked about the mythical Irish warrior Fionn Mac-Cumhaill, and of Cúchulainn and the hound of Culann, but he had less information about Ireland than he had about Wales.

Jesse had made it sound as if he had just stumbled across the information, but everyone in his group knew that it must have taken him hours, and none of them missed the way he'd smiled at

Rosie when he told her about Owain Glyndwr. He'd talked about stone cannon balls and then said he'd found a reference to Harlech Castle in some writing that was done in 1468. Jesse had made a photocopy of the writing, which he gave to Rosie.

> "Kyng Edward," wrote the chronicler John Warkworth,
> "was possessed of alle Englonde, excepte a castelle in Northe Wales called Harlake."

Rosie had shown the writing to the rest of her group, and on another day they would have joked with her about the attention she was receiving from Jesse, but she was white faced and there were dark shadows beneath her eyes.

"Is everything okay?" Rachel Gordon had whispered.

Rosie had nodded. "I'm fine."

"I also found this," Jesse had said, continuing with his show and tell. He'd held up another piece of paper on which he'd written "Llyncodd y llygod y llaeth."

"It's a Welsh tongue twister," he'd explained.

"What does it say?" Rachel had asked.

"The rats swallowed the milk!" Jesse had said, making noises in his throat and putting his hands around his neck as if he was being strangled.

Rosie had laughed and Jesse grinned. Rosie had told him that her Aunt Sarah was in the hospital. He'd known Sarah Llywelyn since he was five years old and he'd been to the Llywelyn's house many times when he was younger to play with Rosie. Sarah had always helped them make forts under the kitchen table so they could play while she baked cookies for them to eat.

So when Jesse stopped by one day with some papers from his Dad for Rosie's father just after Sarah got stuck in the elevator, he'd not been prepared for how fragile Sarah had become or how strange. Sarah had smiled at him as she always had, but there were tears in her vacant eyes, and she'd kept repeating over and over, "Where's our Rosie?" "Have you seen our Rosie?" and Rosie would say, "I'm here," and "It's okay," and Jesse had not known what to do or what to say.

Rosie was so grateful to Jesse for helping her with her research on Wales. Her Dad had said Jesse was a "brilliant boy" and destined for a law degree from Harvard, but Rosie just couldn't see it. Jesse? A lawyer like her Dad? Or like Jesse's father? He was cleverer than that, even if he was not clever enough to tell her how much he liked her. He'd kissed her once on the mouth, but he puckered up as if he was kissing his mother or sister, and his lips had smacked together making a loud sound that had made her laugh, and he'd got upset because she'd not taken him seriously, and he'd not tried again, even though he thought she might like another kiss, especially if he put his tongue in her mouth.

"In English it's unusual for there to be two "L's" together at the beginning of a word. Can you think of any examples?" Rosie had heard Margaret saying to Rachel. Margaret, who liked her students to call her by her first name, looked around at the students in her class, "Anyone? A word beginning with two ll's in English?"

"My name," Rosie had said, before Jesse got a chance.

"Llywelyn," Margaret had smiled. "I believe Llywelyn is a very old spelling of a very old Welsh name. Have you found out anything about your family's Welsh ancestry Rosie?"

"I didn't even know my name was Welsh until yesterday."

"How did you find out?"

"You told me," Rosie had said, sounding irritated. She liked Margaret but sometimes she bothered her. "You were talking about us studying the history of our names and the countries our names came from. You said Llywelyn was a Welsh name."

"Your parents have never talked to you about Wales?" Margaret hadn't forgotten. It had never occurred to her that Rosie might not know her family was Welsh. She had smiled, ignoring that Rosie was annoyed with her.

"No," Rosie had snapped. "My Dad grew up near London, in Ashford, Kent. I always thought he was English. That's all I know."

"And your mother?"

"She was adopted when she was five."

Margaret had nodded, hiding her concern. She knew Sarah had been hospitalized and that Rosie was having a difficult time. She'd shifted topics. "Tell us what you've found out about Wales."

Rosie had talked about Big Pit and the Blaina riots. She'd been surprised to find that the rest of her group was interested in what she had to say. She'd told her group that the miners were so poor that they didn't even have bathrooms in their houses. She had explained that their toilets were outside and that they used to have to carry buckets of water with them to the outhouses, which were sometimes halfway up a hillside. She'd been surprised at how "Rosie's Umbrella" had helped her with her research, which she was not thinking about when she read and re-read the story. She had taken pleasure in sharing the information about the miners that was such a complicated part of her own history.

"If they didn't have bathrooms, where did they shower?"

"How did they wash their clothes?"

One of the girls held her nose.

"Your questions are going to have to wait until tomorrow," Margaret had said. She never ceased to be amazed at how childlike and how grownup her students could be. Silly, serious and sad, that's how she'd describe the thirteen and fourteen year olds she'd taught for so many years, but with big hearts and insights into life that were often as profound as they themselves were endearing. She'd been pleased that Rosie had gathered so much detailed information about miners' lives.

"Rosie maybe you can find out more about how the miners and their families lived," she'd said. "It's important that we go beyond what history books tell us about castles. No offense Jesse. We do need to know about the great achievements of men like Owain Glyndwr, but we also need to know about the histories of local people." Always focused on getting students to work together, Margaret had continued, "Rosie, you could make a strong contribution to your group if you produced a report on the lives of coal mining families in South Wales."

After school Rachel had walked home with Rosie through the Public Gardens. Rachel's mother was going to pick her up at Rosie's house around six. On Friday afternoons in summer the Gardens were always filled with people. Tourists from other countries had been taking photographs, mothers and fathers playing with their young children, men and women in business suits walking leisurely home, college students sitting under trees writing in the margins of their text books and, even on this unseasonably chilly day, couples had been lying on the grass, some of them kissing.

Rosie had pointed out the Beacon Hill Dogs' Club to Rachel.

"They meet every day," she'd told Rachel, "So their dogs can play."

They'd walked along Charles to CVS at the other end of the street. In the store they'd made their way to the aisle where beauty products were on display.

"This is what I use," Rachel had told Rosie, taking a pretty plastic container of Apricot Scrub off the shelf.

"Okay, I'm going to get it." Rosie took the Apricot Scrub and dug in her pocket for the money she had brought with her.

"Wait," Rachel had said. "I want to look at the eye shadows. My Mom said when she was young she used to buy *Maybelline*."

Rosie's mother didn't wear make-up. Mary had red-brown curls like Rosie, and they both had green eyes and freckles. Her father was always teasing them. He said the only difference between them was that Mary had laughter lines around her eyes and Rosie had more freckles. Rachel's mother didn't have any freckles. She wore mascara and carefully applied eye shadow and she used a lip liner to shape her beigy-pink lips. Rosie thought Rachel's mother was beautiful.

"Your mother lets you wear her eye shadow?" Rosie had asked, trying not to sound surprised.

"Not out!" Rachel had laughed. "But she doesn't mind if I experiment. She gave me some money to get some. I think she's fed up with me using hers." Rachel had spoken in a deep voice and tried to sound as sophisticated as her Parisian Argentinian mother. "Rachel. *Chanel* is too expensive for you to play with. Go to CVS and get some make-up of your own."

"She told you to go to CVS?"

"No. Not really. But she did say that when she was young she used to practice putting on make-up. "

The two girls bent down in front of the Maybelline display stand and had looked at the eye shadows beneath the liquid foundations and the mascaras. The eye shadows came in tiny plastic compacts, which contained two, four or six tiny palettes of color.

Bright and soft blues, deep greens, light browns, dozens of colors, even an iridescent shocking pink which Rosie thought would make anyone wearing it look sick.

"How do you choose?" she'd asked Rachel.

"I don't know. Let's take this one." Rachel had picked a palette with four colors in it. She'd read, "Iced Raisin, Ruby Shimmer, Silver Surf and Pink Opal. They sound like the names of a rock group."

"You're Iced Raisin and I'm Ruby Shimmer," Rosie had laughed.

Rachel had also picked out a black mascara and the two friends paid for their purchases. Then they'd run in and out between the people on Charles, up Pinckney, slowing down only when they were out of breath halfway up Pinckney by Louisburg Square.

"Don't you think it's strange that you don't know anything about your family history?" Rachel had asked, without realizing that in the last few weeks this had become a real problem for Rosie.

"I know more about your history than I do my own," Rosie had said.

Rachel was Jewish. Her father's Grandparents emigrated to the United States before the Russian Revolution in 1917. One of her Great Aunts had written about her Great Grandparents life in Russia, about the pogroms, and how they had fled to the United States. Her mother, who was also Jewish, met her father in Paris where she was studying at the Sorbonne. Her family was originally from Russia, but they had emigrated to Argentina where she'd grown up knowing nothing but privilege. Now there was no one left in Buenos Aires where they had made their home. Rachel's mother never went back to Argentina, and Rachel's Great Aunts and Uncles had all come to the US so that all the family could be together.

Rosie often stayed over at Rachel's house, and every year she was invited to their Seder. In CVS Rosie had suddenly felt a connection to Rachel and her family that she'd never felt before. She had a sense of longing and loss that she had never had before. It was as if her family history had been erased and they'd been left un-memorable. She imagined that Rachel's family must have similar feelings, but she did not try to share these thoughts with Rachel. She'd no idea how she would put them into words. She knew Rachel couldn't imagine not having a history. She also knew that Rachel felt sorry for her and it made her uncomfortable, as if there was something wrong with her.

"Come on," Rachel had said, running past the workmen's trucks, "what are you going to try first, the Iced Raisin or the Ruby Shimmer?"

"All of them!" Rosie had laughed, running after her friend.

"That's why your Mom doesn't want you to wear make-up!"

When Mary had come home Rosie and Rachel were sitting in front of the television in the downstairs den, eating large bowls of mint chocolate chip-ice cream, and wearing Silver Surf and Pink Opal eye shadow and lots of mascara.

"What do you think?" Rosie had asked her mother, looking at her through thick black lashes.

"We thought the Ruby Shimmer was too much," Rachel had said, hoping that Rosie's mother wasn't going to be upset with them.

"Don't move!" was all Rosie's mother had said, "I want to take a picture!" And with that she had gone upstairs to her office to get her camera. Mary had not seen her daughter smile in weeks and she felt a rush of relief.

Rosie had smiled at Rachel, and when her mother came back down the two friends were sitting on the couch together. Both giddy and silly, they had posed with their tongues out and their eyes crossed while Mary took a picture.

"Now a smiley one that I can give to your mother, Rachel."

The two girls had smiled. Rosie's green eyes surrounded by Silver Surf and Rachel's brown eyes edged in Pink Opal.

"You are both very beautiful," Mary had told them, and for a moment Rosie thought her mother was going to cry.

"Go get some ice cream," Rachel had said to Mary. "There's time. My mother is picking me up at six."

They had just finished their bowls of ice cream when they heard a car horn. Rachel's mother was outside and her green Mercedes was blocking the road, and there were several cars behind her. Another horn honked repeatedly. It was a taxi driver. They'd rushed outside and Rachel had run around the front of the Mercedes and jumped in next to her mother.

A quick "hello" and a quick "thank you."

"I hope Rosie will come and stay with us this summer when we go to the Cape," Rachel's mother had called out as she put the car into gear and moved slowly off down the narrow street.

Rosie and her mother had been still standing there when the honking taxi had stopped and Tom Llywelyn had climbed out with his briefcase and a suitcase. They'd waited while he paid the taxi driver and asked for a receipt.

"Sorry," Rosie's Dad had said, with a weary smile as the taxi driver ignored the speed bumps and sped away. "There was no need for him to sound his horn." He'd rushed out of a meeting in New York, into a cab to LaGuardia, onto the Delta shuttle to Boston, into a cab, sat in traffic in the Callahan Tunnel and finally crossed Cambridge Street onto Beacon Hill.

"Long day," he'd said. He was a tall grey haired man who was once skinny like Rosie, but now was slightly overweight. He had taken off his suit jacket in the taxi, and his tie was pulled loose and his shirt collar undone.

"You look beautiful," he'd said to Rosie, noticing her eye shadow for the first time. He'd given her a quizzical look as he stooped to pick up his briefcase and suitcase. "I hope you didn't go to school like that."

"Of course not," Rosie had said.

Sarah at the back of her father's car waving at her flashed through Rosie's mind creating an unwanted space for the elevator shaft to fill her head.

Rosie compulsively began to count.

"One - two –!" Memory on top of memory. "Three-four –!" "Black hole gaping. "Five–six– Rosie! No! Leave it!"

Rosie covered her face with her hands. She wanted to sleep, but she was stuck in a wakeful state of rapid thoughts and the reluctant desire to remember, in case, like Sarah, she should forget.

After Rachel had gone, Rosie had washed her face with the Apricot Scrub and changed out of her jeans. There was no time for her to check her email before they'd left. They were going to *Toscano*'s on Charles for dinner. When Rosie had come downstairs her mother was standing in the hall wearing a green sleeveless blouse and black silk pants putting on her best black coat. Rosie had thought she looked lovely, even if she didn't wear make-up. Rosie had on a short denim skirt, a white T-shirt, and she was carrying a grey sweatshirt.

"Is that what you're wearing?" her mother had asked.

"She looks just fine," her Dad had said.

"Let's go," Rosie's mother had said, smiling and shaking her head.

Together they'd walked down Pinckney under the trees and in the glow of the light from the hundred year old gas lamps that never went out. At the bottom of the hill they'd turned left on Charles past Gary Drug to Toscano's, where they'd been greeted like old friends. They'd made their way between diners who talked and joked, their faces lit up in the candlelight. They'd sat at a table near the window, which Rosie loved because she could watch the people passing by on the street. The waitress had recited a long list of "specials" as she always did, and had waved her hands expansively as she described each special dish. Rosie had watched, admiring her long silver fingernails, and she'd decided that she would get some silver nail polish the next time Rachel came over. Her father ordered a bottle of red wine, one of his favorites, and a soda for Rosie, and a large plate of antipasto, as he often did to share while they waited for their dinners.

They ate as if nothing had happened, as if Sarah had left for her night shift at the hospital. Rosie's parents had talked about work, her mother's faculty meetings and her father's lawsuits and depositions. Rosie had stared out at the people who walked along the street. She had thought about Sarah in the hospital and about the other Rosie Llywelyn, the real one, not her. She'd wondered if it would be too late to write to her Aunt Sarah when she got home. She had looked at her parents and for the first time she saw them as strangers, separate from herself, distant, unknown and unknowing. Even though she was sure Rosie Llywelyn was dead, she had tried to imagine her living in Australia, growing old without her family, or like Rachel's mother in the United States while everything that happened to her as a child was in Argentina. Like Sarah, she'd thought, with her childhood memories of Wales, only Sarah's memories of what had happened to Rosie Llywelyn were too painful to remember.

"Maybe she's in prison." Rosie had thought, considering the possibility. If she'd done something terrible that would explain why her family never spoke about her. "Maybe they cast her out and vowed never to mention her name again," she'd said to herself, sounding like Beth in *Little Women*. "But if she'd done something terrible why did they give me her name?"

"How's school?" her father had asked, not once but twice, before she realized he was speaking to her.

"I'm going to trace our family history back to Wales," Rosie had said, looking at her father, watching him intently as he drank some wine and put down his glass.

"I heard. What have you found out?" He had been unable to resist asking, even though he'd known he was going to regret it.

Rosie had thought it was a loaded question. "Margaret wants us to study our family histories and so I'm going to find out something about my Welsh ancestry. I didn't even know that Llywelyn was a Welsh name." Rosie looked directly at her Dad. "Why didn't you tell me your family came from Wales?"

The "my-your" separation had not been lost on Tom. Rosie had disconnected, at least to some degree. Their waitress arrived before he had time to think through how to respond.

"Your entrées are on the way." she had said, as she picked up the empty antipasto dish. She'd smiled at Rosie. "Would you like another soda?"

"No thank you."

Rosie's question had reverberated in Tom's head, bringing back memories of events that he had spent his whole life trying to forget. It would have been easier if he'd suppressed them like Sarah, but when he was tired what had happened would come back. He'd lived with the horror of it his entire adult life.

Tom had leaned back in his chair staring blankly at a painting of an Italian farmhouse that hung on the whitewashed wall of the restaurant. Rosie had been surprised by the expression on her father's face and she had waited a moment before, disregarding how sick he looked, she'd asked again, "Why didn't you tell me?"

Tom had tried to fathom out if Rosie was asking him about Wales or about what had happened in Wales. What had she found out? Had Sarah talked to her before she was hospitalized? No. Sarah wasn't making any sense. But he was sure that Rosie knew something. She wasn't just asking innocent questions. Old memories banished rational thought. He was back in Wales. A boy. There was laughter. His sister smiled at him. *Rosie!* There were screams. Angry voices. He was breathing rapidly and he could feel a tightness in his chest. He'd reached for his wine but changed his mind and drank some water instead.

The waitress had returned with their dinners.

"Wonderful!" Mary had said, looking at the waitress and smiling

For a moment they'd sat in silence.

"I know more about Rachel's family than I do my own," Rosie had suddenly said, sounding petulant, but her voice faded away as she looked again at her father's face. He'd looked the way he had when she had fallen off her bicycle and hit her head on the pavement and the doctor in the emergency room had said she had a concussion. He'd looked like that, anxious and apprehensive. He'd asked if she was going to be all right. He'd been afraid. It was that kind of look only worse.

The pain in Tom's chest had subsided but he was sweating

and he did not feel well. Mary had reached across the table and put her hand on his. It was not Rosie's fault. *He* had asked her about school and now she was just asking him a question for her school project. That was all.

"There's not much to tell," he'd said, shrugging his shoulders. "You know that I grew up in England. You know that your Grandfather worked in a bank in Ashford, in Kent." He'd looked at Rosie and given her a worn out smile. "What more do you want to know?" But Rosie had known that he was cutting her off. His "there's-nothing-more-to-tell" answer had been too simple. She'd known he was really saying, "Don't ask me about Wales. I won't answer your questions."

"I don't understand," Rosie had said, ignoring her father and challenging her mother. "Why won't Dad answer my questions?" And then, knowing it would cause trouble but unable to stop herself, Rosie had blurted out, "Why did you tell me it was okay to ask Dad about Wales if you knew it would make him angry?"

Mary had wanted to slap Rosie. "Eat!" she'd scolded. "Eat!" She'd looked at Tom. Her eyes had filled with tears. She'd shaken her head and taken her hand off his, but he had quickly caught it and had held on to it, and as her hand came to rest on the table he had covered it with his own.

Rosie had watched the color rise on her mother's face. She could feel her remorse, hear her silent apology. She'd looked across at her father and even though she'd no idea what he was thinking she knew that his message to her mother was that it was okay, and for the first time she'd understood how much he loved Mary.

Rosie had remembered her Dad had once told her that when you love someone you don't need words to communicate. He had said that sometimes words just get in the way. She had been teasing him because he was so quiet, and he never talked for the sake of talking. At the time she'd thought he was just making an excuse for all those times when he'd seemed to be ignoring her, but now she suddenly understood what he'd meant. He didn't need words to communicate with her mother and her mother didn't need words to communicate with him. It was almost as if they were one person and she knew that there was nothing she could do or say that would ever come between them.

Rosie had tried to imagine the silent conversation that was taking place but couldn't. She'd decided they shared a secret they would not tell, a secret so unspeakable, so devastating, that it separated her from them. She'd felt lonely and, although she would never admit it, she'd felt afraid.

"What could Rosie Llywelyn have done?" Rosie had asked herself, side stepping her fear that she was dead. "Why won't they talk about her?" But she still did not tell them about the email messages she'd received. Instead she'd filled the silence with a less threatening question.

"But if Grandad's name is Llywelyn he must have come from Wales."

Even so it had been too much for her mother. "Rosie!" Mary had thrown her daughter an exasperated look. "Let's talk about this another time!"

Tom had taken a deep breath. "Your Grandfather left Wales after the Second World War, when he came back from North Africa in 1946." His voice was low and tight as he tried to stay in control and not shout at Rosie. He'd wanted to push his chair back and walk out of the restaurant, but he tried to keep calm. Mechanically he'd taken a bread roll from the basket and he'd broken a piece off and put it in his mouth.

After a few moments he'd continued. "There was nothing to go back to," he'd said, which was true. "He didn't want to work in the coal mines. He'd been to the grammar school, which was unusual at that time. Grammar schools were – are – the equivalent of our high schools." He'd known that he was rambling, just filling the conversation with left over words. "Dad went. Most of his friends didn't. They left school when they were fourteen and went down the mines."

Tom had picked up his glass of wine and drank. "Anyway, he got a job selling insurance in London. Then he moved to Ashford in Kent where he worked in a bank. That's all there is to it. There's nothing more to tell. End of story."

"What about my Grandmother?"

"He married her before the Second World War. She left Wales with him in 1946, and as you know she died in 1956."

"How did she die?"

"Rosie, that's enough!" her mother had said, ending the conversation. "Eat your dinner or we'll just have to leave and take you home."

"I'd like another soda," Rosie had said, letting her mother know that she was going to stop asking questions.

Back home Rosie had turned on her computer and checked her email. There had been two messages. The first was from Rachel:

hey ruby shimmer girl! r u coming to the cape? we're going soon as school ends ... hope u can come!! ice raisin.

Rosie had smiled, for a few seconds she forgot what was happening to her family and thought about her friend. Rachel's parents had a big old rambling summer-house right on the beach and she loved staying with them. The house was always filled with her mother and father's distant cousins and ancient Aunts, who came from Russia in 1905 before the revolution and from Poland and Czechoslovakia after the Second World War.

Sometimes there were old Aunts from Argentina who now lived close by, elegant and beautiful, even if they were ancient and frail. They spoiled Rachel and made a fuss of Rosie. They sat on the verandas of the big old house telling stories to anyone who would listen to them. Rachel and Rosie always listened. Sometimes the story tellers, the old Aunts in big sun hats, and the old Uncles with their trousers rolled up would follow them onto the beach and paddle in the sea. Rosie had wished she was there right now, jumping waves, holding hands with Rachel and one of her ancient Aunts.

Lulled again by happy memories Rosie made herself return to her quest.

> **Hiya My Lovely. I expect your Dad is home. He called me and said you might go to Toscano's. Did you tell him about "Rosie's Umbrella?" It's alright if you did. I haven't told him yet but he knows I'm writing stories. I have been searching for information for you about our name on the Internet. Did you know that Llywelyn ap Gruffydd otherwise known as Llywelyn-the-Last led an uprising at Tretower Castle in 1263, or thereabouts?**

Rosie had bit her bottom lip.

> **Hiya Aunt Sarah. Thank you for finding out about our name. I will write about Tretower in my report, but I think it will be mostly about the lives of mining families in Wales. Someone asked about taking showers. Margaret said it was an important question. Not sure why. Rachel came home from school with me. We went to CVS and bought makeup. Wish you'd been here. You would have laughed at all the makeup we had on. I know Rachel would have liked some of your lemon barley. Dad came home just as she was leaving. We went to Toscano's, but it was not the same without you. I hope you can come home soon. Why doesn't Dad want to talk about Wales? He got really upset and Mom shouted at me. I didn't mention your story about Rosie's umbrella. I was too scared to ask about her. It's as if she never lived. I hope my writing about what's**

happening here doesn't make it any worse for you. Do you think it is okay for us to write about Rosie? Will the doctors be angry? Sorry to ask. I am just worrying about everything. I love you very much, Rosie.

When Rosie had typed her name she'd suddenly realized that Sarah had stopped calling her Rosie. She was "Luvy," or "My Lovely" or "My Darling Girl." She didn't know what to think about no longer being "Rosie." She'd felt confused. She'd thought about the conversation she'd had with her mother and father in Toscano's. She'd never known either of her Grandmothers and she wondered how her father's mother had died. She imagined the other Rosie Llywelyn with a Lizzy Borden knife running around the house with her arm above her head and the knife in her hand. She could see an old lady with grey hair. Rosie shuddered. She felt she was in someone else's nightmare and she wanted to wake up.

Darling Girl, The doctors know I am writing stories and they keep telling me it's important that I try to talk about the things I remember so I am sure it is fine that we are writing to each other. I just hope I am not upsetting you too much. I love you very much too.

Rosie had smiled. It was so good to read that Sarah loved her, even if in her Aunt's mind she was no longer Rosie. "Maybe it's just too painful to call me Rosie," she'd thought. "Maybe." Rosie had stopped thinking about it and started writing.

You're not upsetting me Aunt Sarah. I am upset that you are not here, but that's different. Are you going to send me another story about your sister?

This time it had been Rosie who did not use the other Rosie's name. She'd thought about it for a moment and it gave her some inkling of how difficult it must be for Sarah.

> Yes I am going to send you another story my lovely.
> I like writing them. I lose myself when I write, or I
> find myself. Both, I suppose. It is wonderful to be that
> little girl again before terrible things happened and
> she forgot who she was and everything about her life.
> Sometimes I feel as if I never lived, as if I am a figment
> of your imagination, just words on your computer
> screen, a cyberspace apparition! Sorry! I am trying to
> make you laugh! But it's the truth. If I can't remember
> me I am not even a memory, and if I can't remember
> my childhood I can't remember Rosie. I can't bear to
> think of it. I have to remember. That's why my stories
> are so important.

Rosie had thought carefully before writing back. She had to
remember Sarah was in a psychiatric unit in the hospital. She'd
wanted to write, "Tell me what happened to Rosie! Why do you
keep going on about her umbrella?" But she didn't.

> You are much more than a memory to me Aunt Sarah.
> I will always love you. I'd like to read your next story.
> I've read the first one over and over.

Rosie had sat and waited.

> Thank you for being so patient my lovely. I'm trying to
> tell you about Rosie, but it's not easy. Sometimes I get
> muddled. There are so many stories. Without my stories
> I am not even a memory. I think I wrote that already. It's
> a thought that goes round and round my head. Keeps
> me writing. I worry that if I stop writing I won't exist,
> and neither will our Rosie. I'm attaching the next story.
> This one is funny. Families are full of funny stories that
> they don't tell other people, but as we are family I want
> to share this one with you. I've called it "Grandad's
> Bath." Write back when you've read it.

Rosie had smiled, thinking that even when life is sad it could still be amusing. She remembered the questions some of the kids in her class had asked when she talked about coalminers and their families. She would be able to tell them how they managed without showers. Surprising herself, she'd suddenly laughed. She'd saved the attached file and had been so engrossed in printing it out that she hadn't heard her Dad knock at her door.

"Rosie. Can I come in?"

"Sure." Rosie had said, still musing on the quirkiness of the situation.

Tom had thought the lightness he heard in her voice, so different from the way she had spoken in the restaurant, was meant for him. He'd smiled awkwardly at his daughter as he entered the room. He'd looked apologetic. "I'm sorry about tonight," he'd said. "It's been a long week. We did go to Wales a few times when I was a kid but I don't remember much about it."

Rosie had left Sarah's story printing and she'd walked over to the bed and picked up Max. She'd stood there silently stroking his head. Of course, she'd known he was lying. She'd given him a long silent enigmatic look. Tom had walked across the room to where Rosie was standing and stroked Max's back.

"I think we're all on edge because of what's happened to Sarah," he'd said.

"I miss her," Rosie had replied, her voice trembling as she spoke.

"Me too."

"Why can't she come home?" Rosie had asked, suddenly feeling as belligerent as she did in the restaurant. "I'll take care of her."

Tom had shaken his head and Rosie had thought he was

going to avoid the question. She hated it when her Dad was silent and refused to answer. He'd cleared his throat. "Sarah is ill Rosie," he'd said, without looking at her. "She needs psychiatric help." He'd hesitated before adding in a low voice, "I think she could try and kill herself."

Rosie hadn't known what to say. She'd not considered the possibility and she was not prepared for such total honesty, or the anxiousness she could hear in his voice. She'd sat down on the bed and her Dad had sat down next to her.

Tom had continued to stroke Max.

"Is that why you sent her away?"

"Yes." He'd leaned forward, his elbows on his knees. "I was worried that she would kill herself and you'd come home and find her. "

This was not the conversation Tom had intended to have with his daughter. He could feel the tightness returning to his chest and he was beginning to sweat. "I kept imagining you coming home from school and finding her dead." His skin had become blotchy and he was having trouble breathing. Abruptly, he had got to his feet. "You've got to understand, I don't want her to die. I had to stop her." There had been tears in his eyes. "I'd never forgive myself if anything happened to her."

It had been the first time Rosie had seen her father cry.

"Sorry," he'd said, fumbling for the right words and trying to laugh, "I just came up to apologize for being so grumpy in the restaurant." He'd walked over to the printer to give himself time to catch his breath. The last thing he had wanted was to fall apart in front of his daughter. But Rosie had dropped Max and was there before him, grabbing the pages.

"What are you printing out?"

"Just some notes for my report. I'll show it to you when it's finished," she'd said, as Tom leaned forward and kissed the top of her head. She'd put her arms around him so that Rosie Llywelyn's story was behind his back.

"Sarah will be okay."

"I hope so."

"She'll be okay," he'd repeated, giving Rosie a squeeze. "It's getting late. You'd better get to bed."

Rosie had waited for her Dad to close the door before she'd sat back down on her bed. She could see her father's face as he'd talked about her Aunt Sarah and she'd wondered if Sarah was really going to try to kill herself. It was too much. She didn't want to think about it. Didn't want to think. She had Sarah's story in her hand and she made herself comfortable.

Rosie looked at her watch. She expected her Mom home at least an hour ago but she was not surprised that she was late and did not dwell on her absence. She remembered the second story and she thought about her father on the night they had gone to Toscano's, in the restaurant and afterwards in her room. It seemed such a long time ago that her father had told her he thought Sarah was going to kill herself.

"Seven – eight – nine – nine –," she could hear the anguish in her father's voice as he shouted "Rosie!" Tears were rolling down her face. "Ten – ten!" she felt herself falling and it frightened her so much she stopped counting.

"How do you explain that you are falling when you are lying in bed?" Rosie asked Max. She tried to take slow breaths.

She had printed another copy of the second story, even though the one she had hidden behind her father's back when she had given him a hug was on top of a pile of them in her desk drawer.

She wanted to read the story but it took her a moment before she found the courage to begin. It was her double take on reading, "Rosie said" at the beginning of the first story had changed her life. Nothing would ever be the same again. This one was different. The first time she read it she had found herself drawn to the other Rosie. The more she read it the more connected she felt. Now when she read it she was in the story. She'd become Rosie living in Wales and her life in Boston seemed strange.

Leaning back on the pillows she drew her legs up and tucked the comforter around them. With a sigh, she began to read.

Grandad's Bath

"Rosie," Grandad shouted a whisper up the stairs. "Have our Sarah while I have a bath. She can come back down when I've finished."

"Come on Sarah," Rosie called quietly, as she sat up in bed and leaned back against the pillows. "Come and cwch with me."

I started up the stairs, and as I passed the twist at the bottom I heard our Grandad shut the door. It was quiet for a moment. I had stopped climbing and I was standing there in the dark. I held my breath and waited. Rosie knew I was holding my breath in temper and for a moment she said nothing. Then, with a rush of air I was climbing again, hitting each step with my angry footsteps, and Rosie said I was making enough noise to wake old Florrie Lewis who lived next door, let alone our Nan and our brother Tommy who were asleep in the front bedroom.

"Be quiet Sarah," Rosie shouted in a whisper as loud as our Grandad's, "you'll wake up our Nan and Tommy."

When I reached the top I stood in the doorway scowling at Rosie. I was a furious little thing with a stubborn chin.

"Come on, there's a good girl," Rosie said. "We can have a cuddle until Grandad's had a bath. Then we'll go down and have a cup of tea with him."

"Why can't I stay down with him?" I asked, still angry that I couldn't stay downstairs with my Grandad.

"You're getting too big," Rosie said, and then to make her feel better I told her, "I had to stay upstairs when I got to be a big girl like you."

"Why?"

"Because I stared at him when he took his trousers off I suppose."

I looked down, "He looks so funny," I said.

"Not really," Rosie smiled, "it would be awful if we all looked the same now wouldn't it."

I smiled too and took a run at the pile of lumpy old mattresses and grabbed for the blankets to help me up. Laughing I crawled, hands and knees, to the top of the bed and got under the covers beside Rosie. Then we slid under the blankets and giggled wicked thoughts in delicious contentment.

While we were hid beneath the bedclothes, Rosie told me about the time when she was a little girl and she watched our Grandad wash himself in the old zinc bath. She said that each morning she'd lie in bed and wait for him to come home from the night-shift at the mine, and when she heard him moving about in the kitchen she'd make her way down the dark narrow stairs, watch out for the twist at the bottom, and feel for the latch to open the door. She said as the door swung open she'd see our Grandad sitting in his chair having a whiff – smoking a pipe of tobacco and drinking tea. She said although he was a tiny man he seemed enormous to her. Covered in coal dust and steaming from working in water, she said he seemed magical and strange. She told me he would look up and nod at her as she stepped down into the room, and then he'd point with his chin and his pipe to the chair on the opposite side of the fire.

Rosie said she would cross the room and climb onto the chair, and there she'd sit drinking the tea that he tipped in his saucer for her. Then she'd watch him as he got ready for his bath. He'd pour water from the giant iron kettles with shiny brass lids that were bubbling on the fire into the old zinc bath that he'd carried in from the back yard. She said he'd take off his old jacket, his Welsh flannel shirt and woolen singlet, before he sat back on his chair, to untie his boots and undo the leather yorks that kept his trousers close to his body and out of the water. Rosie explained that once the yorks were untied, he'd kneel down on the floor beside the bath, and begin to wash the coal dust from his body. He'd take a half-pound of white kitchen soap, rub it on a flannel and then rub the flannel on his head. Little black streams formed in the wrinkles on his face and trickled down onto his neck, and as they went, Rosie said she could see underneath the familiar pinkness of our Grandad's head. The muck and grime was washed away, and he'd polish his bald spot on the towel that was warming in front of the fire on the brass rod of the mantelpiece.

Rosie told me he washed his top half and scrubbed it so clean that it seemed disconnected from his lower half, which was still encased in his steaming trousers. The smell of the damp cloth drying on his body filled the room with the workings of the mine, and of the stall deep inside the ground which was the place where our Grandad worked on his knees with a mandrill and shovel to cut the coal from the narrow seams of the Kay's Slope coalface. Rosie said once his top half was clean he'd stand up, turn his back to her and unbutton his trousers, drop them to his knees and then sit down on his chair to pull them off his legs. She said they were stiff and crusty and our Nan said it was useless to wash them, they were too dirty for that. He just put them on a kitchen chair with the legs dangling over the back so they would continue to dry and be ready for the next night.

Rosie was whispering now. She said then he used to turn his back again, this time to unbutton his long johns and pull them off. She said the blueness of his coal dust body left him not quite naked and as he turned he held his hand over the place that he didn't want me to see. Then he'd step into the bath and lower himself carefully into the water so that none of it would slop over the top onto the floor. Rosie said he'd sit facing the other way and sometimes she would soap his back making patterns in the navy blue bubbles. She told me his skin was stretched tight and it did not give under her fingers. It wasn't soft and fleshy like our Nan's whose belly wobbled when she laughed, it was firm and springy and pulled white over the bumps of his spine.

Rosie said when his back was as clean as his front and his feet were soaped and rinsed, Grandad would raise himself up out of the water and stand to wash between his legs. Then she would look at the things that dangled from his body. They were wrinkled and soft and much darker than the blue white skin of his back or the pinkness of his head, and when he washed them with the soapy cloth they moved around and then swung free as he bent down to rinse the cloth in the murky water of the old zinc bath. She said each day as she watched her fascination grew, and she would stare at him as he washed them, wondering if working down the mines had made these strange things grow.

But one day, Grandad spoke to her sharply and told her to turn her head when he stood up in the bath, but her curiosity got the better of her and she would stand with her back to him bending forward to look at him upside down through her legs. She told me that to her surprise our Grandad knew she was still looking, and he must have told our Nan because she told Rosie she couldn't go downstairs when he first got home. Rosie was told to wait until he'd had his bath. She said he'd call her when he'd finished.

"Rosie," he would whisper up the stairs and she would climb out of bed and hurry down. There he'd be, sitting in his chair, pink and clean in his Welsh flannel shirt, smoking his pipe and drinking tea. He'd nod as Rosie stepped into the room and put his tea down so that he could help her onto his lap. Then he'd pour some of the darkly brewed mixture into a saucer and together they'd sit sipping their tea, enjoying the quiet before the morning began.

The bedclothes were growing hot and stuffy and I forgot our Grandad and his old zinc bath as I tried to escape from the tangle of sheets.

"Do you think we can go down now?" I asked as I wriggled my way to the top of the bed.

"Grandad will call us when he's ready," Rosie said pushing back the bedclothes before we suffocated.

Downstairs I could hear our Grandad raking the coals in the

fire, making it hot for our Nan to cook breakfast when she went down. Then the door at the bottom of the stairs opened and Grandad called up.

"Sarah, come and have some tea," he said, "and you Rosie."

When Rosie finished re-reading the story she had no compulsion to count. Max was purring and she had grown comfortable under the comforter. Beacon Hill was still lit by gaslight and she sat up for a few minutes looking out of her window at the shadowy glow in the late afternoon that the gas lamps made before sinking back on her pillows.

She thought about Sarah writing "Rosie's Umbrella" and Grandad's Bath. She'd been immersed in discussions about stories since she first went to school, and Rosie based her analysis of Sarah's stories on what she had learned from Margaret. She'd studied different genres, fables and fairy tales, even pop-fantasy and science fiction. They had discussed magical realism and that had intrigued Rosie.

She threw the comforter back and got a copy of "Rosie's Umbrella" out of her desk drawer and then settled back under the comforter. She thought about Sarah writing as a young child and as an old woman at the same time, as she tried to make sense of the lost memories that were suddenly filling her head.

Margaret had made sure all her students knew the difference between story and narrative. "Rosie's Umbrella" was definitely a story, non-fiction but still a story, Rosie decided. "Grandad's Bath," was more complicated, part story and part narrative. Rosie thought it read a bit like a school report. She was sure Sarah had revised and rewritten the piece many times to get so much detail into the text. She wondered if her Aunt had written it with multiple purposes in mind. She wanted to help Rosie understand what had happened to her and to Rosie Llywelyn so many years ago in Wales, but she also wanted to help Rosie with her school report. "Grandad's Bath" was both childlike and grown-up.

Rosie was puzzled by the changes from third person to first person. In the first story Sarah had written about herself in the third person, but in the second she had written in the first and third person.

First, second, Rosie had no difficulty analyzing the stories as she would have done if she were given the assignment at school, but she realized now that the shifts had been a clue and that she had missed the warning Sarah had sent her about a tragedy that was yet to come.

"Four – five," Rosie couldn't help herself. She was Rosie Lly-welyn in Sarah's stories. She was in Wales. Her Nan cooked on an open fire in their kitchen and she carried buckets of water with her when she went to the toilet out the back. She could see her Grandfather bathing in an old tin bath in front of the fire, and she imagined herself as Rosie Llywelyn with her back to him bending over to look at him between her legs – as if he wouldn't know she was watching him as he stood up in the bath.

Rosie shivered and pulled the comforter up higher. She could feel the hair on the back of her neck stand on end and she was shaking. She was in her own room, awake and imagining that she was in Wales with her Great Grandfather, sitting by the fire, drinking tea out of his saucer. *She* was the other Rosie Llywelyn. It was more than a dream. She was not asleep. She was convinced the memory was real.

"Whose story is it anyway?" she'd asked out loud, when she'd first read the story, shattering the silence that filled the room.

"What if there's only one Rosie Llywelyn?" Her voice had trembled.

Max looked at Rosie and then the door as if he expected Tom to come back into the room.

"What if Sarah made the other one up?" Rosie had said, getting off the bed and staring at her computer screen. "What if Rosie Llywelyn is just a figment of Sarah's imagination?"

"When was this?" Rosie asked herself, shaken by the awfulness of the memory. "Before the elevator or afterwards? Which elevator? The one in Mass General where Sarah worked?"

"No! No!" she said out loud. "Don't count! Oh please, don't count!"

When Rosie had first read Grandad's Bath she'd immediately sent Sarah an email:

Aunt Sarah, Are there really two Rosie Llywelyns?

It was a while before she'd received a response from Sarah:

My darling girl, there really are two. I'm not playing tricks on you. All that's happening is that you're finding out about your own family, about events that took place before you were born. You're coming face-to-face with your own history. Did you imagine that it was you in the room with your Great Grandfather? Both your Great Grandfathers were coalminers *and* your Grandfather. He worked in a mine for a short while before the Second World War started in 1939.

Rosie had written back:

Why didn't my Dad tell me that? Why does he keep lying to me?

Sarah had written back:

It's complicated Luvy. There's so much he doesn't want
to remember. I've been trying to remember the happy
times as well as the sad. When I think of Wales I think
of the little coal-mining village just over the Coity
Mountain from Blaina, between Blaenavon and Brynmawr, where my Grandparents lived. They were your
Great Grandparents and they lived at 5 Fair Mount on
the Garn. Garn-yr-erw really, but we all called it the
Garn. It doesn't exist anymore. I read when the mines
closed they bulldozed the tiny miners' cottages into the
ground. No one cared about the stories held tight inside
the walls just waiting to be told. It makes me sad that
so many people lived there and now if you drive by all
you can see is the little road that was out the back. The
people are gone and no one remembers them except for
me. Why don't you write about Garn-yr-erw for your
school report? Then if your Dad has forgot you can help
him remember.

Rosie had thought if she learned more about Wales she could
talk to her Dad and perhaps he would then help her understand
what had happened to Sarah. She'd decided to give up on the more
difficult questions and to focus on her school report instead. She'd
liked the idea of writing about Garn-yr-erw, the village in which
her Great Grandparents lived. Her report on Wales would be like
a history of her own family, and maybe if she concentrated on her
schoolwork she could get the other Rosie Llywelyn out of her head:

Okay Aunt Sarah. Thanks for helping me with my
homework. Maybe it will help me understand why Dad
never told me about Wales. So tell me about the Garn.

Sarah's next email had arrived quickly:

Well my lovely girl, I'm not sure where to start. It's different when I write a story. I have a lot of time to think about it – and correct my grammar and spelling!

Rosie had written just as quickly:

Don't worry about typos. Who cares! I don't notice them. Imagine we're talking.

Rosie had watched the screen. A minute or two later the next email had arrived from Sarah:

If that's okay — I'll just write and you decide if you want to use any of it in your school report. I'm thinking … there were four rows of miners' houses, with two rooms up and two rooms down. I can see them as I write! There were also two rows of whitewashed cottages and several small farms.

Rosie:

Maybe you could draw a map of the Garn — could you do that?

Sarah:

I could! It's so strange. I haven't thought about the Garn since I was a little girl but now that I remember I can see the cottages and the road going up over the top – that's what everyone called it! During the Second World War a miner used to stand all night at the top of the road holding a broom handle — in the dark it looked like a gun. If someone came over the top from Brynmawr the miner had to shout, "Halt! Who goes there?" What a funny thing to remember!

Rosie:

I thought Brynmawr was in Pennsylvania?

Sarah:

Named after the Brynmawr in Wales I suppose. Our Grandad used to take Rosie and me to the Brynmawr market. Tommy would come with us sometimes. We'd buy some crackling for a few pennies from one of the stalls and we'd walk around sucking it.

What's crackling?

Pig's skin – the rind on roast pork.

Gross!!!

Haha! I can see your face my lovely. When you were little you used to say you were a two-meat vegetarian and that you only ate chicken and salami — definitely not roast pork! Don't think I could eat it now but it did taste good back then and I need a bit of a laugh!

I remember being a two-meat vegetarian. I don't eat salami any more. I suppose I am now a one meat vegetarian. Rachel is vegan, and Jesse. This summer I am going to give up chicken. Tell me about the people who lived in the Garn?

On the Garn. Everyone said, "on the Garn". Our Nan called it "down home".

Why do you keep writing *our* Nan and *our* Grandad?

Family. Everyone in the family had "our" added to their name. We always said "our Nan" and our Nan always called me "our Sarah". Your Dad was "our Tommy" and then there was "our Rosie". Poor Rosie.

Rosie had felt as if an electrical surge had passed through her body. She typed quickly:

What happened to her?

I don't want to write about it. I don't remember. Ask me another question.

Rosie had sighed and shaken her head. She'd wanted to write, "Please tell me!" but she did not. Instead she wrote:

Tell me about the people on the Garn.

It was a few minutes before Sarah wrote back:

Everyone knew everyone else in the village. Many people were known by the place they lived or worked. There was Annie Field Farm, Away Mary Gunter, Freddie Waenavon, and Thomas the Pit. .... It's coming back to me! Then there were people who were known by what they did – like Jennie the Milk who kept cows for milking.

We'll have to call you Sarah the Nurse!

There. You made me laugh again. That's me! Your Great, Great Aunt Lizzy took care of people when they were ill, but they didn't call her Lizzy the Nurse. When I was a little girl she was very old. There was something about her that made her special. I remember I was a little bit scared of her. If anyone had a problem they ran and got Aunt Lizzy. Many times she delivered babies before the mid-wife arrived and when people died Aunt Lizzy always laid them out.

Aunt Lizzy sounds like you Aunt Sarah. I would like to think I am like her.

She was really special. Our Nan used to say she could talk to the dead. Aunt Lizzy would say, "We're going to have bad news" and a few days later someone on the Garn would die. The women in our family have always talked to the dead. Sorry. Our Nan —your Great Grandmother – used to say that. You won't want to write that in your school report will you?

It would make it interesting! Do you remember any-

thing about the mines?

All the houses belonged to the collieries. That's the way it was. None of the miners owned their own houses. There were two collieries in the village, Garn Drift and Kay's Slope. Neither of them had a mineshaft with a cage that dropped the miners thousands of feet underground. No, it was more like a tunnel that went slowly down into the ground—that's why they were called Garn Drift and Kay's Slope. I can see the gaping hole in the side of mountain that was the entrance to Kay's Slope and the drams being pulled out of the mine by horses.

Like the Mines of Moria in Lord of the Rings!

You never cease to amaze me my lovely. Yes, like the Mines of Moria.

But no wizards!

In the nineteenth century they mined iron ore as well as coal where your Great Grandparents lived.

Tell me about the mines.

Our Grandad worked in Kay's Slope deep inside the mine—all his life. The deeper the coal seams the better the coal, so your Great Grandad had to walk a mile or more in the blackness before he reached the coal seam. He was ten years old when he started and seventy when he stopped digging. All those years underground.

Rosie wondered how Sarah knew that her Grandfather worked as a miner until he was seventy if he was still digging coal when whatever happened took away her memory. She began to type, "How do you know …" and thought better of it and hit the backspace.

Tell me about the miners' families.

The miners' wages were very low in those days and many of them were unemployed. They often went hungry. I remember that Mrs. Luff used to take her son Georgie's suit to the pawnshop on Mondays and fetch it back on Fridays so he could wear it when he went out on Saturday night. Oh dear! I'm not sure what to write! This is so disorganized. Am I boring you? We've been at this for hours! You should go to bed. We'd better stop.

You are not boring me! And I'm not tired. This is better than castles and sheep! If we stop now I'll just keep thinking of more questions! Margaret wanted me to write about coal miners and their families so you are helping me a lot. I can organize it later. Margaret will help me. If you are not too tired why don't you just write about what you remember?

I'm not tired. Writing to you is a bit like being a child again in Wales. Ask me another question.

Where did you shop?

Our shop was called the Co-op. There was just one. The Co-op was owned by the colliery and it had everything we needed—not like now when we all need so much! Everybody had a number. Our Nan's was 1232 — I don't know why I remember that. I used to like counting — I don't want to remember counting. Ask me another question.

Rosie had not understood why counting was a problem for Sarah when her Aunt had first written to her about Wales, but she did now. Her heart was banging against her rib cage and she started counting.

"One – two! Read the next question! Don't count! Read! Go on, read it!"

What did the miners do if they didn't have any money?

We didn't use money for very much. We used tokens. We called them checks. Our Nan had to buy the checks from the colliery and she used them at the Co-op to pay for the milk and bread that was delivered to our door.

So the miners worked in the mines, got paid, and then they gave the money back?

They did. The colliery owned the row houses where they lived so the rent was taken out of their wages, and they owned the Co-op so the only way the families could buy food was to buy tokens, which they used in the shop. Ask me another question.

How did our Nan cook?

I remember we cooked on the fire Luvy. Even on the hottest summer day the fire was never allowed to go out. Every night before he went to work our Grandad would bank the fire with small coal and then put an iron – not sure what it was called. It looked like a shield. The blacksmith made it for us – you could see where he had hammered it. Our Grandad hooked it over the top bar of the grate so the iron bars at the front of the fire that held the coal – I'm not describing it very well — were covered to stop sparks flying out at night. I think it was called a damper but I'm not sure — I do remember that the small coal was put on to damp the fire—make it burn more slowly.

It might have been called a damper — it would have cut off the oxygen to the fire so the coal would burn more slowly. Like a barbeque – if you block the air-flow.

My lovely you are too much for me. How do you know so much!

I don't know how my Great Grandmother cooked on

an open fire all her life!

But she did! Incredible when you come to think about it. There were ovens each side of the fire – two on one side and one on the other. She had big kettles that sat on top so there was always hot water and if she wanted to boil potatoes she put the pot on the fire. Your Great Grandmother did all her baking in the ovens but she used to say she would rather take care of the chickens — she got more pleasure watching baby chicks hatching than baking cakes.

I think I would have liked my Great Nan! It must have been hard cooking on the fire. All that coal to carry!

And the ashes to rake!

Did the mine owners give them the coal?

Not them! The miners had to pay for it. Our Grandad was allowed one ton of coal every month, which cost seven and six.

Seven and six?

Seven shillings and six pence. The money was taken out of his pay packet along with the rent. Fancy that! First he had to go underground, wade through the water that seeped into the mine, crawl through tunnels on his hands and knees in the darkness — except for the dim light of his miner's lamp. When he got to the end of the tunnel he had to dig coal out of the side of the mountain with a shovel and then he had to pay seven and six for it!

How do you know that?

There was no television and your Great Nan and Great Grandad didn't have a radio. Besides, children listen when adults talk. I think we forget as we grow up. Memories get piled up. But my memories have been bottled up and it's as if they happened yesterday.

I don't think I will remember much about what my Mom and Dad say. They only talk about work and they are always rushing.

I hope you'll remember all the times we've spent together — especially all our conversations about the books we've shared.

I won't forget. I'll still have you and all the books! I think I will remember my Mom talking to me on the telephone and my Dad getting in and out of taxis coming and going to the airport!

You'll remember more than that. Your Mom and Dad love you. They work hard. In Wales life was hard but it was different when I was little without a television or radio, and your Great Grandparents didn't even take a newspaper. People actually sat and talked to each other — sometimes for hours — and I loved to sit on our Nan's lap and listen. Even when I was playing with our Rosie and our Tommy in the front room I would keep one ear tuned to what was being said in the back room where the big fire was.

I do that. I listen to Dad upstairs in his office and Mom in her office. What I like best is listening to you singing! Hope you come home soon.

Me too. My Lovely it's midnight! You have to go to sleep!

Just a little while longer!

I remember in the evening before our Grandad went to work, we sat around the fire. He never learned to read but he often told us stories. He used to make up stories about two boys called Pat and Mike who were always getting into trouble. Our Nan would tell us about her childhood. Her father was a foreman at the mine and she had her own pony and trap. Often neighbors would come in and sit by the fire and talk about what was happening on the Garn — the good things as well as the bad.

How did our Nan and Grandad get all that coal?

The coal was tipped out the back. There was a little lane tamped down with grit that came up with the coal from the mine. The coal was delivered by horse and cart and dropped in the lane. Johnny Sebourne — I remember his name! He was unemployed — I don't know why he was not working down the mines — would shovel it into the coal cot for a shilling and our Grandad would give him a couple of buckets of coal as well. What else do you want to know Luvy? I've got my second wind. Ask another question.

Where did you wash your clothes?

We washed them in the back room where we lived. We had a little kitchen with a big square china sink with a cold-water tap. It was more like a walk in closet, just big enough for two people to stand up in. I remember helping our Nan get the plates that she kept in there on the shelf and carrying the cups that were hung on hooks above the shelf. The cups were all different and I thought they were very pretty, but I didn't like it in there because it smelled bad. It was dark and damp – and even though our Nan was always cleaning, coal dust settled on everything and made it dirty. I can smell it now. It was nasty — like an old shed with a leaky roof filled with wet coal. Quick! What else do you want to know?

Washing! How did you do the washing?

Right. Every Monday, Florrie Lewis — who I wrote about in my first story — used to help our Nan do the washing. It took all day. Everything got dirty very quickly.

Do you remember what they did?

They picked up the rag rugs and hung them outside to air. Then they brought in the zinc bath and put it on two kitchen chairs and filled it with water from the big black kettles with brass lids that were always bubbling on the fire. Then the iron boiler was put on the fire and the whites were boiled. After that, the whites had to be put into blue water in the zinc bath, and then they were starched.

How did you dry all the towels and sheets?

If the weather was good we hung them out the back, but more often than not our Nan and Florrie hung them on racks that they lowered on pulleys from the ceiling and then raised up — even so grown-ups still had to bend over to walk under them. They dried quickly because of the fire, but on Mondays and Tuesdays there were nearly always racks of steaming washing in the kitchen. Our Nan hated the racks of washing — when she was a girl her washing was done for her — but I liked the smell of clean clothes drying. Silly really, I used to think the washing looked pretty hanging up above our heads like sails on a boat or flags hung up for a celebration.

I can imagine that. Did Florrie Lewis help out on other days?

On Fridays she would come back and clean through the house with our Nan. I expect it sounds odd that a coal mining family had help in the house, like the maids on Louisburg Square, but it was not really like that.

Tell me about Florrie Lewis.

The story of Florrie Lewis is one of the stories I listened to in the evening sitting by the fire. I remember it as if I heard it yesterday. Florrie was a spinster — she didn't have a husband but she had a son. Years ago on the

Garn, any young woman who was having a baby was quickly married in the little country church at Llanwenyth. But Florrie wasn't that fortunate. She wouldn't tell anyone who was the father of her baby, and so her mother used to beat her and refuse to feed her.

Did she tell?

No. Florrie never told anyone whom she had been with. Then when she gave birth to a baby boy her mother must have forgiven her a little bit because she helped bring him up —but she still wouldn't give Florrie anything to eat, not even a slice of stale bread.

How did she get food?

People in the village had to feed her. She worked for food. On Monday mornings she had toast and tea with our Nan and then she would eat a cooked meal with us after she did the washing. Someone fed her on Tuesdays and another person on Wednesdays. By Friday she was back with our Nan. She'd eat with us and our Nan would give her a little package of food for Saturday and Sunday. We should stop writing my Lovely. It's almost one o'clock.

Are you tired?

I am getting tired.

Do you think we could continue tomorrow?

I'm not sure. I'm a bit precarious.

Let's continue a bit longer then all your memories about the Garn will be on paper and you can read them if they help make you feel better.

Not sure it is that simple my darling girl. All right, just a little longer. I'd like to remember the good times.

Tell me about the cuckoo clock. You wrote you'd suddenly remembered the cuckoo clock.

And apple tarts! I remember how our Nan made apple
tarts. But the cuckoo clock! That's a story! How could
I have forgotten that! The cuckoo clock hung on the
wall above our Grandad's old wooden chair – it looked
like a rocking chair only it didn't have rockers. When I
was three or four years old I used to stand on the arm
of the chair and wait for the cuckoo — I'm smiling as
I write my Lovely.

A happy memory!

Remembering does make me happy — chuckle actually. Our Nan used to tell me to get down, that I'd hurt
myself, so I would wait until she was out the back and
then I would get up on the arm of the chair and wait for
the cuckoo to come out of the clock. It popped out and
said "cuckoo" every quarter hour, but it would pop in
and out on the hour — one cuckoo at one o'clock, two
at two o'clock, and three at three o'clock. I used to love
that! Counting again. I don't want to count.

Don't count. Rosie whispered to herself as her heart beat
faster. Read!

I can see you standing on the arm of the chair waiting
for the cuckoo!

I would watch and wait and try and catch it. Then one
day when our Nan was out I climbed up and stood on
the arm of the chair and I caught it! But then I couldn't
get the little bird back into the clock! I was still up on
the arm of the chair when our Nan came back.

Was she angry? Did she tell you off?

I was so upset she lifted me off the arm of the chair and
sat and cuddled me. I wailed and she just kept saying
"There, there."

I wish I'd been with you Aunt Sarah. I wish you were here. I'd like to cuddle with you – "cwch" – that's cuddle, right? I'd like to cuddle up and watch a movie. Tell me what you did all day?

We amused ourselves really. I remember that our Rosie used to take me to watch the horses being brought up from Kay's Slope mine. The miners had made a ramp into Big Pond and they would lead the horses down the ramp into the water to wash off the coal dust before they were fed and stabled.

I would have liked to watch that.

Our ponies were lucky. The ponies that went down Big Pit never came up. They spent their whole lives working underground in the mine, and they went blind in the darkness. At the end of their shift, when they had finished hauling drams of coal, they stood in stalls cut out of the rock. Sad really. There was no sunshine in their lives. Now what was the question?

What did you like to do?

Oh yes. In summer on hot days we used to swim in Big Pond and we used to fish. Then Tommy would come too.

Tell me about fishing with my Dad.

He loved to fish and we used to love it when he came with us. Back then you could buy a long cane at the Co-op for a penny. We used to use sewing thread for a line, a goose feather for a float, a bent pin for a hook and wet bread for bait. I'm laughing as I write! Do you know we actually used to catch fish with our feathers and wet bread on pin hooks! Tiddlers! We used to put them in a tub of water and when we got tired of fishing we would put them back in the water and watch them swim away.

I love that. What did you do in winter?

In the winter when we visited our Nan and Grandad for Christmas, Big Pond would be covered with thick ice. Our Grandad made us each a sled and the blacksmith at the colliery — who couldn't hear anything or speak a word — made us iron runners for our sleds.

Wonder what happened to them?

I don't know Luvy. I think we wore them out! The blacksmith also made us gliders — nobody would know what they were now — they looked like pokers. He made one for each hand and we would take our sleds onto Big Pond and dig our gliders into the ice and move along and bump into each other.

I wish I'd been there with you.

Me too! When it got dark we would go back home and sit by the fire and our Grandad would tell us stories before he went to work. Luvy, I have to go. Let's stop while we are both so happy. It's the middle of the night. You have to go to sleep. I'll write another story for you tomorrow. I love writing to you my darling girl.

Night-night. I love you Aunt Sarah. I hope you come home soon.

Me too! Love you!

"Rosie!" Mary had said, making Rosie jump. A sleepy Mary in a long white night gown and pale blue kimono was standing in the doorway of Rosie's room.

"You're supposed to knock!" Rosie had scowled at Mary. "Please! Don't just walk in here!"

"What are you doing up!" Mary had responded ignoring Rosie's protests. "It's two o'clock in the morning!"

"Sorry. Is it late?" Rosie had asked, softening her tone, as she'd hastily moved the mouse to close down her computer. "I just finished."

"It's two o'clock in the morning!" Mary had said again, as if she couldn't believe that Rosie was still up. "You can't still be working on your report on Wales!"

"Sorry," Rosie had said again. "Did I wake you?"

"No," her mother had said. "I thought we might have woken you. We just got a telephone call from the hospital. Apparently they've lost Sarah. She's been missing for several hours."

"I'm sure she's okay," Rosie had said, feeling a little uncomfortable that she could not tell her mother that she and Sarah had been writing to each other. She wasn't sure Sarah would want her mother to know, and she was worried that there would be no more stories if she found out.

"Come on now, get into bed or you'll never get up tomorrow!" Mary had said.

Rosie had climbed into bed and her mother bent over and kissed her, then she'd walked out of the room. When she reached the doorway she'd looked back at Rosie. The light on the landing behind her cast a dark shadow on her face.

She'd looked troubled and spoke hesitantly. "Rosie, please don't ask your Dad any more questions. It was wrong of me to tell you to ask him about Wales. Nothing good will come of it. Sometimes things happen that it's better to forget."

Mary had not waited for Rosie to reply, and she'd quickly changed the subject as if she was trying to bury what she had just said. "Why don't you go to the library tomorrow and get some books out on Welsh castles? You could add it to the stuff Jesse gave you on Harlech Castle."

Mary had smiled. She didn't want to leave Rosie with sad thoughts in her head. "You know you could write an amazing report. There are at least seven hundred more castles in Wales."

"Okay. I'll go to the library tomorrow and I promise I won't ask Dad any more questions." Rosie had smiled as she blew her mother a kiss. "If you call the hospital I bet they've found Aunt Sarah." Mary had smiled back, even though she'd still looked troubled as she quietly shut the bedroom door.

In the distance Rosie could hear the low rumble of thunder. She'd watched the rain beating against her windowpane and thought about the Garn and her family in Wales. There was so much she wanted to know about them, about what had happened to Rosie and Sarah. She'd thought for a moment and she'd realized she had to include what had happened to her Dad. Another clap of thunder, much closer this time, had made her jump. Max had stood up, stretched, and remembering wet nights in back alleys, he'd pushed his way under the covers and curled up against Rosie's back.

"No more questions." Rosie had mumbled to herself as she drifted off to sleep. There was another roll of thunder. Distant. Far-off.

"D'you wanna go fishing?" she'd heard someone ask. She'd put wet bread on a bent pin. Tommy was there catching tiddlers and Sarah was paddling her feet. Rosie saw the Swan Boats from the Public Gardens in Big Pond and people waving and throwing peanuts at them as they fished.

Max was hot and braved the weather. He'd curled up on the top of the comforter and quickly gone back to sleep.

Rosie saw a small child in a coffin and a woman in a long back dress standing over her. One by one children were coming in through the front door of the miner's cottage. They walked around the table and looked at the little girl laid out in her Sunday school dress. Her skin was deathly blue and she was lying with her hands together on her chest as if she was praying.

Solemnly, the children stared at her as they kept moving around the table. Then one by one they left by the same door that they'd come in. And all the time that they were there the woman in the long black dress stood still, silently keeping watch over the dead child.

A baby screamed. The bronze statues of the ducklings were pecking at Rosie's heels. The mother duck had grown. She was as big as Rosie. Bigger. She lowered her head and stuck her neck out as she hissed and flapped her enormous wings. Rosie put the umbrella up and held it behind her as she ran away from the mother duck.

There was a loud clap of thunder.

Rosie was in her Great Grandmother's kitchen. Florrie Lewis was doing the washing.

"Can we go swimming?" Tommy asked.

"Yes," our Nan said, "but be careful and don't come back here if you drown."

"Nan, how could we do that?" our Tommy asked. "We couldn't come back if we drowned now, could we?"

"Well mind you don't then," our Nan said.

Rosie had pushed the covers back. Max had protested. He was tangled in the quilt and he scrambled to free himself as lightening illuminated the room. There was another clap of thunder right overhead. Rosie had sat up. Her heart had been beating fast, she could feel it thumping, hear her blood pulsing, audibly fizzing. She'd tried to breathe, her mouth had been dry, and she'd gasped for breath. For a moment she had not been sure where she was, or whether she was awake or still asleep. When she was younger she used to call out to her parents and they would come running up or down the stairs into her bedroom, put their arms around her and tell her it was just a dream, and her mother would stay and sleep in her bed with her. But she was too old for that now, and the dream was too complicated, too real. They would know what had upset her. They would guess. Her heart had steadied and she'd taken a deep breath. She'd got out of bed and gone into her bathroom for a glass of water.

"Who was the little girl in the coffin?" she'd asked herself. "Who was the woman in black? Did someone drown?" Rosie had sat on the edge of her bed. "And Robert McCloskey's ducks!" She'd mused. "I understand how the mother duck became so fierce. And how they ended up in my dream about Wales, because of Sarah and Rosie's umbrella, but why were the people in the Swan Boats throwing peanuts?" She'd smiled at the absurdity of how these trivial details of her own life had got mixed in with things that her Dad did when he was a kid. She went over to her bookshelves. Tucked in next to Louisa May Alcott's *Little Women* she'd found a much-loved book with tattered pages that was falling apart.

Rosie had sat on the floor by her bookshelves and she'd turned the pages of Robert McCloskey's *Make Way For Ducklings*. Even though it was years since she'd read the story, she was sure that somewhere near the beginning of the book there was a picture of one of the Swan Boats. Rosie found the page. She'd read the text that went with the picture. "But the people on the boat threw peanuts in the water." She'd looked at the picture. Somehow finding *Make Way for Ducklings* in her dream had made it seem less threatening. She'd taken the book over to her bed and she began to read the story and look at the pictures. There was the pond in the Public Gardens, the State House, which was around the corner from her house, Louisburg Square and the Charles River.

Rosie had tried to stay awake. She'd been safely wrapped up in her own memories and she didn't want to go back to sleep. She'd tried to forget about Wales and instead she'd remembered going to the Public Gardens to feed the ducks with her Mom when she was a little kid. For a while she'd got lost in the tiny details of her own daily life. She'd thought about all the things she'd taken for granted and never thought about much before, before she had found out there was another Rosie Llywelyn, before she had read her Aunt Sarah's stories, before she knew that her family came from Wales. Rosie had drifted off to sleep again before Mrs. Mallard waded ashore and waddled up Mount Vernon Street.

On the Saturday morning after Rosie and Sarah had been up until two, Rosie had come downstairs and found her mother in the kitchen making banana pancakes with walnuts sprinkled into the batter.

"I was going to call you when the pancakes were ready." Mary had said. "D'you want to get the maple syrup?"

Rosie had gone over to the fridge and she'd looked among the bottles of ketchup and salad dressing for the syrup. "Where's Dad?"

"He's gone to the hospital."

"Is Sarah okay?"

"She's fine," Mary had told her, looking at Rosie. She'd thought it was a little odd that Rosie did not seem to be that concerned about what had happened last night to Sarah. "They eventually found her," Mary had told her daughter. "She had a toothache and couldn't sleep, but she doesn't want to see a dentist. Your Dad is going to take her."

"Is he going to bring her back here?" Rosie had asked, hoping she was going to be able to see Sarah.

"It depends on whether or not he can find a dentist who will see her on a Saturday," Mary had said. "If he can't find a dentist near the hospital I think he'll have to bring her home so she can see her old dentist who is on call this weekend and said he would see her. But I don't think the doctors will be happy about that."

"I hope he brings her back here."

"We'll see. Don't get your hopes up," Mary had said

"I hope he brings Aunt Sarah home."

"He might. If he does it won't be until late this afternoon."

"I wish she could come back and live with us."

"Rosie, you know that's not possible." Mary had given Rosie a troubled smile. "Someone has to be with her all the time. What would she do when you were at school and I was at work?"

"I think she would manage." Rosie had put the maple syrup on the table. "Anyway, I don't think Sarah is sick. I think some of the things that she says make perfect sense. It's just that we don't understand what she's saying." She'd glanced over at her mother and frowned. "Or, at least I don't."

Mary had stirred her coffee. "Why do you say that?"

"I don't know," Rosie had said. "Maybe we're the ones that are crazy." She'd stuck her fork into the stack of pancakes. "What d'you think?"

"I think you should eat your pancakes," Mary had said, pushing the maple syrup across the table. She'd put a pancake on her own plate and changed the subject. "What are you going to do this morning?"

"I thought I'd walk up Boylston Street to the library like you suggested." Rosie had stuffed another fork full of pancakes in her mouth. "Maybe I'll find some books on Welsh castles."

"Don't eat like that," Mary had said, shaking her head.

"Mother!" Rosie had said, smiling with her mouth full.

Smiling back, Mary had rolled her eyes and shook her head, glad to have a moment that was a throwback to Rosie's childhood. "Would you like me to come with you as far as the Public Gardens? We've eaten out so much this week we've got tons of stale bread."

Rosie had remembered her dream.

"D'you remember when we used to go every Saturday morning to feed the ducks?" Mary had asked her.

Rosie had begun to choke and her mother had quickly poured her a glass of milk. Rosie had gulped between splutters.

"Are you all right?"

"Sure," had been all Rosie could say, as she'd caught her breath. It was as if there was an invisible thread that joined her to her mother. It was often like that. Something would happen and her mother would know. Rosie wondered if her mother had known she'd had a dream about the ducks. Did she know that she and Sarah were writing to each other? Did she know that Rosie knew both her Great Grandfathers were coal miners and lived in Wales? What did she know?

"Rosie? I'm speaking to you. Rosie!"

Startled, Rosie jumped.

"You're not listening," Mary had said apologetically, realizing that she had spoken sharply. "D'you want to feed the ducks before you go to the library?" she'd asked again.

"Sure," Rosie had said. She had taken another pancake and

covered it with maple syrup.

"Great!" Mary had said, sounding pleased. "I just need to make a couple of quick phone calls when we've finished breakfast. I can be ready in about fifteen minutes."

Rosie had gone up to her room when she finished her pancakes and turned on her computer:

Hiya Aunt Sarah. Last night I had a dream about Wales. I want to ask you about it. Please write back.

Rosie had sat and waited hoping that Sarah would write back, but she thought her Dad had probably already picked her up. Rosie had logged off her computer and she'd gone downstairs. Her mother had been in the kitchen filling a plastic bag from DeLuca's grocery store with half loaves of stale bread.

"Ready?" she'd asked Rosie, who had her back-pack just in case she found some books on Welsh coalmines at Boston's Public Library.

"I feel like a little kid again," Rosie had smiled at her mother.

"Me too," Mary had said. "Come on."

They'd both been wearing jeans and sneakers so they'd walked quickly down Pinckney, cut across Louisburg Square and headed down Mount Vernon.

"I think Robert McCloskey got it wrong," Rosie had said to her mother.

"Got what wrong?" Mary had asked.

"He says the ducklings went *down* Mount Vernon. But they didn't. They went *up*. We're going down and we're going in the opposite direction."

Mary had no idea what her daughter was talking about. "When did you make this discovery?"

"Last night. The thunder kept me awake so I read *Make Way for Ducklings.*"

"Rosie, you never cease to amaze me."

"He wrote that when they left the Charles River they went *down* Mount Vernon." Rosie had explained. "Well, from the river to the State House is *up*. The ducks were at the bottom of the hill so you would say 'they made their way *up* Mount Vernon.' You would only say 'they went *down*' if they were going towards the river."

Mary laughed as they turned left on Charles Street. She would rather discuss whether Robert McCloskey's ducks went up or down Mount Vernon than answer all the difficult questions Rosie had asked about Wales. She hoped Rosie had decided to give up on all that and write about castles instead.

They'd crossed Beacon Street and walked into the Public Gardens. The crowds around Robert McCloskey's ducklings were different on Saturdays. There were always lots of moms and dads who lived on Beacon Hill and didn't get much time to spend with their kids during the week. They sat their babies and small children on the bronze statues and took pictures. This morning there was one Grandfather who was trying to take a picture of the mother duck and her eight ducklings with a small child sitting on every duck's back. His wife stood beside him offering encouragement.

"Get that one," the Grandmother had said. "That's a great shot."

"Look this way!" said the Grandfather.

"Look at me!" said the Grandmother.

"Cheese," said the little girl on the back of the mother duck.

"I'm going to run out of film," laughed the Grandfather, as he took the picture.

"Brenda! Look at Mommy!" a mother said.

"Andrew!"

"Good," said the Grandfather as he took the last shot.

When they had reached the pond, Mary gave Rosie a half loaf of stale bread out of the DeLuca's bag. Mallard ducks were swimming towards them, moving fast, propelled by their webbed feet. Some ducks were already out of the water. Rosie had crumbled bread for them to eat and then threw larger crusts into the pond for the Mallards who preferred the safety of the water. Mary had some stale French bread, which she'd crumbled for the pigeons that had joined the ducks. A sparrow had flitted between the bigger birds and quickly grabbed a crumb before a pigeon could peck.

"That was brave," Rosie had laughed. "Look." She'd pointed at a pair of Canada Geese who were spending their summer on the pond as they glided gracefully towards them. She had lobbed some large crusts towards them but some Mallards skimmed across the water and the big birds just watched as the ducks gobbled up the bread. The Canada Geese had continued swimming deliberately towards them. Rosie had tried again and this time a piece of bread landed on the water right in front of them. One of the geese had slowly bent its head and scooped up the crust. Rosie had concentrated on the other goose. Another lucky shot. There were pigeons on the bench behind them and Mary quickly dug into her bag and brought out the last few crusts. Sparrows and starlings gathered together, even though they didn't like each other very much, hoping for a few crumbs. Rosie had a little bread left and she crumbled it up and scattered it on the grass. Birds surrounded them and it had made them laugh.

People passing by had stopped and watched. Rosie's hair was lighter and brighter in the sunlight and so were her mother's red-gold curls. For a moment they'd stood there and watched as the Mallards made their way back into the water and swam off.

"Do you want me to come to the library with you?" Mary had asked.

"No," Rosie had said. "You'd better go back in case Dad calls to tell you what's happening with Aunt Sarah. I'll be back around one." She'd suddenly thought Sarah might be there already. "You don't think he'll bring her home this morning do you?"

Mary had shaken her head. "No. He has to see one of the psychiatrists around ten thirty. Then, if they'll let him, he wants to take Sarah to the dentist."

"Could they stop him?"

"It's complicated," Mary had looked serious. "We signed all those papers."

Rosie had suddenly felt sorry for her mother. Whatever tension there was between them had passed. "Will you wait so we can have lunch together?"

"I most certainly will," Mary had said, feeling for the first time that Rosie was beginning to understand how difficult it had been for them to hospitalize Sarah. She'd pulled a face. "You know, Rosie, sometimes I wonder who's the mother and who's the daughter."

Rosie had smiled.

Mary had watched Rosie as she took the path around the pond

and headed for the Boylston Street exit of the Public Gardens, then she turned to walk back home with the intention of stopping at Starbucks for a cup of coffee on the way.

Rosie had walked quickly. She passed two of Boston's park rangers on their huge Belgian Draft horses and she thought about the pit ponies in Wales wading into Big Pond to wash the coal dust off their backs before they were taken back to the stable to be watered and fed. She'd imagined the ponies in Big Pit spending their lives underground hauling coal and slowly going blind. She was out of the Public Gardens, on Boylston, waiting to cross the street. She'd passed the Women's Educational and Industrial Union, and when she'd reached the next intersection, she'd crossed just before the lights turned red, and hurried by FAO Schwarz. Ahead kids had been riding skateboards, jumping up on benches, turning high in the air, whizzing fast, weaving in and out of tourists, and crashing. Rosie had walked on as an empty skate board flew by.

The black shining glass of the John Hancock Building seemed to reflect coal dust in the sunshine, casting dark shadows on Trin-

ity Church and Copley Square. One more intersection and she'd
reached the Boston Public Library. Rosie had visited the children's
section since she was a tiny child, but in the winter Margaret had
brought her class to the library and showed them how to research
topics that were obscure and about which there was very little information. The massive stone building filled a city block. Rosie went in
through the main entrance and turned right when she got inside.

"Can I help you?" the librarian at the Social Science Information Desk had asked, looking at Rosie over half-glasses with purple
frames.

"Have you any books on coalmining in South Wales?"

"I expect so." The librarian had looked back at her computer
screen. Rosie had waited. The librarian had typed a series of keys,
peered expectantly at the screen and then hit some more keys. She'd
looked up and smiled at Rosie.

"There are different data bases, nothing so far," she'd said. "I'm
not sure where to go next." She'd peered back at the screen. "Coal
mining. Wales. We don't have anything listed." She'd sat back in her
chair and taken off her glasses. "I'm astounded. We don't have any
books between 1980 and the present." She'd stood up. "We'll have to
look in the research index at books that were published before then."

Rosie had followed the librarian as she went into the next
room and sat down at one of a bank of computers. She'd been in
this room before when she'd come to the library with Margaret. The
librarian, who was now totally focused on her quest, typed in the
subject as 'Coal Mining Wales' and three references appeared on
the screen. She'd turned around, looking triumphant, "we do have
three books. Let me just try 'Coal miners Wales.'" Another reference
had appeared. "Four! Not many out of ten million books!" She'd

smiled at Rosie as she'd shown her how to fill in the request form, and Rosie had thanked her, even though Margaret had already shown her when she'd brought her class to the library.

Rosie had taken the request forms to the book delivery desk where another librarian had told her to fill in a seat number in the upper right hand corner of each form. Rosie had thought of her Great Grandmother's Co-op number and she decided to sit in seat twelve or thirty two. Twelve had been taken so she wrote down thirty-two. The librarian had given the forms to another librarian who had gone back into the stacks, which were closed to the public, to look for the books.

Rosie had sat in seat thirty-two and waited. For a moment her mind wandered back to the Public Gardens. She'd enjoyed feeding the ducks with her mother. It brought back memories of when she was a little girl. She thought about then and remembered now, feeling safe then, not feeling safe now, knowing her family then, not knowing any of them now, not even Sarah. Back and forth, then and now, she realized how much her life had changed.

At school Margaret had told her class that Martin Luther King said all life is interrelated and that whatever affects one directly affects all indirectly, and Rosie remembered because she had quoted Martin Luther King in her report on Nelson Mandela.

"No one's story," Margaret had said, "can stand alone. Every story is part of another." She'd talked with them about a Russian scholar called Michel Bakhtin. She'd told them that Bakhtin had written that their lives were like novels, that their stories were their own, but that all their stories were interconnected.

"Living," Margaret had told them, "is like turning the pages of a book, but there is neither a first nor last word – no beginnings and no endings."

"Your stories," she'd said, "had many chapters way before you were born."

Everyone in Rosie's class was used to the way Margaret talked to them. They'd learned to take the ideas she shared with them and puzzle over them for future conversations – which they knew would take place at some unexpected moment – possibly in the middle of a science experiment or when they were painting a mural or in comedy hour when they wrote jokes and skits and were expected to perform them. They wanted to be ready. It was a mind game they played with Margaret, and with each other. They wanted to outsmart her, and score points – imaginary ones – against each other.

"This is my page," Rosie had said on one such occasion. "There might be others on this page, but it's not the same for them as it is for me."

"And why do you think that is so?" Margaret had asked, smiling at Rosie.

"Because each person on my page will see it differently to me," Rosie had said, without a moment's hesitation. She'd thought about it and spoke as if she was sure of what she'd said.

"Am I on your page?" Jesse had asked, and the rest of the class had laughed.

Rosie knew Jesse liked her, loved her, maybe, but this had not been about that. He'd been trying to knock her off kilter, to interrupt her as she presented her argument, so he could score points, and then present a counter argument, that the class would accept or reject and argue about. The class understood the game and there'd been raucous laughter. Then quiet. They'd waited. All eyes had been on Rosie.

"Yes," Rosie had said, making eye contact with Jesse and speaking slowly. "You are on my page."

Without thinking Jesse had stood up and taken a bow. Rosie had looked over at Rachel. It was a girl moment, a bright eyed, smiling moment of triumph, that Jesse had caught as his head came up. He'd looked around the room and then at Margaret who gave him an eyebrow raised, quizzical look. Jesse had reddened. He'd known his response had been personal, an impulse that had nothing to do with the intellectual challenge. He'd shrugged and sat down knowing the battle would not be so easily won.

"How could you not be on my page?" Rosie had continued, looking straight at Jesse, trying to help him get back into the game. "We've been in the same class since kindergarten and we played together when we were little kids"

The class had waited, but it had been Jesse who had been knocked off kilter – or so it seemed. She'd waited while he'd tried to focus.

"Even though we are on the same page, we see the page differently," Rosie had continued, enjoying the moment, "my page – which I admit you are on – is not the page that you think you are on. You will never see the page the same as me. You cannot look through my eyes and see what I see."

Jesse had raised his arms and bowed again – this time at Rosie, who was smiling because she'd held her ground, presented her argument.

"And, who knows," she'd said, "what will happen when I turn the page."

The class had laughed, stamped their feet and clapped, and Margaret, had raised her hand to quiet them, and then she'd made the most of the moment, by taking them back – and forward in their thinking – to Bakhtin. She'd told them he'd written that at any moment in the development of a dialogue there were immense boundless masses of forgotten meaning.

Margaret had looked at Rosie and then at Jesse. "Which," she'd said with a knowing smile, "I'm sure we all agree is definitely true in this case."

Again, there had been clapping and stamping of feet, which Margaret had quickly ended by putting her finger to her lips and calling for "hush".

In the library Rosie had thought about what Margaret had said as she'd sat waiting for the books that she'd requested. She'd remembered being with her mother in the Public Gardens, the page that they were on before Sarah had got stuck in the elevator and fainted, before she knew there was another Rosie, before Sarah – before Sarah? What had Sarah remembered? What had happened to the other Rosie?

"I'm the replacement," Rosie had muttered to herself, "The spare. She should be an old woman, but she's still a child, living her life through me." She'd thought about the moment when her life changed.

"Someone turned the page," she'd said. "This is not my page," she'd said, more loudly than she had intended. "This is not my page!"

Rosie's thoughts were racing. She was sitting on her bed surrounded by Sarah's stories and by the email conversations they had had about her childhood in Wales. She thought about feeding the ducks with her mother and going to the library. She remembered the moment in the library when she'd realized that she was no longer on her own page. She was living on the page that belonged to another Rosie, who had lived far away many years before she was born.

Thinking back, she remembered sitting in the library waiting for her books, her thoughts wandering back to school, to Margaret and to Jesse. She wondered now if Jesse had actually conceded because he knew that Sarah had been hospitalized and that it was really Rosie who was off kilter. Thoughts flashed so fast she couldn't catch them. She was in the Public Gardens with her mother, in the library, at school, flirting with Jesse, falling, holding on to the old umbrella, and Margaret, holding on to Margaret, grabbing at her academics, grasping for meaning.

When Margaret had talked with them about Bakhtin and "the immense boundless masses of forgotten meaning" she'd written it in her notebook. Intuitively, she'd known it was not some abstract idea that actually described her present situation.

Rosie remembered that on the day that Jesse had asked if he was on her page, Margaret had given them each a quote from Bakhtin to put in their backpacks to read when they went home. Rosie had forgotten about it. She rummaged in her backpack. The quote was on a crumpled piece of paper at the bottom of her bag. She smoothed it out. Margaret had read them the beginning of the quote in class.

"There is neither a first nor last word," Rosie read and then continued reading.

"Even the past meanings, that is, those born in the dialogue of past centuries, can never be stable, finalized, ended once and for all. They will always change, be renewed, in the process of subsequent, future development of dialogue."

She thought about her quest for her own truth and for a moment she felt Bakhtin was on her page.

"Did Margaret know that when she gave us the quote?" Rosie asked herself. Margaret had given the quote to the whole class so was it just that she knew this was a moment when they were all searching for their own truth? She'd read the last sentence of the quote.

"Nothing is absolutely dead," Rosie whispered, "every meaning will have its homecoming festival."

Margaret had taught them to read deeply, to try to find connections to their own lives in the complicated quotations she presented to them. "Read deeply," she always said. On the day that she'd given them the quote from Bakhtin, she'd said, "Remember, there is no prize for getting to the end of the quotation, only for getting the meaning of a phrase or sentence and being able to put into words what it means to you." She'd looked over at Rosie, "How it fits or doesn't fit on your page." Rosie had smiled at Margaret, and Margaret, still holding her gaze, had said, "Try to imagine the ways in which your lives are part of the past as well as the present. See if you can find connections between what Bakhtin is saying and your own lives."

"Even past meanings," Rosie read again, more slowly this time, "that is," she focused, "those born in the dialogue of past centuries," she thought of her Aunt Sarah's stories and the emails about her childhood in Wales, "born in the dialogue of past centuries, can never be stable, finalized, ended once and for all."

"I didn't understand what Bakhtin meant before the emails from Aunt Sarah," Rosie thought to herself, "now I get it." She was not sure she could put it into words, but she understood what Bakhtin meant, except for the homecoming festival.

She thought quickly of Jesse. She knew he could have come back at her and told her that there are always others on our page, that we do not see what they see, and that if we cannot see what they see, the page can never completely belong to us. Pages are always shared – with members of our family, our friends, and those who lived before us. He could have challenged the idea that it was her page, because it clearly was not. Ironically now, she thought there were two Rosie's on her page.

"This is not my page" Rosie had whispered in the library, loud enough to break the silence and making people sitting motionless at the huge tables near her look at her in annoyance.

"Sorry it's taking so long," the librarian had whispered, having arrived after Rosie had made everyone jump. "You look very pale. Are you sure you're alright?" She thought Rosie looked as if she might faint or be sick.

"I'm okay," Rosie had said. She'd got her notebook out of her backpack and put the smoothed out piece of paper with the Bakhtin quote inside it. Then she'd searched at the bottom of the bag for a pencil.

"Right," the librarian had said. "I'll go and find out why it is taking so long to get your books. By now we could have printed them."

Rosie had tried to keep her thoughts in the library and not think back. She'd looked around the enormous room with its high brick ceiling and long numbered tables.

The man across from her had looked up and he'd given her a reassuring nod. Rosie had imagined him saying, "Don't worry. Everything will be okay."

She'd pressed her lips together and raised her eyebrows as if to say, "Apologies for making so much noise."

The man had smiled and shrugged "that's okay" and returned to reading his book.

"Here you are," the librarian had said cheerfully, as she put four books on the table in front of Rosie. "I had some help finding them," she'd whispered, continuing without taking a breath. "One of the other librarians said you're the second person who has been searching for information about Wales and coal mining families. No one in years and then two people in two weeks! Well, it might be a bit longer than that," she'd said, "maybe three weeks."

Rosie had wanted to interrupt, but didn't. Totally convinced it must have been Jesse, she'd finally asked, "Was it a boy, my age?"

"A woman, I think Daisy said," the librarian had looked over her glasses at Rosie, "the librarian's name is Ms. Blake," she'd said. "She's finishing up what she's doing and coming to speak with you. I think she has some more resources that might interest you." The librarian had smiled and patted the pile of books on the table. "See what you can find in these. I'm sure she won't be long."

"Okay." Rosie had said, realizing it was better to wait than to ask any more questions. Besides she'd already made up her mind that the woman who had come to the library looking for information about Wales must have been her Aunt Sarah. Rosie had stopped feeling muddled.

"Sarah must have been here before Dad took her to the hospital," Rosie had said to herself. "What was she looking for?"

A shiver ran down Rosie's spine that was so strong her whole body shook. She remembered that her Aunt used to say that "shivers up" mean something good is going to happen, but "shivers down" mean someone has just walked on your grave.

"But I'm still alive!" Rosie used to tell Sarah.

"It's a sign of foreboding," Sarah used to reply, nodding her head, screwing up her eyes and looking around as if the devil himself was creeping up behind them. Then laughing out loud she'd say, "My lovely girl! I'm teasing you! It's an old wives tale!"

"But what if it isn't?" Rosie had asked herself in the library, "What if it's a sign that something bad has happened? Or," she'd reasoned, shivering again with a distinct feeling of uneasiness, "something bad *is going* to happen!"

She'd thought about her Dad telling her he was worried Sarah would try to kill herself.

"It's a sign of foreboding," Rosie had whispered out loud, looking around to make sure no one had heard. "I never understood the meaning of the word," she'd thought, feeling chilled and filled with apprehension, "but I do now".

Rosie had tried to concentrate.

"Aunt Sarah must have sat here," she'd thought, looking at the four books on the table. Two of them had identical red covers and looked as if the spines had never been cracked, but Sarah must have opened them, she'd thought. "Whatever our reasons for reading we'll have both turned the same pages and just possibly landed on the same page."

"You might not know what you're looking for," Margaret had told them, "but you will know when you find it."

The first book had been about colliery closures and social change. She'd flipped through the pages and sighed. The writing was small and uninviting. At first she'd struggled to understand what the author was trying to say.

Margaret had told them again and again that sometimes there is interesting information even in the most uninteresting of books.

"One small gem of an idea," Margaret said, "sometimes that's all you are trying to find." She must have said it a hundred times. "It's a quest for a nugget of information so rare you have to search every paragraph, every sentence, until you discover where it's hiding."

"The period surrounding the announcement of a colliery closure is one of great uncertainty," Rosie had read and then she'd scanned the lines of text. The sentence ended three quarters of the way down the page. Every page was the same. Forgetting Margaret's advice Rosie had become increasingly annoyed with the writer.

"Aunt Sarah makes the lives of miners and their families come alive," she'd muttered to herself, as she'd tried to pretend she was Sarah looking for information in the book. She just couldn't imagine Sarah reading it. She closed the book and picked up the next one that was equally stiff covered and off-putting.

"Maybe Sarah wasn't looking for anything in particular," she'd thought to herself, "maybe she just wanted to find out as much as she could about coal mining in Wales to fill in the gaps in her memory."

The second book had also been about mine closures. She'd scanned the introduction and then skipped through the book reading pages at random.

"The demand for coal was maintained in between the First and Second World Wars."

"The population in the coal mining valleys continued to decline."

Rosie had made some notes and for a few moments her feelings of foreboding had faded. Again it had been Margaret with her insistence on primary sources, the search for legitimate accounts, and making accurate notes, that steadied Rosie.

"Investigate!" Margaret always told them, "Don't accept second hand opinions! Get the facts! Find out for yourselves!"

Rosie and the other students in Margaret's class had quickly got the message. All it had taken to quickly shift the class into research mode was for a few students to make abysmal presentations of unsubstantiated opinions weakly strung together, followed by other student presentations filled with gems of ideas that sparkled with well supported facts. It was a badge of honor to find the most obscure document and the least known fact.

Two years of such intense research had helped Rosie as she studied the text in front of her, but Margaret had also tempered her enthusiasm for research with the advice that there were times when a book just had to be abandoned, left on the shelf for another search.

Rosie had taken some notes and then snapped the book shut. She might have taken more notes for her school projects if Sarah's visit to the library hadn't filled her mind, but probably not.

"Look for resources that inspire you," Margaret always told

them.

The third book had been filled with diagrams of the segregated settlements in which the miners and their families had lived in one of the coal mining valleys of South Wales

When Rosie had first studied the diagrams she was convinced Sarah would have looked at them closely. This was the gem, the nugget of information she was searching for, and it was as black and shiny as a nugget of coal.

"All the houses belonged to collieries," Sarah had written in her emails. "That's the way it was. The rent was taken out of the miners' wages."

Rosie had read the emails so many times she remembered them almost word for word.

"We didn't use money for very much. We used tokens. We called them checks," Sarah had written. "Our Nan had to buy the checks from the colliery and she used them at the Co-op to pay for the milk and bread."

"Our Grandad was allowed one ton of coal every month which cost seven shillings and six pence. The money was taken out of his pay packet along with the rent. Fancy that! First he had to dig the coal out of the mountain and then he had to pay seven and six for it!"

Staring at the diagrams Rosie's thoughts had once again bumped into each other. Sarah's first-hand account of the segregation of miners and their families fitted with the closed circles of segregated houses depicted in the diagrams, except on the Garn the miners lived in rows of houses close to the mines that were called Garn Drift and Kay's Slope, and to Big Pit with its deep mineshaft that was not far from the Garn but closer to Blaenavon.

Rosie had studied the diagrams and copied several of them into her notebook. She drew the circles while other thoughts and revelations cascaded through her mind. It had been as if drawing the circles was changing who she had been. For the first time she'd thought of herself as the Great Granddaughter of coal miners who lived in a segregated settlements, separated from the rest of society because they were poor and worked down the mines.

Rosie had found her own history was deeply embedded in the struggle to stay alive and survive the misery of the mines. She'd studied the Civil Rights Movement. She knew about segregation, but she never imagined that she'd come from a segregated community.

"Coal dust made the families black," she'd thought to herself, wondering what Margaret would say if she said that.

For Rosie, until this moment in the library, *segregation* had been about racial injustice, but it had suddenly become much more than that. She considered it now to be human injustice.

Rosie had left the book open at the page with the diagram of the segregated coal mining settlement on the table and made some notes.

"Document the facts," Margaret always told them, "but don't forget to include in your account what you think about them."

She'd looked at her watch, worried about the time and getting back in case her father brought Sarah home. Several people had come into the cavernous room, an old man bent and frail, and a very tall young woman in a long green skirt with a flowered top. She had green streaks in her short black hair and for a moment Rosie tried to imagine herself with green streaks amongst her red curls, and the image made her smile.

"I'd look like a bunch of flowers," she's thought to herself.

The young woman with green streaks in her hair had been carrying a very large leather bound book, which she'd put on a table at the other end of the room, Then she'd helped the old man shuffle into position so that he could sit down on the chair she'd held steady behind him, as he settled in to read the *Boston Globe*.

Rosie had turned back to the table and she'd picked up the fourth book and opened it to a page in the middle of the book.

"It's like Hell there now!" a miner was quoted as saying on the first page that she read about halfway through the book. "You'd have a coal-mandrill which was very light and very sharp with a long blade like a stiletto. You had a shovel, and then you had a seven-pound axe."

Rosie had remembered her Great Grandad using a mandrill in Sarah's story about him. She'd imagined him on his knees with a mandrill and shovel to extract the coal from the narrow seams of the Kay's Slope coalface.

"You'd work until the rock would be kind of like a layer on you," she'd read in the book as if her Great Grandfather was talking to her, "where your own skin had been taken off. And it would get stiff like, as if you'd baked it in clay, till you put it into the bath in the night; and it would start to burn and come off."

Rosie had started taking notes.

She'd decided that she would have a section in her report on how coal miners in Wales dug the coal. She'd written how huge steam-driven fans were used to ventilate the mines, how a "cage" was lowered into deep pit mines to take the men deep underground to the coalface, and how the cage was raised to bring the drams of coal and the men back to surface when their shift was done.

"In the quiet of the stall where there were no sounds except those made by themselves, a barely heard crack or a faint trickle of dust from the roof would warn them they must take some action," she'd copied, "either put up more support timber or, if they interpreted the warning sound more urgently, move quickly out of danger before the roof fell down or the place caved in."

Rosie had flipped through the pages looking for an uncut diamond, a shiny nugget of coal, but all she found were devastating facts. What caught her attention were the chapters of the book that described what happened to the miners who spent all their lives digging coal in the dark damp tunnels so far underground.

"It is well known," she had read and copied, making sure she included the bibliographic information, "that miners develop silicosis". She'd made notes about the symptoms of "pneumoconiosis," which include "dyspnoea" which means shortness of breath, "a cough" which is "almost always present," and in the "late stages" "signs of heart failure or tuberculosis."

Rosie had lost herself in the facts and figures that accompanied the text. So many miners injured, so many died, but the others, the lucky ones, gasping for breath, lived out what was left of their lives when the mines were done with them. She'd thought of Sarah and what she might have said if this was just a school report, if she hadn't got stuck in the elevator, if she had not become *un*stuck.

"You must be Rosie Llywelyn!"

Rosie had jumped. The young woman with green streaks in her short black hair had been standing a bit to the side of Rosie, but mostly behind her.

"Sorry if I made you jump!" The young woman had looked around to include everyone sitting near Rosie in her apology. She'd nodded her head and said, "Shall we sit over there so we won't disturb anyone?"

Rosie had gathered her books, put her notebook on top of them, slung her backpack over her right shoulder, and carried the books to the table where the young woman with green streaks was opening the huge leather bound book of newspapers that she had brought with her.

"I'm Daisy," she'd said, as Rosie reached the table. "Daisy Blake." She'd held out her hand and they shook hands, and as they did Rosie had seen the circles of what looked like writing tattooed on her wrist.

"They're ancient Runes," Daisy had whispered, holding out both hands and turning them so Rosie could see the Runes. "You read them from right to left. They remind me of my history and keep me constant in my beliefs."

"I've heard so much about you, not only from your Aunt Sarah, Ms. Llywelyn, but also from Margaret." She'd given a little laugh, "Does anyone call Margaret by her last name? I know her students don't and she always introduces herself as just 'Margaret'".

"Actually," Daisy had whispered, "Margaret was talking about her class, and Sarah was taking about you and mentioned Margaret, so that's the connection!"

Rosie had been going to say something about why Margaret's students called her by her first name, but the librarian shifted topics and continued by telling Rosie how she had helped Margaret with the preparations she had made to bring her class to the library to do their own research on their Civil Rights project. "But, I was on maternity leave when your class came to the library with Margaret." She'd said, looking sad that she had missed it, and then smiling again. "I have a baby boy," she'd said, "William, like Shakespeare!" she'd laughed. "Well that's what I tell the children when I read them stories, actually it was my Grandfather's name."

"Aunt Sarah?" Rosie had said, nothing more.

Daisy had immediately looked concerned. "Sarah came into the library about three weeks ago, just like you asking for books on coal mining in Wales." Daisy had spoken conspiratorially as if she knew there was a mystery. Rosie had wondered if Sarah had told Daisy that she had become undone, that her family had fallen apart, that there were secrets that Rosie did not know.

But she had quickly realized that Daisy knew very little except that Sarah was trying to trace her family history.

"I was working at the Social Science Reference Desk when she first came into the library," Daisy had said. "She seemed a bit lost."

"My Aunt has not been well," Rosie had said.

Daisy had reached out to her and clasped her hand. "She loves you very much," she'd said. She'd pointed at the open book on the table in front of them. "I got goose bumps when I saw you studying those diagrams. Sarah was fascinated by them too."

Rosie had felt as if someone was walking on her grave.

"It's for a school project," Rosie had said. "But my Aunt must have been in here before that. I didn't start the project until after she was admitted to the hospital."

"Oh, I hope she is alright?" Daisy had said. She'd seen the look on Rosie's face and didn't ask any more questions.

"I made her some tea on one visit," Daisy had rushed on, not wanting to pry or put Rosie on the spot. "We're not supposed to of course, but I'm not very good with 'not- supposed-to's'!"

Rosie had liked Daisy and joined in the deflection of the conversation away from Sarah. She'd grinned, "I don't expect librarians are supposed to have tattoos!"

"We're supposed to cover them up," Daisy had grinned back, "but it's a bit confusing because they are runes and the other librarians like to decipher them!"

Rosie had looked more closely at Daisy's wrists. Daisy had looked at them too, then impulsively pulled Rosie's notebook towards her.

"Can I write in it?"

"Sure," Rosie had said, turning the page.

Daisy had picked up Rosie's pencil and she drew what looked like a capital M only the cross strokes literally crossed, making what had seemed to Rosie to be an x between two straight lines.

"This is the starting point," Daisy had said, "It's the symbol for the self. Its essence is water. Your relationship with yourself is primary, like water you must be willing to change. The Rune means to me that I must strive to live the ordinary life in a non-ordinary way. This is what it says in *The Book of Runes*. Take heart, in the life of the spirit you are always beginning."

Rosie had wondered if Daisy knew that she felt as if she had lost herself, that somehow what was happening to Sarah was happening to her too. Daisy had written another symbol. It looked like a lower case n with the horizontal at the top sloping to the right with the right vertical much shorter than the left.

"This is the Rune for strength, for womanhood. It's the Rune that reminds us that new life comes of old. When there is a death experience we must seek amongst the ashes for new perspectives and new birth. It's important that we are creative and we adapt."

Rosie had been unnerved by how close to her own experience Daisy had come in the Runes she had chosen to share with her.

"I'm going to share one last Rune, because I have something else to show you," Daisy had said, drawing again in Rosie's notebook. This Rune looked like an uppercase R. "It stands for a journey, communication, union and reunion. The journey is the soul's journey, it's about healing, trusting yourself to take the journey, and if you have begun, to continue on."

"Thank you," Rosie had said, as if she had been blessed, and without thinking about it she'd put her arms around Daisy and hugged her.

"Do you realise we're both named after flowers!" Daisy had said, as the moment passed, and Rosie had laughed.

"I was imagining myself with green streaks in my hair!" Rosie had said. "I'd look like a bunch of roses!"

"Ahh!" Daisy had laughed, her eyes going up. "Claude Monet. Giverny. I was reading books on Monet with some children this morning and we painted water lilies." She looked down at her green skirt and flowered top. "When I sit on the floor my skirt looks like a lily pad," she'd looked up again, "but the green streaks were done with the paint we used." She'd laughed. "It's a long story! Don't ask! No time to go home and wash it out!"

Rosie had laughed and then her eyes had rested on the enormous book of newspapers on the table.

"I've had this book in my office for the last couple of weeks in case your Aunt Sarah returned to the library," Daisy had said. "We really didn't find a lot of information about coal mining in Wales when she was here, which is strange really. I'd have thought there would be more, so when I went to see my Uncle Harry I rummaged around in his old books and manuscripts. He's a Sanskrit scholar, which is probably why I became interested in Runes. Anyway he collects old newspapers and he has copies of all the London *Times* newspapers between the First and Second World Wars! Each year is bound in leather like this book! They are very beautiful. Most of them are boxed up, but when I went to see him I told him how little I'd been able to find in the library on coal-mining in South Wales and he jumped up."

He took me by the hand into his study," Daisy had smiled. "There on his desk was the book of newspapers for 1936. In it were three newspaper articles about the coal mining valleys of South Wales. One was about the King visiting, the other two about the mines closing."

"He knew the month and the exact day that the articles were published!" Daisy had said. "We looked at the articles together and then he said I could borrow the book!"

"He knew you'd take care of it," Rosie had said, smiling at Daisy. "Isn't that what librarians do? Take care of books? Still it was very nice of him."

Daisy had pushed the big book of 1936 newspapers towards her. "I was going to surprise your Aunt Sarah." She'd glanced at Rosie, again not asking questions.

"She's in a psychiatric hospital," Rosie had said. "Actually a psychiatric unit of a hospital."

Daisy had looked upset.

"I don't think she belongs in there," Rosie had said, without any display of emotion. "I think she just remembered something that was very terrible and they locked her up."

"Something was troubling her," Daisy had said, biting her lip, unsure if she should say anything. "But she was very focused on finding out more about the lives of coal mining families in South Wales. It's possible that you will find out something that will help her in these newspaper articles or in your other research."

Rosie had agreed.

"You were both on the same page in the book you were studying," Daisy had reminded her. "Look, I'm going to leave you here with the newspaper articles. There's also this folder of articles on the Blaina Riots that I'd put together for Sarah. She was interested in them. You can take the folder home. Just let the librarian know when you've finished with my Uncle's big book of newspapers and she will put the book in my office."

She'd looked at her watch, "Goodness! Is that the time! I have to go! My babysitter has to leave early today."

Rosie looked at her watch and realized it was almost one o'clock and decided she'd stay for another thirty minutes.

"Please come back," Daisy had said, giving Rosie a hug. "I hope Sarah comes home soon," and then as an afterthought she asked, "By the way, did you find your umbrella?"

"Was Aunt Sarah looking for it?" Rosie had asked, visibly shaken.

"We looked for it together," Daisy had replied, slowing her departure, knowing that her question about the umbrella had upset Rosie. "So many umbrellas get left in the library but we couldn't find your umbrella."

"My Aunt was looking for her sister's umbrella," Rosie had said, quite calmly, again without any visible emotion. "There were two of us you see, two Rosie Llywlyn's, my Aunt Rosie is dead, so now there is just me."

Daisy had also been visibly shaken and without thinking she'd given Rosie another hug.

Rosie's eyes had filled with tears.

"Please come back," Daisy had said, and needing something more to say she'd added, "there are copies of the newspaper articles in the folder."

"Thank you," Rosie had said. She'd closed her eyes and with a tremor of a smile she'd nodded, a Rune of a gesture to let Daisy know she was okay.

Rosie remembered she'd looked at Daisy's notes in the folder before she'd read the articles in the 1936 book of the London *Times* newspapers. She smiled to herself thinking of Daisy. She thought about the green streaks in Daisy's hair and the lily pad skirt she'd been wearing because she'd been reading books on Monet and painting water lilies with children.

For a moment Rosie thought about Daisy without intrusive thoughts crashing into what she was thinking. It was as if she was holding on to her memories in the same way she had held on to Daisy's notes. She didn't want her thoughts of Daisy to go. She knew what she really wanted to do was hold on to Daisy. The folder was on her desk and she picked it up. It had comforted her then as it did now that Daisy had written a note to her Aunt Sarah.

Opening the folder took her back to the library. Daisy had written in a blue pen and her handwriting was a mixture of script, italic, and print that lolloped across the sheets of yellow lined paper torn from a note pad. It had taken Rosie a moment to decipher Daisy's writing, but then she had found it easy to read.

Dear Sarah,

I had another look for your umbrella. Alas I did not find it. However, I did find time to do a little research on the Blaina Riots and on the plight of children in South Wales during the depression. I had no idea that the conditions in the coalmining valleys were so bad.

George Orwell got it right in "1984"!

I've included a quote from the Prime Minister, Neville Chamberlain, who said, "the devastation in the coalfields can only be compared with the war devastation of France".

Capitalism is in crisis! Rich men have always preyed on the poor and historically they've shown no mercy. I was surprised to find there is very little written about what happened to the coal mining families in South Wales.

History records the exploits of great men, but not the exploitation of the poor. We know very little of their lives or what happened to them. It is why it will happen again, and sooner than we imagine, I fear.

I know you are particularly interested in what happened to the children. I did find a few references. In 1932 there was an inquiry into nutrition in the mining valleys of South Wales, and in the report there is a description of the children in Rhymney, which is just a few miles from Blaina.

The children were described as "small with a tired expression, lacking bright sparkling eyes and with no tone to the skin".

Cruel. I think of my little William and my heart breaks. Thank goodness for you Sarah, and all those who care about what happens to our children. I really enjoyed talking with you and having tea! Please come back and see me.

Good luck,
Daisy Blake

Rosie had wondered if Daisy meant for her to read the letter. She had no idea but she didn't think Daisy would mind that she had read it. She'd looked through all the copies of pages from the books and articles Daisy had put together for Sarah. Some of them were just one or two pages of much longer texts, and Daisy had written the bibliographic information at the top of each first page. She had also underlined words and phrases as well as whole sentences,

Rosie had quickly read the underlined words:

distressed areas … hunger marches … bitterness … hopelessness. … unemployment reached colossal levels … loss of income suffered by many unemployed families forced the older sons and daughters out of the parental home. … the National Government was accused of destroying family life.

Daisy had also drawn a line in the margins to indicate longer passages of relevance.

"Unemployment benefit is not a living wage," declared the Prime Minister, Ramsey MacDonald on 25th August 1931. "It was never intended to be that."

Practically all this property is unfit for human habitation - a good many houses are back-to-back or without through ventilation, the sanitary arrangements are of a primitive type and in some cases shared between houses.

Except those suffering from industrial diseases, whilst the men of the towns looked their age, the women of the communities generally looked older than they were. The children of the valley were particularly badly affected by the Depression. The infant mortality rate doubled from 56.6 per 1000 children less than twelve months old in 1930 to 118.8 in 1934.

If they survived the early years of life, these children had little to look forward to. In 1935, the Monmouthshire County Health Department reported that 80 percent of Abertillery's schoolchildren were physically incapacitated to some degree. Only ten percent were in normal health.

Daisy had included information on Blaina and these pages were held together with a red paper clip. She had stuck a post-it on the first page on which she had written, "Hunger marches not riots!" Other than that she had not made any notes or marked any passages. Rosie picked up her pencil. She underlined dates, places, and the number of people participating in the hunger marches.

January 1935 a rally at Merthyr ... attracted 40,000 people. In Pontypridd a few days later 20,000 people marched in protest, and other such marches and rallies occurred regularly as the previously contained anger of the unemployed flooded out onto the streets.

On Sunday, 3rd February 1935 ... at least 300,000 people had been on the streets of South Wales on marches and rallies.

In Blaina and Nantyglo a rally organized for Thursday, 21st March 1935 was witnessed by young children from the mountainside above the road who reported many thousands of people peacefully marching when a police whistle blew from amidst the ranks of police. Many who participated in the rally were injured by the police, who beat them with their truncheons. After the police dispersed the crowd they left the wounded lying on the road, and among them were many women and children. Estimates put the total number of seriously injured at around 200.

Rosie knew her Great Grandfather had played in the Blaina Brass Band and he would have been a young man at the time of the Blaina hunger march. She'd wondered if he had participated, but did not spend much time thinking about it. She'd been worried about the time and getting home to see Sarah, and she'd decided to read the rest of the documents when she got home. Even so she'd taken a quick look at the big tome that belonged to Daisy's Uncle Harry.

The articles were about the King of England's 1936 tour of the coal mining communities in South Wales. Rosie had become familiar with the names of the mining towns and she recognized some of them even if she was not sure how to pronounce them, including Brynmawr, Ebbw Vale, Llanelly, Cymbran.

The King had visited Blaenavon, which was the nearest mining town to Gan-yr-erw. She'd scanned the articles quickly and had been surprised to read that the government response to the plight of the miners and their families was to establish a "Policy of Transference".

"The Government aimed at easing the situation by transferring able-bodied men and juveniles to other parts of the country," Rosie had read. She had drawn in her breath as she'd read about "the social loss to the nation of having on its hands a lumpen people." She knew what "lumpen" meant.

The next sentence she'd read was that the "King left Padding-
ton in a private special train consisting of two sleeping cars, two
saloons, and two first-class coaches". It had occurred to her that if
she had been alive at the time she would not have been travelling
with the King of England, she'd have been weak and malnourished,
and possibly even lying in the road bloodied and bruised after being
hit by a policeman's truncheon in Blaina.

Rosie had left the library at 1:45 in a hurry. She'd wanted to see Sarah and started running, other than that she had no memory of the journey home.

"How's Aunt Sarah?" she'd called out as she opened the front door.

"Not good!" her mother had shouted from the kitchen. "The dentist did some root canal work this morning, but she has to go back and see him next week because her wisdom teeth are impacted!"

"Sounds awful! Is Dad bringing her back here?"

"They wouldn't let him." Mary had said, knowing that Rosie would be upset. "In the end she saw a dentist at the hospital."

Rosie had dropped her backpack on the kitchen table.

"Fuck!"

"Rosie!"

Rosie had mouthed the word again. There had been nothing else she'd wanted to say, except to shout at her mother that Sarah did not belong in the hospital and she wanted her to come home. Rosie had kept silent, knowing it would just make matters worse.

Mary had been sitting at the table with a stack of student papers and a cup of coffee. She'd gone back to the paper she was reading and for a few minutes they had sat in silence.

"I hate the end of the semester," Mary had said, suddenly standing up and taking off her reading glasses. She took the backpack by one shoulder strap and lifted it off the table and let it drop a little too quickly to the floor.

"If my laptop had been in there you'd have broken it," Rosie had said, scowling.

"Your laptop is on your desk."

"What were you doing in my room?"

"Looking for Max," Mary had said. "You shut the door and he was inside."

Rosie couldn't help herself. She'd rolled her eyes and smiled. Mary had smiled too.

"Ooops," Rosie had said. "Hope he didn't need to go."

"Smells fine," Mary had said.

Rosie opened the fridge and looked inside and then shut the door without taking anything out. Instead she took the last banana in the bowl on the table, and then she went back to the fridge and took out a carton of milk, got a glass from the cupboard and filled it.

Mary had started reading again. "All I do is read students papers," she'd said. "Sometimes I think they just pull their ideas out of thin air. Look! This one doesn't even have one reference!"

"You sound like Margaret!" Rosie had groaned. "Fortunately,

I have a lot of references."

"For your report?"

"On coal miners and their families." Rosie had pulled a face. "I have a lot of stuff."

"No castles?" Mary had asked, trying to be humorous, and then worrying that Rosie would take it the wrong way.

"No," Rosie had said. "No castles, but I do have a King on a train." She'd smiled and shook her head. "Don't ask."

"Then you probably don't need what's in that package," Mary had said.

"What's in it?"

"A peace offering from your Dad," Mary had said. "After we went to Toscano's he phoned Peter Cornwell in Brighton, and asked him if he could send you a study about coal mining families in Wales Tom remembered Peter had found at Sussex University."

"England?"

Mary had nodded.

"Why did he do that?" Rosie never ceased to be amazed by the odd behavior of her parents. "And who's Peter Cornwell?"

"Your Dad went to university with him. They've stayed friends."

"He never told me he had a friend called Peter Cornwell," Rosie had said. "He never tells me anything."

"Well anyway," Mary had said, ignoring the comment. "Your Dad remembered talking with Peter when he saw him in London last year about some study that had been done in Wales. Peter's in television and he'd been doing some research in – they call it the Mass Observation Archive – at Sussex University."

Mary had pushed back her chair and picked up the carton of milk Rosie had left on the table. "To cut a long story short," she'd said. "Peter told your Dad about some study that was done in Blaina in the 1930's or 40's. Your Dad called him. Peter made a copy of the study and he sent it DHL to you."

"Seems an awful lot of trouble for a school report."

"It's probably just your Dad's way of letting you know that he loves you."

"His way of not having to talk to me about it," Rosie had said. "'Here, just read this report!'"

"Rosie, that's unkind!"

"Sorry."

Rosie had eaten the banana and she'd grabbed an apple from the dish and headed upstairs with the package. "I'd rather he took me to a baseball game!" she'd shouted down at her mother.

"He has tickets for the baseball game next Saturday."

"Gotta finish my report," Rosie had said. "Tell him I can't go."

Mary had got up from the table and went out into the hall and stood at the bottom of the stairs. "Rosie!" she'd shouted. "What about lunch?"

"Later!" Rosie had yelled back, looking over the banister and holding out the apple for Mary to see. "When you've finished reading all those papers!"

Rosie had turned on her computer and logged on. There was a message from Jesse, another from Rachel, and even one from Margaret to remind her group that they were presenting their preliminary findings of their family heritage projects in class on Monday, but there was no message from Sarah. Rosie wrote messages to her friends, and then she had written to her Aunt:

Hiya Aunt Sarah, I need to talk to you. Please write!

She'd waited. Nothing. She'd tried to send another message but her computer froze. She pressed keys and clicked the mouse. Nothing. She'd shut it down and started it back up. She'd logged on and sent another message. She had wanted to tell her Aunt about the little girl in the coffin, and she had questions about her school report. She hoped Sarah was all right.

Feeling lonely, Rosie had left her computer and sat on her bed. Per usual, Max had jumped up and made himself comfortable beside her. She'd opened the DHL package and found a thick stack of papers and a note from Peter Cornwell.

Dear Rosie:

Your Dad said you might be interested in this report on Blaina. The young woman, whose name unfortunately does not appear on the report, went to Blaina in 1941 and lived there for three months. The report was never published, but it has always interested me. The whole point of the study was to document the voices of the ordinary folks. What a radical idea! Anyway I hope it's useful. Good luck with your school report. Tell your Dad to bring you to England some day. You'll like it – and I know you'll love Wales.

Best Regards,
Peter Cornwell.

Rosie had looked at the report. It was a copy of the original, which had been written on a typewriter over fifty years ago. The ink was smudged and much of it was difficult to read. She'd sat on her bed leaning back against the pillows. Max had padded around then climbed onto her lap. Rosie had rested the report against Max and began to read. Much to her surprise it read like a novel. The young woman who wrote it described the houses in which the miners and their families lived, and her descriptions had reminded Rosie of her Aunt Sarah's stories.

When Rosie had finished reading the report she'd pushed Max off her lap and got off the bed. She'd sat down at her computer and with a few clicks created a new file on coal mining families in South Wales and created a new document. She'd then typed all the bibliographic information at the top of the page just as Daisy had done on the documents she had given her.

Rosie had typed "Coal Miners' Houses." She planned to write an introduction, but right now all she was interested in doing was copying the bits of the report that seemed to be important. She imagined the young woman visiting the miners in their homes. She pretended that she was the young woman and she wrote.

> The first house was one of a group of eleven standing back off the road and opening onto a big muddy fore-court. The water closets stand away across the court and in front of the houses. In winter the forecourt would probably be squelchy with mud and water. At the rear is a retaining wall against a pit-tip. The tip is pushing down and gradually the retaining wall is breaking up.

Rosie had lost herself in the young woman's writing. It was like being there. She imagined the tremendous pressure of the pit-tip and the wall collapsing on the houses killing the miners and their families who lived in the eleven dilapidated houses.

> The second house visited was one which had become a back house. It had once been a four-roomed house with good sized rooms, a staircase rising between the two back and two front rooms. At present, it is occu-pied by two families, both using the same stairs. There is, naturally, no bathroom, but there is also no indoor lavatory. There is no adequate inside sink, but the back house has a small tap just behind the backdoor.

"No matter what else, every house should have its own lava-tory," Rosie typed, quoting one of the tenants. "It's only healthy."

"The third house was a cellar dwelling," Rosie had looked back and forth from the computer screen to the text.

> Two rooms only and a pantry, which backed against the earth. These cellars were originally meant to be

store houses for the rest of the house and not lived in for any length of time. This particular house was nicely furnished and obviously a source of pride to its owner. The brass was highly polished and the curtain clean, and the floor newly washed. The young girl who was tidying the house looked hurt and angry at a comment not intended to be overheard: "These places aren't fit for anybody to live in."

Rosie had wondered what the sociologist would have thought about her Great Grandmother's house, and for a moment she'd imagined that she was the tenant being interviewed by the sociologist. She'd stopped at another description of a cellar in which a woman and child were living without permission from the collieries.

The child seemed ill and apathetic, and the woman, dirty and in ragged clothes looked like a wild beast, ready to fight for her right to stay in the house.

Rosie had continued reading and copying sections of the report, but she'd kept thinking about the sick child, and in her mind she could see the children walking around the table looking at the little girl who had died.

She'd reached a section on "Work Conditions" and started a new section for her own report. The sociologist had included the comments of miners on working in the mines and Rosie copied them.

Mining is hard work – a continual strain – over time it takes the energy out of a person.

Conditions aren't too good, really. You get harassed from morning to night. You can't do more than with one pair of hands.

Life is always at stake. Even when you're going down each day, there is always the possibility of the rope breaking.

The way you're treated seems to shatter all your hopes. You start work when you're 12. Often you work fifty years underground and you're worse off at the finish than at the beginning.

When you're a miner, you feel as if you're a goat on a tether, you go round and round in a small space, and never get any further.

The miner can never feel the same as other people. The fact he's covered in coal dust. My wife's ashamed when she sees me in these clothes. If we were going together in the train, you and I, the guard'd open the first-class carriage for you and a third class or the guard's van for me.

Wherever you go, if people know you're a miner, you're looked down on. It's best to keep quiet about it.

Rosie had sat back in her chair. She wondered if she'd misunderstood what was going on. "Is my Dad ashamed that he comes from a coal mining family?" she'd asked herself. "Is that why he won't talk about it?" She'd read on, writing down what the miners and their wives said. At the end of the report the sociologist wrote a postscript, which contained the comments of a miner's wife about her life when her husband was out of work. Rosie had decided to end her note-taking with the miner's wife.

My husband was three years out. It became terrible. We saw the children failing before our eyes. Father and I would say we didn't want things – to let the children have them. We could see the children getting weaker. My eldest girl became ill. They said she had tuberculosis.

Again Rosie had thought about the little girl in the coffin on the table in the miner's cottage.

What we were doing for our children, dozens of others were doing. Mothers and fathers going without. You could see the look on the women's faces, the starvation look, the cheekbones and the eyes. We know, here in the mining villages, what it means when a woman looks like that.

There 'ave been times when I've had no shoes to go out in, and I've had to stay in the house.

I used to sit up to 2 o'clock on a Sunday to wash the children's clothes and iron them so that they could go out again on Monday – go to school tidy. They used to go to Sunday school, but they were too shabby at last, I had to stop it.

Now, things are a little better. You meet a smile now and again instead of cheeks pinched in and people worried to death.

Rosie had included the entire account of the plight of the children in her notes.

When Rosie had first read the accounts Peter Cornwell had
sent her that were written by the sociologist and also the miners
and their families in Wales she'd thought about the 1936 *Times* use
of "lumpen". She did exactly the same again now, sitting on her bed
after school the night in the hospital.

One of Rachel's very old Great Uncles had used the word
when she'd stayed with them on Cape Cod last summer. For some
reason it had upset one of Rachel's Great Aunts who had taken off
her glasses and used them to point at Rachel's Great Uncle, and she
had told him off, not mincing her words, and he'd become so angry
his whole being seemed to change and he'd shouted at Rachel's Great
Aunt. And as ancient as she was, she'd stood up and she'd not been
intimidated. It had been as if lightning had passed between them.

Rosie had heard the words "lumpenproletariat" and Karl Marx,
and later when Rachel's Great Uncle and Great Aunt were sitting

together laughing and drinking tea, they'd asked Rosie to join them. They'd both apologized. Rachel's Great Aunt had explained the origins of lumpenproletariat, which they shortened to "lumpen". They'd talked about Engels, Marx, and Trotsky, and from what Rosie had gathered from their much too detailed explanation, the lumpen were people too poor and too demoralized to be of any good either to society or to the revolution to overthrow the very rich ruling elites, who Rachel's Great Uncle and Aunt explained cared only for themselves and lived lives full of selfish indulgence.

They'd explained, agreeing on every definition, that "lumpen" meant people who were miscreants and outcasts. People, who were declassed and degraded, often reduced to begging on the streets. Rachel's Great Uncle had quoted Marx.

"He described them as vagabonds, discharged soldiers –" he'd said.

" – And discharged jailbirds –," Rachel's Great Aunt had chimed in.

" – Escaped galley slaves, porters, organ grinders, ragpickers, tinkers, beggars," Rachel's Great Uncle had said, eyes gleaming, smiling at Rachel's Great Aunt, who'd clasped her hands together finishing the sentence with "in short, the whole indefinite, disintegrated mass, thrown hither and thither, which the French call la bohème!"

Mystified, Rosie had asked, "So what were you arguing about?"

In a chorus and once again looking fierce the two very old people had said, "About how soon before the terrible time at the beginning of 20th Century happens again!"

Realizing they might have been heard they hushed each other and whispered to Rosie that they did not want to upset Rachel's other Great Aunt who had been resting upstairs and who came from Argentina and had suffered much.

"I am convinced in another twenty years people will suffer the way they did in Russia and here in the United States during the Great Depression," Rachel's Great Aunt had whispered. "The rich will be so rich they will destroy the world."

"And the rest of society will gradually degenerate into a lumpen people," Rachel's Great Uncle had said, nodding his head, talking softly and sounding conspiratorial, "but not just the poor – doctors, lawyers, teachers, they will all become lumpen people."

"There will be great suffering," Rachel's Great Aunt had said, "the suffering will be so great it will destroy us all."

"Wait!" Rosie had said, getting exasperated. "You're agreeing again!"

"We *dis*agree on how long it will be *before* it happens," Rachel's Great Aunt had said, smiling at her Great Uncle. "I think it will be no more than twenty years before there is a total breakdown of the economic system here in North America and around the world. The gap between rich and poor is already getting wider." Her smile had been replaced by a look of anguish. "The great acceleration in wealth accumulation by an undeserving few means more and more people are living in poverty."

"A few underserving people are becoming extremely wealthy at the great expense not only the much maligned poor, but also the professional classes," Rachel's Great Uncle had said, his voice filled with emotion. "We know this because of what happened to our family – what happened to us!"

"I'm convinced it will be no more than twenty years before the gap is so great there is a total breakdown in American society,"

Rachel's Great Aunt had said, speaking calmly, "and my very dear friend here thinks it will take a little longer." She'd sighed. "That's all our disagreement is about. We both agree it will happen. We're convinced. But we're not certain when."

"In twenty years it will be 2015," Rosie had said. "I will be thirty-four." She'd looked from one to the other, "What happens then?"

"We don't know," Rachel's Great Uncle had said, looking immensely worried. "I think it will be a little after that, 2017, but *it will* happen."

"We really don't know," her Great Aunt had said, reaching across the little table between the teapot and tea cup and clasping Rosie's hand with her crabbed fingers as if to save her.

"And *we* won't be here to find out," Rachel's Great Uncle had said shaking his head.

Rachel's Great Aunt had looked over the top of her glasses at him and after a few moments of fighting back tears, looking at Rosie, she'd said, "but *you* will be here, and Rachel. You will find out."

"My heart is breaking," Rachel's Great Uncle had said, pulling out a pocket-handkerchief.

"Never mind us!" Rachel's Great Aunt had said, tutting at him. "We're just old –"

" – And wise," Rosie had said, not knowing what to make of what they'd told her.

"My darling Rachel!" her Great Uncle had sobbed. "And Rosie!"

"Hush!" Rachel's Great Aunt had scolded him. "Stop this morose lament! Such theatrics! You should be ashamed of yourself!"

At the time Rosie had felt the conversation with Rachel's Great

Aunt and Uncle was like an improv skit at school. Looking back it seemed more real. She remembered the conversation differently than she had before.

She'd become aware that her memories seemed to be stacked on top of each other, changing shape as they touched, becoming present when they were past, and past when they were present, happening and happened all at once.

Now, home from school after the night at the hospital, Rosie remembered how the descriptions of the lives of miners and their families in Blaina seemed to be harbingers of the future that Rachel's Great Aunt and Uncle had prophesized.

Rosie thought of Margaret talking to them about the importance of becoming *critically* conscious of the ways people are positioned in society, as if they were studying for a Ph.D. and not 8th grade students, whose bodies were changing so rapidly it was almost impossible for them to become anything other than awkwardly *self*-conscious. Margaret had laughed when they'd protested and she'd said they should make the most of the precious gifts their youth had bestowed on them.

"It is a little known fact," Margaret had said, as if sharing a great secret, "that 8th graders are the most socially sensitive creatures on the planet and quite possibly in the universe."

Rosie shook her head as if to get Margaret out of it.

She remembered that up in her room after she had arrived home from the library she'd read what the miners and their families from Blaina had said themselves, and she'd found the folder Daisy had given her and in it the copies of the articles that were published in 1936 in *The Times*. She'd wanted to read the exact sentence in which the word "lumpen" had occurred but had trouble finding it. She'd wanted to read the articles anyway so she started working her way through them underlining words and sentences that she might quote for her report.

At the top of the first article the word "TRANSFERENCE" was written in all caps and below it "THE NEGATIVE WAY WITH DISTRESS". Then in italics beneath was written *Our Special Correspondent records his impression of the present mood of the people, and in particular the effects of the two main policies of transfer and re-employment.*

The first paragraph was about the miners being out of work since the general strike in 1926. The second stated "the Government aimed at easing the situation by transferring able-bodied men and juveniles to other parts of the country."

"Transference as a sole policy," the Special Correspondent had written, "would leave behind an aging, shrinking population, costing the country a lot, anxious to work but sometimes lacking the will. Not particularly heroic or 100 per cent admirable, but undoubtedly brave in endurance."

"In the end one's impression is not of apathy or despair, or the small lazy minority," Rosie had read, "The unemployed have the courage of Houseman's Spartans at Thermopylae, 'where he stands will die for nought.' They may be like the Alcázar defenders without any relieving force, but they put a good face on the business."

The article had ended with *"To be concluded"*.

Rosie had sent an email to Jesse about Spartans at Thermopylae and about the defenders at Alcázar before reading the second report from the Special Correspondent. She'd smiled as she'd pressed send. Jesse would like that. She'd have a last stand battle at the end of her report on what happened to the coal mining families in Wales.

The second article by the Special Correspondent had shaken Rosie. In the first article the Correspondent's descriptions of the miners had resonated with her. She'd tied them to her emails back and forth with her Aunt Sarah and to the personal accounts of the miners and their families in Blaina, but "Transference" had been too abstract and had remained just a word. The second article had changed that.

"Get the facts," Margaret impressed on them. "Facts. Facts. Facts. You need them to present your argument. Otherwise your research papers are nothing more than opinion."

"Since 1931 the South Wales special area has lost 90,000 people through migration," Rosie had read and then copied into her notebook. "The Rhondda, which, with a present population of 134,600, has lost 28,117 (17.3 per cent) since 1921, of whom nearly 20,000 have gone in the past six years."

"There are now (approximately) 1,952,000 people in the Special Area of South Wales," Rosie had copied. "Depopulation may reduce them to 1,603,000 by 1945. This figure includes all ages, and allows for a rise in the over-60 age group from 193,000 to 243,000. So when one turns to the school children the fall is accelerated. Since 1929 the school population has fallen from 122, 278 to 103,819. By 1945 it may be down to 72,000."

In her room after the night at the hospital Rosie had no compulsive urge to start counting when she remembered reading about the miners and their families being forced to leave Wales. The terrible facts were a safe place to be. The English Government put a policy in place to transfer them. It was the cheapest solution. Get rid of them. And that's what they did. Rosie had worked out and written in her notes for her report that 500,000 miners were forced to leave their homeland. They became migrants, "lumpen" in the heroic sense of the word, scattered around the world.

She remembered all the thoughts that had welled up inside her when she'd thought of her own family being transferred, before that terrible night at the hospital. Her Dad had said there was no work so his father had left Wales. It was too much. Aunt Sarah being transferred to a psychiatric unit, her family transferred from Wales. *And* Rosie Llywelyn. The other one. What happened to her? Maybe she wasn't dead.

Now she knew what had happened to Rosie Llywelyn she wanted to count. She squeezed her eyes tight as she'd done when she'd found out her family had been lumpen, no, *are* lumpen, holding on to the past, interrupting the present.

"We are scattered and she is broken," she said determined not to count.

Daisy had come into her mind then, as she did now, when she remembered the moment, and once again she resisted her compulsion to count by re-reading the letter that Daisy had written to her Aunt Sarah.

"Capitalism is in crisis!" Daisy had scrawled in her unruly handwriting. "Rich men have always preyed on the poor and historically they've shown no mercy."

"History records the exploits of great men but not the exploitation of the poor," Rosie read, slipping back into her memories of working on her report after meeting Daisy at the library.

"We know very little of their lives or what happened to them," Daisy had written.

For the first time Rosie had a sense of some greater purpose for her research project. She couldn't put into words how desperately she wanted to know what had happened to Sarah *and* the other Rosie Llywelyn. But she'd suddenly realized that Sarah was not the only one who had lost her memory of what happened when she was a little girl, but hundreds of thousands of people had lost their memories of what had happened to them, and their history had been expunged. No one remembered them. Their memories had been erased and they had been rendered un-memorable.

"I don't know who I am," Rosie had said, as Max rearranged himself on the bed beside her. "I come from a forgotten people, and that gives me something to write about."

She'd heard Margaret talk of how the "collective memory" of the nation is shaped by what is in the history books they read in school. Margaret had told them very often what actually happens is "shoved under the rug".

"Find out what is under the rug," Margaret had advised them. "Look under that very expensive carpet and you will find the truth. What happens to us is hidden there, downtrodden for centuries by very fine leather boots."

Rosie had written "collective memory" at the top of the first page of the 1936 newspaper articles and followed it, pressing more heavily on her pen, with "collective amnesia".

"It is why it will happen again," Rosie had re-read in Daisy's letter, "and sooner than we imagine, I fear." Rosie had immediately heard the chorus of Rachel's Great Aunt and Uncle crying out, "The terrible time will happen again! Our hearts are breaking!"

Rosie had remembered more of what they had said. Rachel's Great Uncle had whispered something about futurism and fanaticism that glorified war and militarism, and the risks of false patriotism, and the dangers of regarding the body-as-machine. And

Rachel's Great Aunt had tried to calm him, telling him to hush but she was crying, her frail body shaking, and she'd said something about the "pantomime of dismantlement", or it might have been "dismemberment", and as their chest heaving crescendo of grief dipped Rachel's Great Uncle had whispered, "What will happen to the Jews? To Black people?"

And Rachel's Great Aunt had whispered, "And to women." Her eyes were filled with tears that her deep wrinkles stopped from running down her face until she closed her eyes and they overflowed and Rachel's Great Uncle used his pocket-handkerchief to gently mop her cheeks.

"The contempt for women will cross all lines," Rachel's Great Aunt had said. "Religion. Race. Rich or poor. Women will suffer as they have never suffered before."

Rose had wondered how she could have forgotten and then suddenly remembered so much of what they had said. Perhaps because it had seemed so unreal at the time, more than a school skit that she was participating in, more like a play she was watching, a Shakespearean tragedy, but she couldn't figure out which one. She'd brought her thoughts back to the moment, and with the echoes of Rachel's Great Aunt and Uncle voices comforting her, Rosie had searched through the copies of the 1936 newspaper articles by the Special Correspondent for the word "*lumpen*".

Searching the columns, she'd read in all of Wales only four factories had opened employing more than twenty-five people, and at the same time five factories were closing. Then there was the sentence about "the prevalent idea that the Welsh workman is born to make trouble," which the Special Correspondent had written was "bogey" and "without justification".

"I didn't make it up," Rosie had thought. "It's here some place."

There was Blaina and Blaenavon and "thin hopes", and the train journey of the King of England, and "saving the expense of supporting the population" which "sooner or later will get beyond the control of the local authorities", and there was *lumpen*!

Rosie read carefully now as she'd done a lifetime ago when she had come home from the library with the folder Daisy had given to her. On this her memory was crystal clear, she could still feel her first response to reading that the Special Correspondent had written it was a Welshman who'd used the word. She'd backed up and re-read, "supporting that population sooner or later will get beyond control of the local authorities, and have on its hands what a Welshman described to the writer as "a lumpen people".

"If he is lumpen," Rosie had told Max, "I am lumpen. My whole family are lumpen people."

"Rosie! Come see who's here!" Mary had shouted up the stairs on the Saturday that Rosie had gone to the library.

"Aunt Sarah?" Rosie had cried, laughing, half question, half exclamation. She'd run out of her room and looked over the banister. In the hall below was her father with Aunt Sarah. "There's my lovely girl!" her Aunt had said, her arms out as Rosie ran downstairs.

Sarah had on a white blouse and a blue cardigan with the grey skirt she'd often worn before she'd started wearing thrift store clothes, and Rosie had known immediately that Mary had sent the clothes to the hospital.

"I missed you!" Rosie had said, as they hugged and kissed.

"Careful," her Dad had said sounding concerned. "She spent all morning at the dentist."

"I didn't like that and I have to go back!" Sarah had told Rosie, with only the right side of her face moving as she spoke. "Awful, it was. My face is all numb."

"I hate that too," Rosie had told her, commiserating as she'd tried to cover up how distressed she was by the state of her Aunt. Sarah had lost weight, her skin was sallow and there were dark circles beneath her eyes. When Rosie had sat writing to Sarah she'd imagined her Aunt just as she used to be, but when she arrived home from the hospital she'd looked so frail, so old.

"I brought my pinny so we can cook," Sarah had said, knowing that Rosie was shocked by the way she looked and wanting to make light of it.

"Not today, Sarah," Tom had told his sister. "The dentist said you have to rest until the medication wears off. You can cook tomorrow."

"I thought they wouldn't let you bring her home?" Rosie had whispered to her Dad.

"I persuaded them," Tom had said, with a smile that was followed by a worried look at Sarah.

"Oh good," Rosie had said, covering it up, grinning at her Aunt. "You're going to stay."

"Forever, my Luvy," Aunt Sarah cried. "Forever!"

"Just the weekend," Mary had said firmly, giving Rosie a look that was more unfathomable than the one she had seen on her father's face.

"We'll see," Rosie had said, grabbing her Aunt's hand and giving it a squeeze.

"I think I'll have a little lie down on my bed," Sarah had said, and Rosie and Mary had helped her up the stairs and Sarah had undressed and put on the nightie that Mary had placed on her pillow. Exhausted, but still smiling, Sarah had fallen asleep holding Rosie's hand before Mary had finished folding her blouse and cardigan and she did not wake up until the next morning.

Rosie remembered on Sunday when she had come downstairs, the kitchen was filled with the sweet smell of apples cooking, and Aunt Sarah, wearing a tattered dress and a pinny covered in faded blue flowers, had been making a pot of tea. She held on to the memory. She could smell the sweet apples. Almost taste them.

"You started cooking without me!" Rosie had said, pretending to scold her Aunt.

"Just apple tarts my lovely girl," Sarah had said, pouring her a cup. "They'll be cooked soon."

"Where are they?" Rosie had whispered, glancing out the window.

"Out on the deck with their coffee and the Sunday papers."

"What are we going to cook?"

"Shall we make some Welsh cakes?" Sarah had asked.

"Okay." Rosie had been amazed at her own stupidity. Her Aunt had made Welsh cakes with her since she was a little girl but she'd never thought about it. "Just because she likes making Welsh cakes," she'd thought to herself, "there's no reason why I should have known she's Welsh."

"I don't know if we have all the ingredients," Sarah had said, looking in the cupboard.

"Can we make enough Welsh cakes for me to take to school tomorrow?" Rosie had asked. "Margaret says we learn better when we eat together"

"Of course, we'll make some with sultanas and some without," Sarah had said, the way she might have said when they'd cooked together on a Sunday morning, before she got stuck in the elevator.

"I'm going to present my 'preliminary findings', as Margaret calls them, for my report on Wales tomorrow," Rosie had said, suddenly worried that she should not have mentioned Wales.

Sarah had stopped looking in the cupboard and turned to look at Rosie.

"Well now, if it's for a report on Wales we'd better make some bara brith to go with the Welsh cakes."

"What's bara brith?" Rosie had asked, trying to cover up her nervousness.

"A kind of fruit loaf." Sarah had told her, opening the oven and taking out two apple tarts. "You cut it in slices and put butter on it. She went back to searching through the cupboards. We'll need to buy some self-raising flour and some sultanas. You're Mom doesn't have any." Sarah had looked around the kitchen. "Now where's Rosie's umbrella?"

"Why do we need the umbrella?" Rosie had asked, filling in her part of their conversation, tense with anticipation.

"In case it rains, my Lovely" Sarah had said, looking a little disconcerted.

Rosie had hesitated, but encouraged by the familiarity of this strange conversation and with her heart bumping and skipping beats, she'd asked the question that bothered her most.

"Why do you always call me Luvy or Lovely?" she'd asked Sarah, almost blurting it out. "Why don't you call me Rosie?"

"Because I don't want to get the two of you mixed up," Sarah had said, her bottom lip trembling. "You know how muddled I get."

Rosie had been annoyed with herself. She'd put her arms around Sarah and hugged her. Sarah had held on tight and when Rosie finally let go she'd looked confused.

"Shhh," Rosie had whispered, as she turned her head to look out the window where Tom and Mary were reading the Sunday papers.

Sarah had seemed to relax and she'd pulled out the chair she always sat on and sat for a few seconds stirring her tea. Rosie had sat down next to her and picked up her cup, and was about to take a sip of tea when Sarah had suddenly drawn in her breath, making an agonized sound as she'd stood up.

"She's gone to Blaenavon to get me some new sandals," Sarah had said, sounding as if she was going to cry. She'd looked down at Rosie as if pleading for help and her eyes filled with tears.

Frightened, Rosie had quickly put down her cup.

"Sandals?" she'd asked, immediately wishing she hadn't said it.

Sarah had started to sob. Rosie didn't want Sarah to start screaming. Her parents would come running in and yell at her and her father would take Sarah back to the hospital. "She'll be back soon," she'd said, putting her arm around her Aunt's shoulders. Sarah had wiped away her tears with her handkerchief and she'd tried to smile. "Come on my Luvy let's go to the Co-op and get some flour and sultanas."

"Co-op!" Rosie had said, grabbing this opportunity to change the subject. Sarah had looked puzzled. "You say 'Co' like 'Joe.' I saw Co-op written down and I read it as 'Coop' – like the Coop in Harvard Square.'" Rosie had known this was a silly conversation but there was a serious side to it. "Now I understand. You're talking about the shop on the Garn!"

"Don't tell your Dad!" Sarah had whispered, fiercely grabbing her arm. He's told me never to talk about the Garn."

"I won't tell him," Rosie had whispered, frowning at the thought of her Dad silencing Sarah. "It's our secret. Come on, let's go to the Beacon Hill Market on Anderson, I think the Co-op has closed."

"Oh, I forgot!" Sarah had said. "It doesn't open on Sundays. The market it is then, my Lovely."

Now that Rosie had promised not to tell, Sarah had talked about Wales. "Our Nan makes Welsh cakes but our Aunt Lizzy always makes the bara brith," Sarah had explained, as they walked to the Market on Anderson Street. For the first time Rosie had realized that Sarah was talking about her Great Grandmother as if she was alive and as if Sarah was still living in her house.

They had walked along with Sarah talking about the Garn as she had in her emails to Rosie. The difference was that when Rosie had read Sarah's emails, she'd imagined Sarah totally lucid, but here she was disheveled and very close to tears, and yet, smiling and enjoying the moment, walking along talking about her early life in Wales.

When they came back Mary had joined them in the kitchen while they made Welsh cakes, so Sarah had stopped talking directly about Wales. Even so she'd said enough for Mary to raise an eyebrow and look hard at Rosie.

Rosie had just shrugged. Sarah had filled a big glass-mixing bowl with a pound of self-raising flour. Rosie had added two sticks of butter.

"We usually use lard and margarine," Sarah had told Rosie. "The lard helps the Welsh cakes stay fresh, but your Mom likes me to use butter."

"Lard is animal fat!" Mary had pulled a face.

"So is butter!" Rosie had teased.

"Yes," Mary had laughed, "but it tastes much better than lard."

"They taste so good," Rosie had said smiling, glad Mary had stopped giving her that look. She'd squeezed the butter between her fingers and began to rub the fat into the flour. "And anyway, you always made them for us even though you used to tell us off for eating too much fat."

Rosie had been aware she was talking as if those days were gone. The three of them had looked at each other, each remembering such a short time ago when they had laughed and joked together, and when their lives were so much simpler than they are now. Then Sarah had turned away and filled the kettle and Rosie had continued rubbing the butter into the flour. For a few moments they'd been lost in their own thoughts.

"They taste much better when they're cooked on an open fire," Sarah had said quietly, breaking the silence. She'd smiled at Rosie as she'd poured half a pound of sugar into the bowl and then added four ounces of sultanas and a teaspoon of mixed spice. "Now then Luvy, break two eggs into that glass bowl"

"And then beat the eggs, right?"

"Right."

Rosie had beaten the eggs with a fork while Sarah made a well in the middle of the flour that was mixed in with the butter. Rosie had poured the eggs into the well and Sarah had used her hands to make a creamy yellow dough dotted with sultanas. She'd formed two balls of the dough and she'd given one to Rosie.

"We'll have to make another batch of plain ones," Sarah had said, "so you have enough to take to school."

Mary had rummaged in the drawer of the kitchen table looking for the rolling pin. "I know it's in here somewhere," she'd said. She'd taken out the telephone directory, a ball of string and some kitchen scissors. The rolling pin was jammed at the back of the drawer with a student's paper wrapped around it. "How did that get in there?" she'd asked, holding it up. "I've been looking everywhere for this!" She'd smoothed out the crumpled paper while Rosie rolled out the dough.

Sarah and Rosie had arranged the Welsh cakes on the griddle and after a few minutes they'd begun to rise. One by one Rosie had turned them over and in a few more minutes they were all done. Sarah had taken them off the griddle and put them on a wire tray to cool.

"We've got to try them," Rosie had said, getting the butter dish out of the fridge. She had laughed, "They might taste bad." She'd buttered one for Sarah and one for herself, and Mary had taken one without butter, and the three of them had eaten them standing together in the kitchen.

"They are so good!" Rosie had said, as she'd buttered two more and taken them out to her Dad.

"I'll make another batch," Sarah had said.

"Let's have another cup of tea first," Mary had said.

Tom had been reading the sports sections of the newspaper. "The Sox won their last three games," he'd told Rosie as she pushed the sliding door open and stepped out onto the small deck that was filled with pots of flowers.

"Welsh cakes," she'd said, as she handed him the plate.

"Great!"

"Did you eat these when you were a kid?"

Tom had looked at Rosie and ignored her question. "Your Mom said you got a package from Peter Cornwell. Any good?"

"Very good," Rosie had said. "Thanks." She'd remembered her promise not to ask questions about Wales, but she'd been annoyed with her Dad for telling Sarah not to talk about the Garn, and for not answering even a simple question about Welsh cakes. Without thinking she'd blurted out "Are you ashamed that you come from a coal-mining family?"

"Rosie! Don't be ridiculous!" Tom had glared at her and Rosie had felt as if she'd been slapped. Very deliberately he'd turned the page of the sports section folded the paper in half and had started reading about the New England Patriots' preparations for the new football season.

Rosie had turned and walked back into the kitchen. "Enjoy the Welsh cakes," she'd said, trying to sound sarcastic and unfriendly.

"I've got tickets for the Red Sox next Saturday," Tom had said, as if nothing had happened.

"I have to finish my research on coal-mining families," Rosie had said, "I don't think I can go. And I'm *not* being ridiculous."

"It's the end of the semester," he'd said, ignoring her last comment. "It won't hurt for once."

"I don't know." Rosie had said, not wanting to argue, but not wanting to give her Dad the impression that everything was okay. "Maybe Mom would like to go."

Sarah had made another batch of Welsh cakes without sultanas and after that she'd made bara brith which had been quick and easy. Half a pound of self-raising flour, four ounces of sugar, four ounces of sultanas soaked in black tea, a teaspoon of mixed spice and an egg beaten in a cup of milk.

"Let's soak the sultanas in orange juice," Sarah had said. "I think your friends might like that better than soaking them in cold tea." Her eyes had shone. "We always use a tea cup, but you can use a measuring cup if you like."

Mary had left the kitchen.

"Who's 'we'?" Rosie had whispered.

Sarah had moved closer to Rosie. "Aunt Lizzy, Luvy," she'd whispered back. "But don't tell your mother." She'd given Rosie a wooden spoon as Mary had walked back into the kitchen. "Now mix it all up Luvy, there's a good girl."

The bara brith had to cook for an hour at three hundred and twenty five degrees. Rosie had looked at the oblong cake tin. "D'you think it will be enough for my whole class?" she'd asked, knowing that Jesse would eat the whole bara brith on his own if he got the chance.

"Well, everybody can have a taste and at least two Welsh cakes," Sarah had said, smiling at Rosie. "I'm going to take a nap."

"You look very tired," Rosie had said, looking intently at Sarah.

"Just a bit," Sarah had said. "I'll be alright when I've had a nap."

Rosie had finished cleaning up the kitchen after Sarah had gone upstairs to her room and Mary had helped her.

"I want to know what happened to Sarah," Rosie had said to her mother, angry and belligerent. "What's going on?" she'd whispered fiercely. "I'm fed-up with everyone having secrets. I want to know what's happening. Why does Aunt Sarah talk as if she is still living on the Garn? Why won't Dad answer any of my questions? You've got to tell me."

"I knew Sarah had been talking to you!" Mary had responded, angrily. "What has she told you?"

"A lot!" Rosie had yelled, looking belligerently at her mother. "A lot more than you!" and in her agitation the glass mixing bowl that she'd been about to put in the dishwasher slipped through her fingers and shattered on the tiled floor.

The remains of the bara brith batter was splattered not only amidst the splinters of glass, but had also somehow managed to reach the walls and cabinets. Shocked by what she had just done, Rosie had stormed out of the kitchen.

Without a word Mary had started picking up the larger pieces of glass. When she'd looked up Tom had been standing in the doorway watching her. She'd pressed her lips together and raised her eyebrows, the pain in her eyes disguised in a hopeless shrug.

"I'll help," Tom had said. "This is my fault."

"It's nobody's fault," was all Mary had said.

"It's my fault," Rosie had said coming back into the kitchen. "I'll do it."

"Let's clean up together," Mary had said, putting her arms around Rosie.

Tom had put his arms around both of them. "I'm so sorry," he'd said.

Rosie had wanted to ask "what for?" but instead she'd said, "I'm sorry too."

She remembered the shards of glass and the splattered batter of the bara brith. She could feel her mother and father's arms around her and she wrapped herself in the memory. She desperately wanted to hold on to them and never let them go. She felt fragile, vulnerable and lost in her own indefiniteness, as if her mind had left her body behind or her body had left her mind. Who she had been she no longer knew, and she did not know who she would become. Her desire to count was overwhelming.

"One – two –"

She tried to focus on the Sunday night when Tom had taken Sarah back to the hospital. She'd wanted to understand how a terrible tragedy had become a part of her life. She'd thought if she tried to remember everything that had happened perhaps she would be able to piece her life together, not "back together", because there was no going back. She knew it would not be as easy as picking up the shards of glass from the shattered bowl in which they had made a bara brith.

"Find your own truth," Rosie said to herself. She thought about Daisy and her tattooed Runes. She found in her notes from the library the symbol for the self that Daisy had drawn and the symbol for strength and womanhood, which is a reminder that new life comes of old.

"Read them from right to left," she remembered Daisy saying. "They remind me of my history and keep me constant in my beliefs."

Suddenly it all seemed to fit and Rosie thought it might actually be easier than picking up shards of glass.

"When there is a death experience," she remembered Daisy telling her, "We must seek amongst the ashes for new perspectives and new birth. It's important we are creative and adapt."

Rosie printed all the emails that Sarah had sent her after she returned to the hospital that Sunday, and she started numbering them but quickly stopped.

"Don't count," she whispered. "Please don't count."

She used paper clips instead and tried to keep them in order, but her hands were shaking and she put them on the bed. Max jumped up on the bed and padded over to the pile of paper and curled up. Rosie sat down on the bed beside him. Max started purring. She picked him up, retrieved the emails, and as she stroked his back she felt herself relax.

"Ashes," she whispered. She thought about her Great Grandfather digging coal, her Great Grandmother cooking on the fire in the kitchen, and Sarah writing that the fire was damped at night but they never let it go out.

Around six o'clock Tom had told Sarah it was time for him to take her back to the hospital. Rosie had brushed Sarah's hair and persuaded her to put on a pink blouse from her second hand bag of clothes, but Sarah had refused to take off her pinny.

"You look pretty," Rosie had told her.

"Never!" Sarah had said, laughing.

"Yes you do!" Rosie had insisted. "I think you are beautiful."

Sarah had looked at Rosie, "You make me feel beautiful my Lovely," she'd said. She'd hesitated, as if she wanted to say more, and then she'd added. "Don't worry about me. I'll be home soon."

"Soon," Tom had said, nodding his head and smiling at Sarah. "Yes. Soon."

Mary had made another bara brith. Rosie had helped her. They'd worked silently together, glad of each other's company. At ten o'clock Rosie had kissed Mary goodnight and she'd gone upstairs to bed. She'd wondered if Sarah had written to her after she had returned to the hospital and she'd checked her email just in case:

> Hiya my darling girl. I miss you already. I hope your presentation at school goes well and that your friends like the Welsh cakes and bara brith. Love Aunt Sarah

> I miss you too Aunt Sarah. Are you sure you're okay? I was so worried about you. You seem so strong when you write to me, but when I saw you today you looked so frail. Did you get the email I sent about my dream? LOVE YOU! Rosie.

> Writing to you has helped me my Luvy. It really has. If I didn't have you I don't know what I'd do. Do you want to tell me about your dream?

> Okay. We were chatting until very late and there was a thunderstorm. I think I started dreaming as soon as I fell asleep. Everything was muddled up. I was fishing in Big Pond. I think it was me but it could have been the other Rosie Llywelyn, your sister, only I was her, if you get what I mean. There was a swan boat from the Public Gardens, and people throwing peanuts. Then there was a little girl in a coffin on a table, and children walking around the table looking at her, and a woman in a long black dress watching over her. And then my Dad asked my Great Grandmother if we could go swimming, and she said, 'Yes, but don't come back here if you get yourself drowned.' What do you make of that?

> It's a strange dream Luvy. I'm worried that I shouldn't have sent you my stories. I'm not sure I should have told you about Rosie Llywelyn.

> You said writing to me helped. It's okay. I'm glad I know. But the dream? What do you think of the dream?

> I can see how the Big Pond got muddled up with the pond in the Public Gardens. My stories and your memo-

ries got mixed up. But the child in the coffin isn't so easy to explain. I don't think we've ever talked about her. You are dreaming about things that happened to Rosie and me.

I was one of the children who walked around the table. Rosie was also there. It was Grethel who died. She was very young and there were a lot of children in her family. Nine, I think. I can still remember their names. There was Elga, Virginia, Molvena, Veronica, Colin, Ingrid and Daffyd. Grethel came between Elga and Virginia. I can't remember the other one.

They were very poor and Grethel was always sickly. I was staying on the Garn when Grethel died, and when I went to Sunday School with the other children we were taken by our Sunday school teacher to say goodbye to Grethel. But I don't think the woman in the long black dress was my teacher. Remember I told you your Great, Great Aunt Lizzy took care of the sick and when someone died she was the one who laid them out? Well I expect that was Aunt Lizzy that you saw in your dream.

Strange! Do you really think it was my Great Aunt Lizzy?

Luvy, I really don't know. As for the conversation between our Tommy and our Nan, I think it's another one of my memories. Whenever we asked if we could go swimming our Nan would say "don't come back here if get yourself drowned." It was just a joke between us.

But how would I know? And anyway I wouldn't say it like that.

I'm a bit worried my Lovely. Do you think people who are closely related can share memories without ever knowing each other? I wanted to share my stories with you but I don't want you to actually experience what happened to me.

What happened to you? Tell me! It doesn't make sense. How can I dream about something that happened to you? Someone must have told me about Grethel and the drowning joke. I don't think it's possible for me to remember things I haven't been told.

You're probably right. But you have to understand how difficult it is for me to talk about what happened. Let's chat about your school report and then I'm going to send you another story. It's about the day that changed all our lives forever.

Rosie had been worried that Sarah would stop writing to her if she'd asked her any more questions about her dream, and so she'd focused on her school report. She'd planned to finish it that afternoon, but when Sarah had come home there was no way she was going to sit in her room to work on it. She'd told Sarah she'd decided to divide her report into two sections. The first section was about the lives of mining families, and the second about the miners and the mines:

I'd like to ask you a few more questions.

Okay. But you have to go to bed soon or else you will be too tired to present your report. When I told you I wanted to share my stories I never imagined you'd be sharing them with your whole class.

Rosie had sent Sarah her notes on the Blaina Report as an attachment to one of her emails, and Sarah had written back that the conditions were the same on the Garn. She'd written about families who lived in one room and of the children, like Grethel, who were sickly and sometimes died:

Aunt Sarah, Were there other families living in the village? The men can't all have been miners.

They were Luvy. They were either miners or they worked for the colliery. No one else lived there. The Garn was a segregated community. There was a Co-op shop that was owned by the colliery. Everyone had a number. Your Great Nan's number was 1232. I might have written that before. She used metal checks, you'd call them tokens, instead of money for milk and bread. There was a post office. Mr. Painter ran that out of the front room of his house. He sold a few groceries as well. He was the only person in the village that had a telephone. He would take messages for nothing. He had twin girls, Beryl and Brenda, and they used to play violins. They worked in the post office in Blaenavon when they were older. One or the other of them used to deliver the messages when someone phoned. There was a welfare hall. Most coal mining villages had one.

Did you go there with my Dad?

I went there a few times. Tommy played billiards there. There was a big hall where we could have dances, a stage for us to put on plays and the billiard room for the miners to use. Then down the road a bit on the opposite side there was the school and the chapel. At the other end of the Garn there was also a pub called the Whistle. After your Great Grandad had finished his shift at six o'clock in the morning he used to go the Whistle and drink a pint of beer with his wet clothes steaming. I used to go to the Whistle on Sundays when the pub was officially closed and sit in the taproom with him and drink pop and "smoke" a clay pipe. Then he would walk me along the road from the mine and when he saw your Great Nan walking up from the Garn he would say, "Go on home now, there's a good girl," and I would walk down the road to meet her.

Aunt Sarah, how old were you then?

No more than three or four, my lovely. I was a very little

girl. The Whistle was built next to the entrance to the mine at Kay's Slope but there was no doctor's office. We had to go to Blaenavon if we were ill.

What if there was an accident at the mines?

The ambulance would come from Blaenavon. I can hear the siren now. One time your Great Nan was washing the dishes in a tin bowl on the kitchen table and we heard the siren go off at Kays Slope. She wiped her hands on her pinny and we went out the front and stood and waited with the other women. I remember we stood for hours. The ambulance came through the village and went up the road to the mine but did not come back. Your Great Grandad worked nights so he was safe in bed, but we still waited with the other women and children. Then an ambulance came down the road from the mine so slowly that we could have walked beside it, but no one called out to ask who was inside it. Too scared everybody was. Then a miner came down the road from Kay's Slope, and told us the name of the miner who was hurt and the women standing around me started crying and waving their hands and I thought it was one of their husbands who had been killed, but it was a miner from the lower row of houses. One of the timbers gave way and the roof collapsed on top of him and the other miners risked their own lives fighting to save his life. The women around me were crying with relief, you see, and great sorrow for the woman whose husband went by in the ambulance and later died, leaving her without a husband and her children without a dad. Living with death on a daily basis left the women and children in a constant state of anxiety. I feel it now as I did when I was a little girl.

That's terrible. I can't imagine living that way.

Sometimes the women lost their minds with worry. I remember Florrie Lewis telling our Nan about the mother of one of my friends who lived a few doors up. "She's gone mad," Florrie said. "Don't stare at her if you go and visit," our Nan told me. I think you should go to bed now Luvy.

Aunt Sarah, were you ever frightened?

Well, you know I was, frightened so much that I lost my memory as well as my mind. I do remember when I was a little girl the coal tips seemed to loom over us whatever we did, casting dark shadows on our lives. Sometimes when I looked at the smoke rising from the side of the tips I imagined it was from the chimney of the farmhouse that I knew was buried beneath all that slag, but I knew it was just the throwaway coal that had caught fire. I used to watch the solitary miners who walked around the edge of the tips looking for a piece of shiny back coal to hide under their arm inside their coats, but I never played on those tips. Each summer they grew larger and larger, from ground advances and spoil creep, towering above us. They really did cast dark shadows over the village, as dram after dram of slag went up the extending conveyer belt and was dropped. "It's tragedy waiting to happen," your Great Nan would say. And when I asked her if someone could be buried alive under the big tips she would smile at me and give me a hug. She did not know then that very tragedy would happen in Aberfan.

Aberfan? What happened at Aberfan?

The coal tips collapsed and buried a school. That's what happened my Luvy. There were heavy rains for weeks and weeks, and dram after dram was tipped and dumped until the enormous mountain of slag collapsed and buried the little school in Aberfan. One hundred and sixteen children were buried alive. I remember reading about it and getting upset but I didn't know at the time that my life had been like theirs. I had lost myself you see. I had no memories of Wales but I remember I was terribly upset when all those children died. They were buried alive. One of them could have been me. Or Tommy.

Or Rosie?

No. Not Rosie Llywelyn.

Rosie stopped reading. "One of them could have been me. That's what it feels like," she whispered to herself, reaching her hand out to stroke Max, as the separation between past and present collapsed like the giant coal tips at Aberfan killing so many children.

"I've lost myself too, Aunt Sarah." Terrified that she might count she tried to focus. She wanted to understand, put the pieces back together and know the truth, although she knew Margaret would tell her there are many truths. She had talked to them that semester about growing up and the loss of childhood.

"If you want to find yourselves," she remembered Margaret telling them. "You must look for your own truth. Find out what you believe and then question it."

At the time Rosie had smiled. Margaret often talked like that, and even though it made no sense to her at the time she listened to Margaret because she trusted her.

Now what Margaret had said was all she had left to guide her. To find her own truth Rosie was convinced that she had to go back and re-read the last story that Sarah had sent her. Even if it made her cry she had to read it, or she knew she would end up like Sarah, stuck in her grief, never knowing who she might have been or who she might become.

"To find yourself you must find your own truth," she said to herself, thinking of Margaret. Comforted, she continued to read. She smiled when she read the next email from Sarah. For a brief moment it was as if she was in the room with both Margaret and Sarah and they were both trying to make her feel better.

> I don't want you to think that we had sad lives, my Lovely. Most of the time we were happy. In many ways we had everything we wanted. We took care of each other and made our own fun. Your Great Grandad played in a jazz band. The miners dressed up in all sorts of odd clothes, and they played anything that would make a noise, from tin whistles and tambourines to paper wrapped around combs. Then, of course, there were the brass bands. Your other Great Grandfather played the tuba. He lived on the Varteg, the other side of Blaenavon. They used to say he had six B's after his name. He was the Best Blinkin' Blower in the Blaina Brass Band! I think I am repeating myself! Then there were the male voice choirs. You had a good many Great – or is it Great Great? – anyway, a good many Uncles who sang in the Blaenavon Male Voice Choir. They used to say that miners sang melancholy Welsh songs because it was the only way they knew how to cry about spending their entire lives underground. Like singing the Blues, I suppose. I think their music also gave them dignity. It was so beautiful.

Rosie had asked some more questions about the miners and

the mines and they continued writing well into the night. Sarah
had told her more about the deep pit mines and about the cage
dropping down the mineshaft:

> The miners used to say that they dropped so fast their
> feet would leave the bottom of the cage and they would
> feel as if they were floating until the cage slowed and
> their feet would be firmly planted ready for the cage to
> stop. I think there are moments when falling must feel
> like floating. But that's enough of that. My lovely girl
> you have to go to bed. You will be half asleep when you
> give your report in the morning. Love Sarah
>
> Good night Aunt Sarah. I love you. Thanks for helping
> me with my report. Margaret said we can present our
> work "in progress" so if I don't finish it is okay. Love
> Rosie
>
> Good luck tomorrow, Luvy. I hope your friends enjoy
> the Welsh cakes and bara brith. You'll find I've attached
> another story to this message. I've called it "Gwenny
> Morgan." I had difficulty writing it. It's a bit muddled.
> It's not so much of a story. Not sure really what it is.
> I'm not sure I should send it right now but if I stop and
> think about it I might never send it. Read it tomorrow
> when you get home from school. I love you more than
> anyone in the whole wide world Luvy. You are the moon
> and stars to me. I'm sorry our lives are such a tragedy.
> Love Sarah

Rosie re-read the last two sentences over and over. She had
some understandings now of what it meant to lose yourself, for past
and present to become mixed up, and for memories to be muddled.
She felt a new connection with Sarah but she was no longer sure if
Sarah had been writing to her or to her sister, Rosie. She had called
her "Luvy" but then she had written, "our lives are such a tragedy."

Whose lives?

"All our lives," Rosie thought, "including mine."

Even though on the night Sarah had returned to the hospital she'd told Rosie not to read the story until after she'd made her presentation, Rosie had printed it and read it that night.

Now she wanted to keep events in the order in which she remembered them, and so she reprinted the story. Max had jumped down off the bed and curled up on the rug. Rosie sat on the floor beside him.

The last story that Sarah had sent her was called "Gwenny Morgan."

Rosie could feel her heart banging in her chest. It was not rapid or fluttering, it was slow like a drum. The first time she had read the story she'd been eager to read it. Gwenny Morgan had been just a character back then. Now Gwenny filled her mind, her spirit, her anger, and despair,

She thought of Margaret to calm herself.

"There are always stories within stories," Margaret had told them over and over again. "A story is different each time you read it."

Gwenny Morgan

Our friend Gwenny Morgan never threw stones. She just watched as we played, fascinated by the way we made fun of the deadly mine shafts that dotted the hills behind our Nan's house. But we never understood the danger. Rosie and I lived in Ashford, Kent and we only spent our summers in Wales, so we never really knew the place as Gwenny did. Even our brother Tommy who was older than all of us and big enough to go on the bus to Blaenavon on his own didn't know it like Gwenny.

It was as if time had stopped still on the Garn and left the coal miners and their families behind in a different time, and so for all our new fangled worldliness we never really understood how dangerous the place could be. That's why we treasured our friendship with Gwenny. She held the key to life in the village and she helped us to unlock the door and slip through the crack into a time that no history book would ever remember and people would soon forget.

Gwenny lived in a tiny miner's house like our Nan's. There were forty houses in the two rows and they stood like soldiers ready to do battle against the giant heaps of useless slag that came up from the mines with the shiny black coal.

"That mountain's on fire," Gwenny warned us, pointing to the smoke that drifted up from one of the heaps. "And there are houses buried beneath that other one over there."

We listened to Gwenny when she told us of the houses under the piles of slag, and we wondered if the coal tips would shift their ground and cover our Nan's house and the other houses that stood in two lines so close to the mountains of slag. Painted black with bright red and blue front doors, the houses seemed to stand in defiance of the mountains of dirt and muck that towered above them.

Each house had two rooms up and two rooms down, which was fine for our Nan and Grandad. There were only two of them now, but in Gwenny's house there were eleven children, *and* Mr. and Mrs. Morgan, their Mam and Dad. It seemed impossible to me that so many people could live in four small rooms, but they did, and there seemed to be order in the friendly chaos that filled their house.

Whenever Rosie went there to see Gwenny she would take me. Mrs. Morgan always seemed to be washing clothes in a zinc bath out the back. She would smile and ask Rosie about our Nan. Then she would ask about our Dad and our Tommy.

"They're very well, thank you Mrs. Morgan," Rosie would say, being careful to be polite.

Mr. Morgan was usually sitting by the fire in the kitchen eating bread and dripping and drinking tea. Mr. Morgan's tea was not black like our Grandad's but milky with lots of sugar, syrupy like, too sweet for me. Watching him heap spoonfuls of sugar into his cup made me pucker-up. Mr. Morgan would nod his head when Rosie and I walked into the back kitchen with Gwenny. He sometimes talked to Rosie, but he never spoke to me.

I never got to know Gwenny's brothers and sisters very well except for Mary, her little sister who was just a little younger than me. Gwenny had a brother, Gwilfa, her baby brother, who she used to take care of when Mrs. Morgan was busy. When Rosie and I visited Gwenny it always seemed like there were children everywhere, on the floor playing, sitting at the kitchen table eating bread and lard with salt on it, running through from the back of the house to the front, and bouncing up and down like the springs that poked out of the sofa in their crowded front room. They laughed and teased, shouted and cried, needing nothing from the outside world, in tune with one another.

I never felt awkward or strange when I visited their home, but Tommy didn't like to go there. He played with Gwenny's bothers but I think there were too many babies in her house. People used to talk about Gwenny and her family and our Rosie told me not to listen to the grown-up talk, but I did listen even if I didn't believe what was said. Dirty they were supposed to be, and stupid too if you listened to the gossip that went up and down the rows of houses on the Garn.

I often wondered, if Gwenny Morgan was so stupid, how come she knew so much more than me or our Tommy or our Rosie? She was eleven years old and could take care of her brothers and sisters just like her Mam, and she knew more about the mines and the hills than any other kid in the village. Skinny and pale in someone else's dress, she looked older than Rosie but she wasn't. They were the same age and as good friends as good friends can be.

Even when one of the miners told our Dad that Rosie and I shouldn't play with Gwenny, we still spent all our time together. Our Dad said he liked Gwenny and he told us not take any notice of all the gossip.

Gwenny had an old-world face and a faraway look as if her thoughts had all grown up, even though she was still a child. She never talked about her troubles and she never told us what she was thinking, except for once when Mary Morgan, Gwenny's little sister, was tested to see if she was retarded. We were climbing up one of the hills out the back of our Nan's, Rosie, Gwenny and me.

"Two women came to see our Mary," Gwenny said.

Rosie looked at me. We'd heard people say the authorities were going to take Gwenny's sister Mary away because Mrs. Morgan was worn out and couldn't take care of her, on account of having too many children.

"Why do they want to do that?" I asked, not knowing what else to say.

Gwenny frowned. "They think our Mary's daft, but she's not!" Then she began to laugh, and even though we didn't know why she was laughing, we laughed with her to make her feel better and to show her that we cared. We were silly with giggles and Gwenny was holding her sides as we stepped on stones to cross the brook.

"They asked Mary to tell them what a puddle was," Gwenny told us, "and Mary said, 'Oh, Mr. Puddle lives at number three!'" Gwenny laughed until tears ran down her cheeks and then she began to cry, "Mary always liked Mr. Puddle."

We were on top of the hills looking down at the two rows of houses and beyond them to the coal tips.

"Look," Rosie said, pointing at one of them. "You can see the smoke."

I was running ahead of them carrying a stone.

"Wait, Sarah!" Gwenny called after me, and she began to run.

"She's going to throw that stone down the mine shaft!" Rosie called after Gwenny, telling her what she already knew.

Rosie and Gwenny were both running and I laughed, but I stopped laughing when they caught up with me.

"Throwing stones down mine shafts," Gwenny said, frowning at me. "Now that's *really* daft, Sarah."

"Retarded," Rosie said, taking the stone out of my hand. "Come on Sarah. Let's all hold hands."

"Rosie?" Margaret's voice had been soft. "Are you ready?"

Rosie could hear Margaret speaking to her as she did on the morning that she had made her presentation. The story of Gwenny Morgan had been fresh in her mind and she'd found it difficult to focus. She was aware that Sarah's stories were unraveling as she tried to write about what had happened to her sister. Gwenny Morgan read more like a journal entry or one of Sarah's emails than a story. On the morning that she had given her report, Rosie had tried to focus on the information about the coal tips and Aberfan but it wasn't easy. The Morgan family had inexplicably become connected to her own and she imagined Gwenny Morgan and Sarah and Rosie Llywelyn playing on the hills and picking up stones.

"Rosie?" Margaret had realized how complicated this assignment had become for Rosie. In past semesters there had been students who uncovered family histories that they had not expected, but she had never had a student who had so little knowledge of her own heritage and who was so deeply immersed or troubled by what she'd found out. Rosie's behavior in school had changed dramatically in the last few weeks. She had always been a hard working student and she continued to work hard, but it was as if all the joy had gone out of her life. She was listless and there was a pallor to her skin that concerned Margaret.

"Rosie?"

The class had waited. No one was joking that day.

Rosie had looked at Margaret, who had given her a reassuring smile as she'd got up from her seat and walked slowly to the front of the room. Rosie had focused on Margaret and what she had told them about finding their own truth and being true to themselves.

Margaret had always given Rosie courage. Together they'd walked the Black Heritage Trail to the African Meeting House on Joy Street, which is the oldest Black church in America. And afterwards the whole class had gathered in Rosie's house–just around the corner from Abiel Smith School–for lemonade and chocolate-chip cookies.

She'd listened as Margaret had told her class that her Great Grandfather had been a slave. Margaret had said he'd taught her Grandmother to read even though as a slave he had never been allowed to learn to read. When her Grandmother was a little girl he had bought her books, and he would sit with her when she came home from school and ask her "What's that word?" and she would tell him and read the stories to him, and he would always make sure she did her homework.

Rosie had always enjoyed listening to Margaret as she talked about her Great Grandfather, but for the first time she felt connected to the story. She now knew about her own Great Grandfather, and in one of her late night email conversations with Sarah she'd learned that he'd also never had the opportunity to learn to read.

Margaret was standing at the side of the room in a long blue summer dress and her hair was in intricate braids, black laced with grey. She'd held out her arms as Rosie had walked towards to the front, not to embrace Rosie but to welcome her and Rosie had raised her eyebrows and smiled at her in an almost lighthearted sort of way.

"Can I pass these around Rosie?" Margaret had asked as she'd picked up the plates of Welsh cakes and bara brith that Rosie had left on her desk. "What's this called? Bara brith?"

"Right," Rosie had said, organizing her notes. "Bara brith."

Margaret had taken a piece of bara brith as Jesse and Rachel took the plates from her. "This is good!" she'd said, laughing. "What's it called again?"

"Bara brith," Rosie had said. "I made it with my Aunt Sarah yesterday when she came home for a visit from the hospital." There had been an awkward moment.

"How is your Aunt Sarah?" Margaret had asked.

"Not good," Rosie had said, looking as if she might cry.

"Say hello to her for us," Margaret had said, not sure if Rosie was going to be able to make her presentation. She'd walked to the front of the room. "Let's do this together," she'd said, softly, and then turning to the class she had smiled with a look in her eyes that they'd all recognized.

"Rosie and I are going to present together," she'd said. "I'm going to talk to you about the Welsh language and then Rosie is going to share with you some of the findings of her research project about coal mining families in Wales."

Margaret had prepared a lesson for later in the week as a follow up to Rosie's presentation, but she'd wanted Rosie on a firm foundation before she made her presentation. More than anything Margaret wanted her classroom to be a safe place for her students, filled with the familiar rituals and routines of teaching and learning.

"Something solid beneath their feet," she had mused to herself as she'd worked on her lesson about the Welsh language for Rosie, "even when the ground seems to have given way beneath them." Later she would remember the metaphor she had used and how prophetic it had been.

Margaret had started by asking the class to listen to a Welsh choir singing "Hen Wlad Fy Nhadau", which she told the class was the national anthem of Wales. She'd put a tape in her old tape player and pressed play.

"They call this kind of singing 'polyphonic," she'd explained as the voices of the choir had filled the room, "but it's got nothing to do with learning phonics when you're a little kid."

The class had laughed, relieved that Margaret had joined Rosie at the front of the room and she'd brought them back to doing school.

Margaret had written the anthem on a large piece of oak tag so that everyone could get some idea of how the Welsh language is written while they listened to the anthem:

> Mae hen wlad fy nhadau yn annwyl i mi,
> Gwlad beirdd a chantorion, enwogion o fri,
> Ei gwrol ryfelwyr, gwladgarwyr tra mad;
> Tros ryddid collasant eu gwaed.

Gwlad, gwlad, pleidiol wyf i'm gwlad,
Tra môr yn fur i'r bur hoff bau,
O bydded i'r heniaith barhau.

"In English, the anthem means 'the land of my fathers is dear
to me,'" Margaret had said, as she'd pressed stop. "It's a land of poets
and singers and famous men."

She'd smiled at Rosie and looked around the class.

"If we wrote the anthem now we might add 'famous women,'"
she'd said, before continuing.

"For freedom its brave warriors lost their blood. My country,
my country, I love my country."

Jesse had postured like a warrior and Margaret had frowned
at him. He was ready for the great uprising of Owain Glyndwr, but
Margaret wasn't finished. She'd picked up another chart and placed
it on the easel. "I thought you might be interested in how some of
the places in Wales got their names."

```
Aber ..........river mouth ..............Aber-fan
Blaen..........source of the river.....Blaenavon
Bryn ..........hill.............................Bryn-mawr
Cwm..........valley..........................Cwm Rhondda
Garn............a heap of stones.........Garn-wen
Nant...........stream........................Nant-y-glo
```

"The name of the place tells you something about the topog-
raphy of the location," Margaret had explained. "Rosie, what was
the name of the village where your Great Grandparents lived?"

"Garn-yr-erw," Rosie had said, "that's how my Aunt Sarah

pronounces it. I think it means a heap of stones!"

"Can you write it for us?" Margaret had continued, smiling, proud of her class because on another occasion they would have laughed.

Rosie had taken a page of her notes to the board and she had written Garn-yr-erw on the board.

"Now. How would you say e-r-w in English?" Margaret had asked, looking around the room.

"You can't say it in English," Rachel had said. "r and w don't go together."

"In Welsh the w is used as a vowel." Margaret had nodded in agreement. "I've made this chart of just the long and short vowel sounds of w and y." She put up another chart.

Margaret had encouraged everyone to pronounce the name of the village where Rosie's Great Grandparents had lived, and Jesse had reminded them of Owain Glyndwr and they had a go at pronouncing "Gleandoorw", but time was getting short and finally Margaret had told Rosie it was her turn to talk.

"I'm about half-way through my report. I've done most of the research. I just have to finish writing it up." Rosie had said as she tried to gather her thoughts. The "heap of stones" had thrown her off. It had reminded her of Gwenny Morgan who never threw stones.

"Rosie?"

"My Aunt Sarah helped me," she'd said, trying to focus. "I also found some books at the library." She looked at Margaret. "Daisy Blake was very helpful," she'd said, somehow finding her courage by just saying Daisy's name. "She said you are friends and to say hello."

"We are friends," Margaret had said, pleased to see Rosie grow stronger.

"The books were scholarly, and I did find a few interesting facts," Rosie had said. "But the uncut diamonds were in the newspaper articles Daisy's Uncle had, which were published in the London *Times* newspaper in November 1936."

Rosie had known she was now on solid ground. She'd done her homework and she did not have to worry about establishing the research base for her report. That helped. But she still had to present it.

"I don't think anyone is interested in what happened to the coal miners in Wales," she'd said, looking at Margaret. "I think that's the problem."

There was a tremor in her voice. She'd suddenly saw her Aunt Sarah walking around her school desk and there was a coffin on her desk but she could not see inside.

The class had waited.

"I no longer know who I am," Rosie had said, "I think I just died."

Thinking back Rosie was grateful to Margaret for helping her get through her presentation and replaying it now helped her hold on to the parts of her life that were separate from the life of her family. She was comforted by her memories of that morning in school and wanted to linger there now in the school version of her family history.

Aunt Sarah and the coffin were gone almost as soon they appeared. Rosie had looked down at her notes and on the spot abandoned the beginning of her presentation.

"I have learned," Rosie had begun, "that I come from a lumpen people."

"I am lumpen," Rosie had said. "My family is not middle class or working class. We come from the underclass that the ruling classes consider has no social worth."

"Between 1935 and 1955 half a million people, that's five

hundred thousand miners and their families, were expelled from Wales. The Rhondda Valley lost the most people. The expulsion was carried out through an official government Policy of Transference. Nobody seems to know about it."

"Basically," Rosie had said without a tremor, "the English Government got rid of the Welsh coalminers because they no longer needed them. They starved them out. And the miners and their families had no alternative other than to leave Wales. And so they scattered around the world with no hope of return."

Margaret had covered her mouth with her hand, and Rachel's eyes filled with tears. No one spoke. The entire class sat still.

"For almost two hundred years," Rosie had said, "in the valleys of South Wales, which is where my family comes from, old men went down the mines long after they were able and young boys accompanied the men long before they were able."

"On my Dad's side both my Great Grandfathers were coal miners," Rosie had said. "I don't know about my mother's side. She was adopted."

"I've found out that my Grandfather – my father's Dad – also worked underground for a short time before the Second World War," she'd looked at Margaret. "I didn't know any of this until Margaret told us to research the origins of our names and I started talking to my Aunt Sarah."

"I've found out that there were two kinds of underground mines." Rosie had said, her voice growing stronger. "My Great Grandfather – the one that I know the most about – worked in Kay's Slope. There was an opening at the surface and a tunnel that sloped underground. My Great Grandfather worked on the coalface for sixty years. Most of that time he worked nights."

Rosie had felt as if Sarah was standing beside her holding her hand as she shared the stories that no one remembered, but she would never forget.

"Sometimes my Great Grandfather walked almost two miles underground before he came to the place where the miners were digging," she'd said. "Sometimes he had to wade through dank and very cold water that seeped into the mine. Sometimes he had to crawl on his hands and knees when he got close to the coal seam before he could start digging. Once he reached his stall he used a mandrill which had a blade that was sharp and pointed like a stiletto, a hatchet and a shovel to dig the coal."

"In one of the books I read," Rosie had explained, "it said miners carried a seven pound axe but my Aunt Sarah says my Great Grandfather always talked about 'his hatchet'"

"The deeper the coal seam the better the coal," she'd said, "and sometimes the seam of coal was so low and narrow the only way my Great Grandfather could reach it was to lie on his side and dig."

"Once the coal was dug it was loaded in drams that ran on rails underground, and pit ponies would pull the drams of coal up to the surface."

Rosie had talked of the mines as if she had been a miner and it crossed her mind that their history had become part of her own.

"The pit-ponies in my Great Grandfather's mine were lucky because when they had finished their shift they were walked up to the surface and washed in Big Pond. Then they were taken to the mine stables where they were fed and watered. They were well looked after but the pit ponies that worked in the coal pits where there was a mineshaft were not so lucky. They were taken underground and they never came up. The ponies were stabled underground. They never saw the sunshine and they went blind living their lives in the darkness."

"To go down a deep pit mine the miners traveled in a cage," Rosie had said, her voice growing stronger. "My Aunt said it was like traveling in an elevator with just a metal grid under your feet so you could look down into the black hole beneath you, and there was nothing between you and the sides of the shaft except for the metal bars which held you in."

"My Aunt told me my Great Grandad said the cage dropped so quickly there were times when the miners felt like they were floating," Rosie had said, "and when the cage reached the bottom, they had to brace themselves as their bodies tried to keep on traveling down."

The class was quiet. Rosie had grown more passionate. It wasn't until she'd begun to speak that she realized how much she had to say, how important her Great Grandfather had become to her, how much she loved her Great Grandmother and her father and mother and Aunt Sarah, and how she wished she knew what had happened to the other Rosie Llywelyn.

"Rosie?"

"Sorry," Rosie had been a little shaken by these thoughts but she quickly picked up the thread in her report. "When miners went underground they had to be careful," she'd said. "Sometimes the timbers that held up the roof of the mine would cave-in. The miners would watch for trickles of earth falling above them or for the creak of timbers that were about to give way."

Margaret and her class had sensed the urgency in Rosie's voice. It was as if some timbers were about to give way and she had to shore them up.

"Then the miners would try to put in new timbers, but if it was too dangerous they would try to get out as quickly as they could," Rosie had said. She could feel the quickening of the way in which she was talking as if they would be killed by what she said.

"Sometimes the roof collapsed before the miners were able to escape," she had said. "Many miners were crushed or buried alive."

"But the biggest danger was methane gas. Methane was trapped in the seams of coal and it accumulated in pockets. Ventilation shafts were dug down from the surface to ventilate the mines, but the gas still collected in cracks and along the roof."

Rosie had everyone's attention. They had all been caught up in what she was saying, the cadence of her voice, and the gestures she made. Even Margaret had been taken aback by the intensity of the way in which Rosie spoke. Margaret's heart had been full and she had to work hard to stop herself from crying.

"Sometimes the miners knew the gas was there because the methane would get inside their safety lamps causing a blue flame to flare. But the copper gauze of the lamp stopped the gas in the air around the lamp from burning."

"My Aunt explained to me that the copper gauze – which I think must have been like the wire mesh in screen doors – didn't get hot enough to light the gas in the air around the lamp. She says there was always some methane in the air and the miners worked in constant danger of an explosion."

Rosie had some handouts on mining disasters. She had given them to Rachel who had passed them out.

"This information comes from a book by David Bellamy who is an artist. He went around South Wales painting pictures of miners and the mines. Anyway, it's my Aunt's book. It's called *Images of*

South Wales Mines. I've included some of the information on disasters from the book in the hand-out, and I've added some more facts
about the mining disasters at Universal Colliery." Rosie had read
from her own copy of the handout to get the numbers straight.

"In 1867 there was an explosion at the Ferndale Pit that killed
178 miners," Rosie had read, pausing and looking at Margaret, who
had smiled at her and gestured for her to continue.

"At mid-day on Wednesday September 11, 1878, at the Prince
of Wales Colliery in Abercarn, 268 miners died in an explosion.
Most of the miners remained entombed," she'd read, adding, "But
93 miners were rescued and 6 of these died."

"By far the worst mining disaster to happen in Wales occurred
in a mining village named Senghenydd, at Universal Colliery," Rosie
had paused, and looked at Margaret. "Seng-hen-id?"

Margaret had nodded.

Rosie had pressed her lips together and given a nod. She'd
looked at the class, her eyes resting on Rachel and then Jesse. Rachel
had smiled encouraging her and Jesse had given her a thumbs up.

"There were two explosions," Rosie had said, before returning
to her handout and reading. "The first on May 24, 1901, killed 82
colliers. But the second explosion was far more deadly. It occurred
12 years later, on Tuesday, October 14, 1913, and killed 439 men
and boys."

"When the first explosions occurred at Universal Colliery the
pit owners were severely criticized in a report published soon after
the 1901 explosion. The pit owners refused to implement the safety
procedures and so 12 years later the second explosion occurred in
which so many miners lost their lives."

Again, Rosie had paused, as if she had been struggling to carry the weight of the miners on her back. "If the pit owners had acted when the report was made available, the miners' lives could have been saved."

She'd read the rest of the list without stopping.

"On March 1, 1927 at the Marine Colliery 52 miners were killed," Rosie had read, looking up from her notes as she added, "March 1st is Saint David's Day, the patron Saint of Wales."

"The last explosion that I have listed was at the Six Bells Colliery on June 28, 1960," she'd said. "Forty five miners died in that explosion."

When Rosie had reached the end of the list of explosions and the deaths of so many miners, she'd felt as if she was on the Garn standing with the woman waiting for the ambulance to go by, not knowing who had been injured or killed. She remembered it as a lumpen moment.

Margaret had known Rosie was struggling but she'd understood that Rosie had to find her own place to end her presentation. The class waited. For a few moments Rosie had stood perfectly still. Then she'd returned to her presentation.

"The miners that were killed were probably killed by the methane," Rosie had said, "which was sometimes called firedamp, but they could also have been killed by afterdamp."

She'd caught Jesse's eye and he'd nodded at her and she knew that he was thinking that this was better than anything she might have found out about Owain Glyndwr.

"Afterdamp is carbon monoxide. When methane burns it makes carbon monoxide. The miners kept little birds in cages underground and the birds would drop to the bottom of their cages and die if there was carbon monoxide in the air. Then the miners would know that they had to get out quick. Afterdamp was a silent killer. After an explosion it would fill the tunnels where men were running to get out and they would drop to the ground dead."

"There's not much more that I want to say today." Rosie's voice had trailed off. "I have more information." The class sat quietly. Rosie had felt they wanted her to say something more. Even Margaret seemed to be waiting.

"When I started my research on Wales my Dad's secretary said there was nothing in Wales except castles and sheep and I told my Mom I'd rather study South Africa." Rosie had smiled, but there was pain in her eyes and for a moment Rachel had thought that Rosie was going to cry. "But I've learned that in some ways South Wales is like South Africa."

Rosie had looked at Margaret. She was not sure if she should say what she was thinking.

Margaret had nodded, and remembering Rosie's report on Nelson Mandela and apartheid, she'd silently encouraged her to continue.

"I think the miners in South Wales were treated like slaves. Men died in explosions, they were buried alive when the roof caved in. They died of silicosis and pneu," Rosie had stumbled, she'd glanced down at her notes, and read "pneu-mo-con-iosis," before continuing, "which the miners called black lung disease. Often when a miner got sick the owners of the colliery refused to take any responsibility. The death certificates were fixed. Miners' families received no compensation and miners' wives and children lost everything, a husband and father, and the little hovels in which they lived."

"In a report I have about a mining town called Blaina it says that miners were sometimes so sick they had to be carried down the mine by other miners. They went to work because if they didn't go they didn't get paid." Rosie's voice had once more filled with passion. "They had to work because the collieries owned their homes and owned the local store. If they didn't work they couldn't buy coal to light their fires, and without the fire they couldn't cook their food."

"My Aunt says that when men were out of work they would walk around the slag heaps looking for a good lump of coal, and when they found one they would put it inside their coats because the owners of the collieries considered that stealing."

"The miners had no rights," Rosie had said. "They lived in segregated communities, they were owned by the rich men who owned the collieries, and that's why I think they lived like slaves."

The room had been silent. Usually when one of them finished making a presentation they would clap, but when Rosie finished they had all just sat and Rosie had waited, unsure if she had said too much. Maybe she had gone too far. She hadn't planned to make the connection between coal mining and slavery.

"Thank you Rosie." Margaret had said. She had walked over and put her arms around her. "I remember when I was at school there was another coal-mining disaster in Wales in a place called Aberfan." Margaret spoke softly, wanting to hold on to the moment, to preserve it for Rosie, knowing that in the life of this young woman a transformation had taken place that went to the very core of who she was, and which in the years to come would shape who she would become.

"I was reminded of it when I made the chart on Welsh place names." Margaret had continued. "Sometime in the mid-sixties a giant coal-tip – or slag heap – collapsed and buried a school filled with children. Many of them died."

"My Aunt told me about Aberfan," Rosie had said. "It was too painful for me to talk about today. There were two coal tips right outside my Great Grandmother's house." She had given Margaret a little smile but there were tears in her eyes.

"Very painful," Margaret had said nodding her head and smiling reassuringly. "You've given us a lot to think about Rosie. Thank you."

Rosie had started to cry. "It's about remembering our stories when governments do everything they can to take them away and make us forget. The Special Correspondent who wrote the *Times* articles in 1936 about the Transference Policy quoted a coalminer who said, 'We are a lumpen people.' That is why I began by saying I am lumpen. If he was, I am."

Suddenly Rachel had stood up, her chair tipping backwards was caught by the girl sitting behind her.

"I am lumpen too," Rachel had said. She'd smiled fiercely at Rosie. "How could I not be? My Great Uncles and Aunts who fled

Russia talk about being lumpen too. My family does not hold with the definition of Marx that the lumpenproletariat is too done-in and too apathetic to be any good to the revolution. They see the term lumpen as a way of blaming very poor people for the wretched circumstances in which rich people force them to live."

Margaret had stood at the back of the class watching the scene play out. Rachel was a force to be reckoned with and the rest of the class looked as if they were getting ready to march.

"My Great Uncle says," Rachel had continued, "by stigmatizing lower working class people as a rabble outside of society, the men in power did not and *do not* take responsibility. They put them on cattle trucks and shipped them out, and it will happen again, my Great Aunt says."

"To be lumpen," Rosie had said, "is to take responsibility for your own history and prove them wrong."

"And hold them accountable," Rachel had said, and with that, seeing the battle ahead, Jesse had pushed back his chair and stood up.

Margaret had started clapping as she walked to the front of the room and more chairs scraped the floor as the whole class stood and clapped.

"La bohème," Rachel had said, quoting her Great Aunt and smiling at Rosie.

Nothing more was said.

Margaret had put her fingers to her lips and then placed her hand on her heart before stretching her arms wide this time as if to embrace her whole class, and with similar gestures the eighth graders gathered their books and left.

Rosie shifted positions. Her eyes were closing but she did not get into bed. She had to get to the end of the story, to the hospital, to the elevator. Thinking about it woke her up, the smell of it, damp, metallic, dirty, cold.

"Rosie! No!" her father cried.

"Don't count!" She put her hands over her eyes and shut them tight. "Please don't count. Think of Margaret. Yesterday." She thought about Margaret saying she had given them a lot to think about and how much more she could have said. She wondered what she would have told them about Gwenny Morgan, but quickly returned to thoughts about Margaret.

It suddenly occurred to her that Margaret hadn't asked her any questions about her family. When Rachel had presented there was a long discussion about her Jewish heritage and the pogroms and about Russia. Margaret had also asked her about Argentina and Los

Desaparecidos and the Madres de Plaza de Mayo.

Rachel had grown up with her own history and she was comfortable talking about her family fleeing Russia and leaving Argentina in the late 1970's. The political circumstances of her family were often part of their dinnertime conversation.

For a while Rosie thought about her friends. She wondered again if Jesse was going to ask her out on a date, and if she would go to Cape Cod with Rachel. For a moment she tried to think of nothing at all, and then without any conscious effort she picked up her own story where she'd left off.

Easing back in gently, she remembered the sun had still been shining when she got home on the Monday after her presentation. Sarah had made Rosie some barley water and she'd left it in the fridge for her before Tom had taken her back to the hospital. Rosie had filled a glass with ice and poured some. She'd sat down at the kitchen table and thought about her presentation. She'd felt good about it. Somehow she'd felt stronger.

She'd thought about Margaret and how she always told them to look for the stories within stories, and she mused on that in her own life. Her mind had wandered back to Gwenny Morgan and her little sister Mary, who was supposed to be retarded, and to their Dad who liked sweet tea. She'd thought of Gwenny's mother out the back doing the washing. She'd imagined her thin and worn out from taking care of all Gwenny's brothers and sisters. Rosie had been sure that the story of Gwenny Morgan contained the answers to many of her questions about Rosie Llywelyn if she could just figure it out.

She had finished the barley water and had been just about to go upstairs to send an email to Sarah to tell her about her presentation when she'd heard the front door slam. A few moments later Mary had walked into the kitchen. She was carrying two bags of groceries from Bread and Circus, which she put down on the kitchen table. For a moment Mary had just stood there looking at Rosie. Her face was flushed and she looked as if she had been crying.

"What?" Rosie had asked, wondering what was wrong. "Is Aunt Sarah okay?"

"Sarah is fine," Mary had said. "Just fine."

"So what's wrong? Are you sick?"

"I'd like you to come up to my office," Mary had said, trying to keep calm. "We won't be interrupted there."

"Who's going to interrupt us?" Rosie had protested. "There's no one in the house!"

Rosie had climbed the stairs and by the time she reached her mother's office on the third floor Mary had already retreated behind her desk. It was the place she was most comfortable.

"I feel like I've been called to the principal's office," Rosie had said, trying to make light of the occasion.

"Rosie, this is serious. I'm not in the mood for any jokes," her mother had gestured towards the easy chair. "Please, sit down."

Rosie had moved the student papers that were on the seat and sat, uncomfortably, on the edge of the chair. "What have I done?" she'd asked. "What?"

"I'm not sure that you've done anything," Mary had said, wondering why she had made Rosie come up to her office instead of sitting down at the kitchen table and having a chat. She knew she was over-reacting. She'd felt as if her life had been bulldozed and she was trying to find bits of herself in the rubble. She'd no idea what to do except to be the professor she had become and not the lost girl she'd used to be. She'd felt vulnerable. Stupid. Retarded. In desperation, she looked around the room at the bookshelves filled with books, at the piles of students' papers on the floor and at her own research notes piled up each side of her computer. Her lip trembled as she smiled, her mind filled with stray memories and old emotions.

"What?" Rosie had shouted, frightened by the smile. "Why are you so angry?"

"I think I'm more upset than angry," Mary had said, making eye contact with Rosie, and suddenly realizing how much her behavior had upset Rosie, she'd added, "And if I'm angry, it's not with you, Rosie. I am not angry with you."

"Then why are you talking to me as if I've done something bad?" Rosie had asked. She'd spoken quietly, but Mary could hear the anxiety in her voice.

"I met Margaret in Bread and Circus."

"She didn't like my presentation?"

"No. She thought you did a superb job." Mary had picked up a pencil and was tapping it on her desk. "She said I should be very proud of you."

"Then what's the problem?"

"I'm sorry Rosie," Mary had said. "I know I'm behaving badly. I am proud of you." Then, as if it wasn't important, she had said, "Margaret told me you gave a lot of credit to your Aunt Sarah for helping you with your report, and she asked me to thank Sarah."

Rosie had looked at her mother in silence.

Mary had started crying.

"So what's wrong with that?" Rosie had asked. "Tell me!"

"I can't!" Mary had been racked with sobs and as grief stricken as Sarah.

"Stop it!" Rosie had shouted. "Or, you'll end up in the hospital with Aunt Sarah." She'd felt trapped in her mother's nightmare. She'd wanted to know right there, right then, why her mother and father had never told her about Rosie Llywelyn.

"Why didn't you tell me I had another Aunt?" She'd blurted out. "Why didn't Dad tell me he had a sister called Rosie Llywelyn?" Rosie had shouted. "You gave me her name, but you never told me about her! What did she do that was so awful that you've kept it a secret all these years!?" Her whole body was shaking. "Why won't Dad talk about her? Why did he lock Aunt Sarah up in a loony bin? Tell me! What did Rosie Llywelyn do?"

"She's dead." Every last drop of blood had drained from her mother's face and her voice had been nothing more than a whisper. "Rosie Llywelyn is dead."

"So what's the big secret?" Rosie's heart had been hammering in her chest. "Why didn't you tell me I had an Aunt who died?"

"She was killed more than forty years ago."

Rosie had tried to concentrate. She felt the way she did at school when she was making her presentation, as if she was standing beside herself. Now, as she looked back, there were more and more layers in the back and forth between her and her mother in her mind.

"Who killed her?" she'd asked, almost as white faced as Mary. "Who killed her?" she'd asked again in a voice no more than a whisper.

"We did Luvy" Mary had said, rocking, her arms wrapped around herself. "We did."

Rosie had stood up, her mother's voice echoing in her head. Luvy. The lilt. She had never heard it before but it had always been there. Suddenly, the pieces had fallen into place. Rosie had looked at her mother as if she was seeing her for the first time.

"Who was Gwenny Morgan?" she'd asked, looking intently at her mother, and then again, "Who was Gwenny Morgan?"

Mary had stopped rocking and she was staring at Rosie.

"Your name was Beresford, right?" Rosie had asked, before her mother could recover.

"Yes." Mary had said, knowing the next question.

"That was the name of your adoptive parents, right?"

Mary had nodded.

"What was the name of your birth parents?"

"Rosie, please!" Mary had closed her eyes and she had begun to rock again.

"Morgan," Rosie had whispered. "You're Mary Morgan, Gwenny's little sister."

Mary had put her head down on her desk. Rosie had sat unable to move. After what seemed like a life-time Mary had lifted her head and looked at Rosie.

"It was all so long ago. Why do we have to talk about this now? If Sarah hadn't got stuck in the elevator none of this would be happening. Maybe it would have been better if I'd grown up with everyone thinking I was retarded. It wouldn't have been any worse than this."

Thinking back Rosie was surprised that she hadn't tried to comfort her mother, but she had not. She remembered the incredible clarity of her thoughts. She'd been determined to find out what had happened and she'd thought about how, in the last story that Sarah had sent her, she'd written that Gwenny Morgan had said, "They think our Mary's daft, but she's not." Lost in thought she had suddenly realized that her mother was talking.

"Poor Sarah," Mary had said, "It wasn't her fault, but she's suffered more than any of us." She'd regained some of her composure and she looked at Rosie. "Many years ago I made a promise to your father," she'd said. "There are some things I can't tell you, but I can tell you how I came to be adopted and how I came to marry Tommy. Then it's up to him if he wants to tell you the rest."

Rosie had nodded and without saying anything else she had sat back in her chair, pulled her legs up, and tucked her feet under her.

"When I was a little girl I was very sick." Mary had pressed the lead of the pencil she was holding into a pad of notepaper. Her fingers had moved down the length of the pencil, and then she had turned it pressing the eraser into the pad. She'd dropped the pencil and rested her elbows on her desk.

"There were eleven of us," she'd said. "My mother was tired, worn out, and it was Gwenny that took care of us. When I was about five someone reported my mother to the authorities. I remember two women coming to talk to her and they asked me questions." Mary had looked at Rosie. "They told my mother they thought I was mentally retarded. They used that term back then. My mother said that they were the ones who were retarded, and she got upset and told the women to leave." Again, she picked up the pencil. This time she began to draw a flower on the yellow lined paper.

"But they came back. And they took me away and they placed me in a foster home." Mary had drawn the flower growing beside two cone shaped hills. As she had continued to talk she'd drawn a little girl at the bottom of the hill next to the flower. "A few months later they discovered my mother had tuberculosis." She drew a sun and black raindrops falling like tears on the little girl. Mary had stopped drawing. "They persuaded her to put me up for adoption, so when I was six I stopped being Mary Morgan and became Mary Beresford. There's not much more to tell. My adoptive parents were very good to me. They were school teachers and we lived just outside London." Mary had tried to smile. "Needless to say I wasn't retarded."

In her only-child-loneliness, Rosie couldn't imagine having all those sisters and brothers. "Why didn't you keep in touch with your real family?" she had asked, hoping that her mother would not start crying.

"There wasn't any opportunity," Mary and answered, grateful for the concreteness of Rosie's question. "The Morgans didn't know who had adopted me. I did go back when I was grown up. It was a terrible time. My adoptive mother and father were killed in a car crash, and a few years after that I went back to Wales. But when our Gwenny, my sister, found out I was going out with Tommy she wouldn't have anything to do with me, and no one in the family would speak to me because of Gwenny."

"I don't understand."

"Rosie, I can't tell you anymore." Mary had pleaded with her daughter. "Please don't ask me to explain. You're Dad's got to do that. I just want you to know that your Dad didn't do anything bad. He's hurt, that's all. I was very young when he used to come to Wales. I was just a baby really. I remember he used to pick me up and carry me on his back when we went for walks with Rosie Llywelyn and Sarah." Mary had given a long ago smile. "It's funny we never called her Rosie, she was always Rosie Llywelyn. Then he left Wales and I was adopted. We didn't meet again until I was twenty. Your Dad had just returned to England to visit your Grandfather after finishing a law degree here in the States. I met him at a friend's house, Peter Cornwell's actually. I knew who he was before he knew me. By the time he'd worked it out he'd already asked me to marry him." Mary stood up. "And, the rest, as they say, is history."

"And Rosie Llywelyn?"

"All I can tell you is that she died a long time ago."

"You said she was killed," Rosie had said, "that you and Dad killed her."

"I know," Mary had said. "I'm not sure why I said that. It was an accident," Mary had hesitated and then she'd said, "I've told you enough. Maybe your Dad will tell you what happened when he gets home."

"Is he going to be late?" Rosie had asked. Thinking back she was surprised at how the conversation they had just had was so easily followed by such ordinariness.

"Probably. He went to New York early this morning. He's taking the eight o'clock shuttle back." Mary had left the safety of her desk and she had held out her hand. "Come on," she'd said. "The groceries are still downstairs on the kitchen table." Rosie had taken her mother's hand as she had unraveled her legs. Once on her feet she had given her mother a hug, and Mary had been grateful to her daughter, who just by listening had helped her begin her own recovery, but the moment quickly passed as Mary felt Rosie stiffen.

"Does Sarah know you're Mary Morgan?" Rosie had asked, moving away from her mother.

Mary shook her head.

"You never told her?" Rosie had asked, incredulous.

"How could I?" Mary had responded, the look on her face pleading for Rosie to understand.

"When Sarah started screaming in the hall I thought you shared a secret that you didn't want me to know," Rosie had said, speaking slowly, her voice no more than a whisper, "but it was Sarah who didn't know you are Mary Morgan and you could not tell her."

Mary had started crying.

"I behaved badly," she'd said, sobbing. "I shouldn't have shouted at you. I was terrified. I didn't know what she'd remembered."

Rosie had seen the terror in her eyes.

"I didn't know what *knowing* I am Mary Morgan would do to Sarah. I just knew what it had done to me, *to Tommy*."

Rosie had put her arms back around her mother and Mary had clung to her.

"It's okay," Rosie had said. Not knowing if it was or could be, she'd just kept saying, "It's okay".

For a moment Rosie had sat not thinking anything at all, just remembering her mother holding on to her. Soon, the counting would begin, she knew that, but just for a little while she wanted to hold on to her mother, however fragile she had become.

At Logan planes had been delayed in landing due to fog. Only one runway was open. Tom had phoned from LaGuardia to say he was going to be very late. Rosie and Mary had eaten supper quietly together. Mary had asked if Rachel had said anything more about going to the Cape when the semester ended. Rosie had told her mother that Rachel had two Great Aunts staying, who had emigrated from Argentina and settled in Arizona, and they were teaching Rachel to tango. Her mother had laughed and said she would like to learn. They had filled the dishwasher together, and then Rosie had said goodnight and gone upstairs to her room.

Rosie had closed the door and walked over to the window. A

car had been moving slowly down Pinckney, and the sound of a bass guitar had grown louder and then faded as the car had disappeared down the street. Rosie had checked her email and smiled. Jesse and Rachel had both sent her messages about her presentation and so had Margaret. She had read them quickly and then she had opened an email from Sarah:

> Hello my darling girl. I'm sorry I'm causing trouble. I hope we can still talk. Love Sarah.
>
> Of course we can Aunt Sarah. Did my mother speak to you? I love you too, Rosie
>
> She did. She was a bit upset. I'm sorry luvy. I shouldn't have sent you my stories.
>
> Yes you should. They are important. They're my stories too.
>
> How can someone so young be so wise? I've never lied to you. They are all true.

Rosie had realized when she first read this message from Sarah that her mother must have been very angry with her. Now she had a better understanding of why she had been so upset. "Poor Sarah," she said to herself as she re-read the interchange between them.

> I believe you Aunt Sarah. Please tell me what happened. How did Rosie Llywelyn die?
>
> We'd been swimming in Big Pond. Gwenny Morgan was there and Mary, but I don't think Mary Morgan knew what was happening. She had been very sick and she had a fever. Gwenny only brought her with us because Mrs. Morgan was too tired to take care of her.
>
> Was my Dad with you?

Yes. Tommy was there. He was giving Mary a piggyback ride, and Gwenny and our Rosie were taking turns carrying me because I didn't want to put my sandals back on and the heather was prickly underneath my feet. The sun was shining and we were all happy. Luvy I'm not sure I should go on. Maybe you should wait until your Dad gets home.

No! Go on! I want to know!

Gwenny said she wouldn't let the authorities take Mary away and we charged up the hill determined to keep her safe. Remember the old mineshaft in my story about Gwenny Morgan? Well Gwenny had been so angry that we had all dropped our stones, but just as we were walking past the mineshaft Tommy gave Mary to Gwenny and he picked up a stone and went over and threw it down the shaft.

Go on!

Then he started counting, one – two – three – four – five. If you counted very fast you could get to fifty but Tommy counted slow. Rosie put me down and we went over – six – and lay down around the edge of the shaft with our heads looking down into the cold black hole – seven. Gwenny Morgan didn't say a word. She'd never told our Tommy off and she was not about to start. We heard the stone hit the side of the shaft and Tommy continued to count, slowly, deliberately, eight – nine – TEN. I've counted it so many times since that day I got stuck in the elevator. Then there was a plunk, a flat dead sound that echoed from deep underground.

Then what happened?

Years before we were born the pond in front of our Nan's house had been drained so the miners could dig tunnels to the seams of coal underneath it. The pond water flooded the tunnels of the old mine and we knew the stone had hit the water at the bottom of the shaft.

Aunt Sarah, tell me what happened next?

The sound fascinated us and we dropped more stones between the planks of wood that were supposed to keep the mineshaft covered and we counted.

Did you drop stones?

Yes but when we started dropping stones with our Tommy, Gwenny got nervous and she told us to stop. She was sitting back a bit, away from the edge, holding Mary who was fast asleep. Then I started to cry. I'd cut my foot on a piece of slate and it started to bleed.

Then what happened?

Tommy picked me up and he carried me away from the edge of the old mineshaft. I hated the sight of blood, especially my own. I've no idea how I became a nurse. Tommy tried to comfort me and Rosie said we had to go back down the hill so she could wash my foot in the spring.

Did you all go?

No. I was crying so much Tommy began to fool around to make me feel better. He picked up my sandals and started throwing them up high in the air, juggling with them to make me laugh, and I stopped crying. Tommy tossed my sandals higher and higher and I started laughing. Then one of my sandals went right over his head. We all watched it spin up, up, in the air and then come plummeting down and land on one of the planks of wood that covered the mineshaft. I'm not sure why the board didn't break, but it didn't. "Leave it!" Gwenny shouted to Tommy, and I started to cry again. Tommy gave me a hug and he told me it would be okay. He said he'd tell our Mam and Dad it was his fault that I'd lost one of my sandals. Rosie said she didn't want Tommy to get into trouble. It was the first week of our Dad's summer holidays, and he and our Mam had just arrived on the Garn. So Rosie said, "Let me see if I can get it with the umbrella."

Rosie's umbrella?

Our Grandad gave it to her. This is so hard. It has taken me so long to be able write about what happened. I have to go on. Are you ready, Luvy?

I think so. I love you.

I know. I love you too. Here goes. We had got in the habit of taking the umbrella with us. Rosie had told Gwenny that I couldn't go in the sun because I got burned easily. I did, of course, but really we took it with us because we didn't like the geese.

Go on Aunt Sarah, finish the story.

"No!" Gwenny yelled, dropping Mary, who was still half asleep. She ran over to where we were standing. "I think I can get it," Rosie said, and with that she lay down with her head over the edge of the mine shaft, and she reached out with the umbrella, but the sandal was too far out.

What did my Dad do?

He told Rosie to leave it too. "Leave it Rosie," Tommy pleaded with her. He sounded so frightened and he caught hold of Rosie's ankles.

"I've almost got it," Rosie said.

"Let me try," Tommy's voice was hoarse, and he kept pleading with her. "Rosie, please, let me try."

Don't stop.

Tommy was terrified and he really tried to pull Rosie away from the edge of the mineshaft. I don't know why Rosie couldn't see how dangerous it was. She was lying with her head and shoulders over the edge. She inched her way onto the rotten plank and then she reached out further with her umbrella over the black gaping hole.

Aunt Sarah you don't have to write any more. I know what happened.

I have to write it my Lovely. I have to reach the end of the story. I just won't send it.

No. If you have to write it I have to read it.

The crook of the handle of the umbrella was touching the sandal. "I think I can get it," Rosie said again. Tommy's hands were tight around Rosie's legs but he was frightened to pull her back in case the plank gave way and he couldn't hold her. "No! Leave it Rosie!" he begged her. "That's far enough."

I'm here Aunt Sarah.

"Okay," Rosie said, letting go of the umbrella that she left on one of the planks so she could inch her way slowly back. Tommy relaxed his grip a bit but he had hold of her until she was safe, kneeling on the ground at the edge of the shaft. But then she leant forward to get her umbrella and she lost her balance. She put her hand down on one of the planks of wood to save herself but the wood was rotted through. It splintered and gave way. Tommy grabbed at her and tried to catch her feet but she plunged into the darkness. I remember our screams lasting forever. Tommy and Gwenny and I were lying on the ground with our heads over the shaft and I remember the cold air, dank and deadly, rising up to meet me. It was just an instant but I remember it, smell it, taste it.

Are you all right Aunt Sarah? Please tell me you're okay!

"Rosie!" "Rosie!" I heard our Tommy shout and Gwenny Morgan screaming. I remember the sound of the boards breaking and the deadly sound of her body hitting the water deep underground. I can hear it now. And she is still there. The mineshaft was too deep and eddies and currents too strong for the miners to find her. It's awful. Terrible. I keep imagining what it must have been like for Rosie. I wish it had been me.

Aunt Sarah. Tell me you're okay!

"Rosie! "Rosie!" I was gasping for breath and again I hit the side. After that I remember feeling as if I was floating which I suppose must have been just before I lost consciousness. I don't remember anything after that. Everything is a blur. I've often wondered if I died before I hit the water. I have no memory of that.

Aunt Sarah! It was Rosie Llywelyn who died!

I love you my darling girl.

I love you too Aunt Sarah.

Rosie was crying as she re-read the last emails Sarah had sent her. It seemed so long ago since she'd first read them, but it was only last night.

"Eight – nine!"

Sarah had become Rosie Llywelyn and Rosie had been so frightened she had paced back and forth from the computer to the window waiting for another message from Sarah. The only thought that had been in her head was that Sarah had become Rosie. She had remembered that her father had told her he thought Sarah might try to kill herself. She'd tried to figure out what Sarah was telling her. Rosie had been terrified that it was too much for Sarah, that she believed it was her fault that her sister had died, and now she wanted to die for her sister. She sent another email to Sarah:

Aunt Sarah! Write to me! I'm worried about you! I love you!

And Sarah had written back.

I love you too. Don't worry about me Luvy. Soon, I'll have to go. But I need your help. When I died your Dad felt it was his fault. I know he felt – he still feels – that he killed me. He didn't. Gwenny told him that he shouldn't have been juggling with Sarah's sandals. Gwenny was hysterical. She shouted at him, punched him with her fists, and kicked him. She said he should have stopped me, and maybe he should, but it was *my* decision to try and get Sarah's sandal. No one is to blame but me. Rosie Llywelyn

Rosie had been terrified. She remembered that she had tried to stay calm, to keep writing, to use her email messages to hold on to Sarah. She'd not heard her Dad arrive home and she'd thought he must have still been stuck in New York at LaGuardia. She'd reasoned that if she missed a message then what would Sarah do? She'd decided she had to keep writing until she figured out what to do. Then there was another message.

Tommy was crying. He didn't try to stop Gwenny from punching and kicking him. He was on his knees looking down into the mineshaft sobbing, and he was leaning forward getting closer and closer to the edge. Then Gwenny caught hold of him and pulled him back. Tommy made everyone swear that we wouldn't tell what had happened. I'm not sure why except I think the truth was too hard for him bear, and maybe he blamed himself so much he couldn't stand the thought of other people blaming him the way Gwenny did.

Rosie had felt relieved. Sarah had returned to writing as herself and not as her sister. She'd wanted to stop Sarah from falling apart and becoming Rosie Llywelyn again and so she'd started writing about school.

Aunt Sarah, this must be so hard for you. I want to tell you about my school report. Let's talk about my presentation. Margaret loved your bara brith and the Welsh cakes we made together.

Luvy, I'm almost done. Tommy told us to say we were walking in the hills and we didn't see the mineshaft because it was hidden by the heather, and Rosie stood on one of the boards and fell. Gwenny agreed. She was trying to comfort Mary who was crying, but Mary had such a high fever she had been asleep when Rosie fell.

For a moment Rosie had stopped worrying about Sarah and thought about her mother. She'd imagined her as a little girl being so ill and waking up to find her sister Gwenny hitting and kicking Tommy and all of them crying.

I think Gwenny agreed because she was worried that if the authorities knew what had really happened they would think we were bad children and use Rosie's death as an excuse to take Mary away. It didn't take much for Tommy to convince me not to talk about what happened. I know now I was traumatized. I had nodded at Tommy and no one realized until the next day that I had lost my ability to speak. I didn't speak again for over a year, and by then our Mam had died from grief and nobody talked about what happened. I actually not only could not speak, I could not remember. I repressed my memories of what happened. It was not until the elevator stopped between floors at the hospital that my memory started to come back.

Aunt Sarah, I know how hard this has been for you. I think you should rest. We can write again tomorrow. Maybe you could ask one of the nurses to bring you some tea. You'd like that.

I am tired Luvy. I brought some barley water back with

me so I could have some of that. You get ready for bed now and I'll just sit here and maybe write a bit more.

Rosie had left her email open and had got ready for bed. She remembered she'd followed her usual routine, washing her face with Apricot Scrub, and then for no reason at all she had put on some of the Pink Opal eye shadow she had bought when she had gone to CVS with Rachel. She'd smudged it around her eyes and added Iced Raisin close to her lashes, and she'd stood looking in the mirror not knowing the girl who was looking back at her.

When she'd come out of the bathroom she'd checked to see if there was another email from Sarah, but there was not. Exhausted, she'd got into bed and Max had crawled under the covers beside her. Rosie had curled up with her arms around him, and the big old alley cat had purred as if he'd known she needed comforting. It was all too much. She'd wanted to sleep, to forget, to be like Sarah, to lose her memory and live her life without remembering.

She'd been drifting off to sleep when her mother knocked gently at her door and came in to kiss her goodnight.

"Are you okay?" Mary had asked her, looking at her eyes but saying nothing.

"I'm worried about Aunt Sarah," Rosie had said.

"Dad will be home soon," Mary had said. "He's been circling Logan waiting for the fog to clear," she'd told Rosie. "He called me from the plane. He said if the fog doesn't clear in the next fifteen minutes they're going to be diverted to Hartford."

"Tell Dad it wasn't his fault," Rosie had said. "And give him a kiss for me."

"I will," Mary had said. She bent over and kissed Rosie on the forehead. "Here's a kiss from me too."

"Catch!" Tommy yelled at her.

"I can't," Rosie cried, as the sandal dropped and disappeared. Rosie was falling.

"One – two – three –"

She heard someone cry out.

"Rosie! No!"

She hit the side of the shaft and her body bounced into the darkness.

A girl about her own age reached out and took hold of her hand. The girl was tall and thin. She had long black hair streaked with red, and the whites of her green eyes stood out against the black coal dust that covered her face. Her blue and white dress hung in tatters, and was blackened by coal dust and smeared with blood. The girl smiled and Rosie could see that in her other hand she was holding her red umbrella.

Rosie looked down.

Her room was filled with murky black water. It had become
the mineshaft flooded when the lake was drained and the girl was
rising up out of the darkness and Rosie held out her hand and the
girl took it and Rosie held on to her and together they floated into
the light.

Rosie looked up at the sun shining above them, and the girl
let go of her hand and was gone, but in the confusion of shadows
that filled Rosie's room, she saw the girl again. This time Rosie saw
the girl standing at the bottom of her bed. There was no coal dust
on the girl's face, no red streaks in her hair, and no blood on her
dress, but she was still holding an old black umbrella.

"Rosie Llywelyn," Rosie had whispered.

"Take care of Sarah," Rosie had heard the girl say.

"Sarah!" Rosie was wide-awake.

Rosie's mind was racing back to the night before. There was
no yesterday and today. She was living the memory and she'd got
to finish it. Get to the end. Out of the ashes of death. The end was
the beginning of whatever happened next. The story. *Her* story. She
would find her own truth.

Rosie had jumped out of bed and turned on her computer. An
email had just arrived from Sarah. Reading the email again now was
as terrifying as it had been the night before. Rosie was no longer
reliving what had happened, she was in the moment living it.

**And now it's not that I haunt them, it's that they haunt
me. I can't rest because no one remembers.**

Rosie, heart thumping, had known immediately that Sarah
had become Rosie Llewelyn again.

It's as if I never lived. There are no pictures of me in

your house. No stories are told about me when I was a little girl, and there are *so many* stories Luvy. Our Nan and our Grandad were wonderful people and the Garn was such a friendly place. But now I'm like the Garn. My bones are like a heap of stones that nobody cares about. No one can visit me, sit on my grave, and talk to me. My body is lost in the tunnels of the old mine, tumbled about, washed up, buried in the stall where our Grandad dug coal, in a place where the timbers have collapsed, and the roof has caved in.

So many stories are lost down the mines. Luvy, my darling girl, tell our Tommy it wasn't his fault. Give him my stories. They're all that's left of me. If no one remembers then I'm not even a memory. Luvy please! If no one remembers I'll keep falling – one – two – three. Over and over I'll stretch out with my umbrella to get Sarah's sandal, and over and over the wooden plank will splinter and I will fall down the mine – four – five. I hit the side – six – seven – and float – eight – before everything is a blur and I am back at the top reaching out – one – two – three – four. That's what happened last weekend when you couldn't reach me. I told you I kept falling apart. Remember?

Rosie had quickly typed, her fingers fumbling on the keys, her eyes so filled with tears she had to wipe them away to see the screen.

I remember Aunt Sarah. I'll try and help you. I'll give my Dad your stories but please don't stop writing Aunt Sarah.

Aunt Sarah, I love you.

Rosie kept repeating her Aunt Sarah's name.

Aunt Sarah, I want you to come home.

Dad said you can come home Aunt Sarah.

Aunt Sarah please keep writing to me.

There was a final message:

I'm tired Luvy. Really tired. I hope you understand. I can't keep on falling. Soon I'll have to go. It's time that I stopped remembering what happened. You remember for me. I love you. Rosie Llywelyn.

"I can't keep falling," Rosie had whispered to herself, clicking the mouse to print. She'd read the last email several times while she'd printed it out. Then she'd read out loud as she underlined with a red pen. "I can't keep falling. Soon I'll have to go. It's time I stopped remembering what happened. You remember for me."

Rosie had run upstairs to her parents' bedroom with the emails in her hand.

"Dad! Mom! Wake up!"

"What's happened?" Mary had asked, sounding more asleep than awake.

Rosie had switched on the light and Mary had covered her eyes.

"Read this!"

Mary had blinked, everything was out of focus, she had reached over and tried to find her reading glasses which were somewhere on the table beside the bed with all the papers and books.

"Your mother asked you what's happened?" Tom had said groggily, eyes still shut, his body circling as if still on the plane. "Can't we sort this out in the morning?"

"No," Rosie had said, exasperated with her father. She'd focused her attention on her mother and found her reading glasses. "Please! Read this email! It's from Sarah!"

"Rosie, tell us what's going on," Tom had said, sitting up. He was now wide awake and watching her gravely. "What's happened?"

It took Rosie no time at all to convince her parents that Sarah was going to kill herself. At first Tom had thought she'd become alarmed because he'd told her his fears about Sarah, but when Rosie gave him the last two email messages that she had received from Rosie Llywelyn he had no doubts that Sarah was about to kill herself.

"Sarah thinks she's Rosie Llywelyn," Rosie had said.

"She asked for my old laptop," Tom had said, speaking rapidly. "The psychiatrist has been encouraging Sarah to write. He told me it's the only way he can get her to communicate. She used one of the nurse's laptops at first and then I gave her mine."

"She's been writing stories and sending them to me," Rosie had told her parents. "She wrote about how Rosie Llywelyn died, how Rosie tried to get her sandal, and how the planks of wood gave way."

A shudder had run through Tom. "I hope we aren't too late," he'd said.

By then Rosie had been running down the stairs two at-a-time to her room.

"Call the hospital and tell them to check on Sarah," Tom had said to Mary, pulling on a pair of old Levis. "Tell them to get someone to stay with her until I get there."

One leg in her jeans, Rosie had quickly checked her email but there were no more messages from Sarah. No time for socks, she stuck her feet in her sneakers, grabbed a sweatshirt, and was on her way down the stairs.

By this time Mary had made the phone call and Tom had found his car keys and he was already going out of the front door.

Mary had run after him and caught up with him just as he was getting into his car.

"She's not in her room," she'd said, trying to catch her breath. "They don't know where she is."

"Tell them I'm on my way," Tom had told her, just as Rosie had flown out of the house and run around the front of the car and jumped in the car beside him.

"Rosie! Get out!" Tom had yelled as he started the engine.

"No! I'm coming!" Rosie had yelled back, putting her foot up to tie one of her sneakers. "I might be able to help!"

Tom had started the engine of the old black Mercedes and shifted into reverse gear. He had left his car on Pinckney and he was boxed in, and it had taken agonizing minutes to extricate the car.

Yo Yo Ma was playing Bach, but Tom had switched the radio off as he'd pulled out onto the street. He'd looked at the clock. 12:40 a.m. A pale round moon had risen above the black silhouette of the rooftops on Beacon Hill. People were still walking along Charles and the lights were on in the Seven Eleven store, but on the side streets there was hardly anyone about.

"If Sarah kills herself it will be my fault," he'd said as much to himself as to Rosie. "Sarah's illness has brought back old memories that I've spent my whole life trying to forget."

Rosie had wanted to tell her father that Sarah wasn't ill. She was traumatized and that was different. She'd read about trauma in one of the reports she'd come across when she was researching the lives of coal miners. But she'd resisted telling her father. It had not seemed important. Maybe. Later.

Tom had driven instinctively. Rosie had sat beside him trying to figure out what they were going to do if they couldn't find Sarah. The gloomy streets had faded into the distance like the underground tunnels of the mines where her Great Grandfathers had worked. She'd realized then that when she presented her research to the class, she had said that both her Great Grandfathers were miners, but she had not known at the time that her mother was Mary Morgan. For a few miles the thought had occupied her. She'd thought again of Grethel. It was as if her mind and Sarah's mind were merging. Sarah's memories had become her memories.

"Dad," she'd said. "If Sarah dies I think I'll die."

"Sarah won't die," Tom had said to reassure her.

Soon they were out of Boston and Tom's hands had closed tightly around the steering wheel as he'd pressed the accelerator. The guilt that tormented him was etched on his face.

"I can't think," he'd said. "I keep remembering what happened. I can smell the coal dust, feel the damp air in the mineshaft, I can see Rosie falling."

"Sarah said that too," Rosie had said, suddenly feeling frightened that her Dad was going to end up like Sarah. The car had swerved and Rosie thought he was going to drive off the road.

"Dad!"

"I can hear Sarah and Gwenny screaming!"

"Dad!"

"Sorry," Tom had said, as he'd turned the steering wheel to avoid crossing over into the oncoming traffic. A split second later and there would have been a head-on collision, but somehow Tom steered them safely back onto the right side of the road.

When they'd reached the hospital the doors to the psychiatric unit were locked, but the security guard was expecting them and he'd quickly unlocked the door and let them in.

Once inside the nurse at reception had paged the doctor on duty who arrived within seconds, walking quickly towards them looking grim.

"We have staff looking for her throughout the hospital," he'd said. He'd tried to reassure Rosie and Tom. "Sarah was in her room at midnight," he'd said. "Nobody has seen her since then."

"Where did you find her the last time you lost her?" Tom had asked, sounding angry at the doctor for not being able to find Sarah.

"She was in the cardiac unit," the doctor had replied, ignoring the way Tom had spoken to him. "She'd found an empty room and was in there with her laptop."

"Have you looked for her there?" Rosie had asked.

"We searched there first," the doctor had replied, looking at Rosie as if he disapproved of her being there.

"Cardiac is in the old wing of the hospital, right?" Tom had asked. "The old brick building?"

"Right."

"Is there an elevator?" Rosie had asked.

"The elevator is off the main lobby and people are going up and down all the time," the doctor had said, looking puzzled.

"Is there another elevator?" Tom had asked, understanding why Rosie had asked the question.

"There's an old service elevator, but it's not in use," the doctor had answered, the look of reassurance leaving his face as it slowly dawned on him why Rosie had asked about the elevator. "The mine shaft," he said. "But the doors are padlocked on every floor."

"Who has keys?" Rosie had asked, urgently. "The keys!"

"I don't know," the doctor had sounded flustered and was red in the face.

"Let's hope all the doors are padlocked!" Rosie had said.

"I'll call security," the doctor had said, turning and running back to his office.

"You do that!" Rosie's Dad had shouted, as he banged on the door for the security guard to let them out of the psychiatric unit. Tom was through the door the second it was unlocked and Rosie ran after him.

Looking back now Rosie understood how the past could become the present, how stories could take place over and over. She remembered that she had felt she was in Wales, even though she had never been there, and had no memories of her own of what had happened to Rosie Llywelyn, or to Sarah, or to her Mom and Dad. It made no difference.

She was there dropping stones down the mineshaft. She'd counted slowly to herself as she ran after her Dad.

"Four – five –"

She'd tried to comfort Sarah who had hurt her foot.

"Six – seven –"

She'd tried to make her laugh. She'd picked up her sandals and started juggling with them.

"Eight – nine –"

She was sure her father had done the same.

They'd run down the corridor that led to the cardiac unit. Both of them had been lost in the urgency of the moment, living whole lifetimes as time moved forward but they went back.

The main elevator was moving between the second and third floors and they'd both known it was unlikely that Sarah was in it.

"Where's the service elevator?" Tom had asked a nurse, as she walked by. Without speaking she pointed down a side corridor

Tom and Rosie had started running. When they'd reached the old service elevator on the ground floor they found the doors padlocked. Tom had opened the door to the stairwell and they began to climb. Rosie had started counting. She had been unable to stop herself.

"One – two – three –"

Her heart was beating steadily as she took the stairs two at a time passing Tom who was breathing heavily as he climbed.

On each floor Rosie had checked the padlock on the elevator.

"Four – five –"

She had been filled with a desperate energy, more lucid than she had ever been.

"Six –"

Sarah's sandal had flown over her head. Her heart had lurched and she'd gulped mouthfuls of air as she'd reached the seventh floor and found that the elevator was still padlocked.

"Seven – eight –"

The sandal fell.

"Nine –"

Rosie had reached out with her umbrella.

"Ten – TEN!"

"Aunt Sarah!" Rosie had cried out, as she'd pushed open the door of the stairwell on the tenth floor. "Leave it!"

"I think I can get it," Sarah had said. The padlock was gone and the doors of the service elevator were wide open. Sarah was on her knees leaning out over the edge of the gaping black hole and in her hand was the old thrift store umbrella.

"Please, Aunt Sarah," Rosie had pleaded, her voice no more than a hoarse whisper, "leave it." Rosie, arms out, had slowly taken a step towards Sarah. The cold dank air from the elevator shaft filled her lungs and she'd caught her breath.

"I've almost got it," Sarah had said, moving closer to the edge and leaning out further.

"Rosie, let me try," Tom had said to Sarah, as quietly as he could. He had been gasping for breath after the heart-pumping climb that had filled him with terror.

Rosie had turned to look at her Dad when he called her name, but she quickly understood that he was speaking to Sarah.

Tom had pleaded with Sarah, ignoring the pain in his chest that was making him sweat.

"Please, Rosie. Please," he'd said as Sarah had inched her way a little closer to the edge of the elevator shaft and she'd reached out for the sandal with her old umbrella.

"I think I can get it."

"No! Leave it Rosie, no!" Tom had shouted as he'd lunged forward and grabbed hold of Sarah.

Rosie had closed her eyes as Sarah had inched her way closer to the edge of the elevator shaft and she'd buried her face in her hands when Sarah had said, "I think I can get it." She'd been sure that both Sarah and her Dad had fallen down the shaft, and she'd started crying when she'd looked up and saw them.

Reliving the moment in her room she was still unsure how they had not both fallen. Tom had moved so fast she had no idea how they had not been propelled forward and plummeted to their death.

Tom had held on onto Sarah so tight she'd dropped the umbrella and they'd lain there together with their shoulders as well as their heads over the gaping black hole.

Sarah had started counting as the umbrella fell.

"One – two – three –"

The umbrella had hit the side of the elevator shaft and Sarah had counted to five before it reached the bottom with a wood splintering crack.

"Dad," Rosie had whispered, holding on to his legs. "Get back. Get away from the edge. Get back."

Tom had been in the kitchen leaning against the sink having a cup of coffee the following morning when Rosie had come downstairs. She'd dropped her book bag on the floor by the table. She went over to the fridge and poured herself a glass of orange juice.

"Did you get any sleep?" he'd asked.

Rosie had shaken her head. "How's Sarah?"

"She's heavily sedated," Tom had replied. "Mom says she tried to persuade you to stay home today but you told her you want to go to school."

Again Rosie had nodded. "When's Sarah coming home?" Rosie had asked Tom. "She should never have been there in the first place."

"Rosie, I did what I thought was best."

"I know."

Tom had nodded.

"The doctor told me they will do a complete evaluation of

292

Sarah in the next couple of days and then I can bring her home."

Tom had wanted to put his arms around Rosie and tell her he loved her but didn't.

"I know how hard –"

"Not now," Rosie had said, cutting him off. "I don't want to talk about it."

"I called Margaret," Tom had said. "She knows what happened."

"Great!" Rosie had said, looking at him in disbelief.

Mary had come into the kitchen wearing a black suit. It was as if nothing had happened Rosie thought.

"If Rosie is going to school I'll go to the university," she'd said. She was ashen and her eyes were red.

Rosie looked at her Dad and regretted the way she had spoken to him. He looked ten years older than he did yesterday.

"Maybe we could talk this evening?" Tom had said to Rosie.

"Sure," Rosie had said. "You going to work?"

"Hospital first and then a deposition," Tom said. "I'm sorry if you didn't want me to talk with Margaret. When your Mom said you were going to school I thought I'd better call her and let her know what's going on."

"It's okay."

"I love you Rosie."

"I know." Rosie had said, "I love you too."

Tom had smiled and Rosie had walked around the table and given him a hug. Then he picked up his briefcase and told Rosie's Mom that he had to go. He'd stopped in the doorway and turned back and looked at Rosie. "What about the ball game on Saturday? Do you want to go?"

"Sure."

Rosie's Dad had smiled at her and nodded as he left.

"I'm going to the hospital when your Dad goes to his deposition," Mary had said as she'd poured some coffee and sat down at the kitchen table. "One of us will be there all day."

Mary had taken a sip of coffee.

"Rosie," she'd begun.

"Not now," Rosie had said, quickly.

"That's what I was going to say," Mary had said, her eyes filling with tears. "It's going to take time. So much has happened. When you want to talk about it I want you to know I am ready to listen. Anytime."

"I know," Rosie had said.

At school Margaret had put her arms around Rosie as soon as she walked into the classroom. "I'm here if you need to talk," she'd said.

"That's what my Mom said," Rosie had said with tears in her eyes. "I want to be here with you and my friends. You're family too."

"Jesse is going to make his presentation this morning," Margaret had said, smiling at Rosie.

"Hope he doesn't spend the whole time talking about castles and battles," Rachel had whispered to Rosie.

Rosie had smiled. Rachel had been trying to keep in the moment. Rosie was sure Margaret had told her what had happened to Sarah.

Jesse had surprised Margaret and the class.

"Yesterday," he'd began, "Rosie made a presentation that can't be beat. Margaret, I know you're always telling us we are not in a competition, but the reality is in the US we all compete. And the only thing that's important to the government is that America is number one in the world."

Jesse did not hurry.

"Up until yesterday I was all for that," Jesse had said. "Battle ready, you might say, programmed to win." Jesse had looked at Margaret, "But yesterday I had an epiphany, as you would say." He'd grinned, "and also, as Margaret would say, I learned that winning isn't everything."

Margaret had smiled at Jesse and rolled her hands to encourage him to go on.

"A couple of days ago Rosie sent me an email and asked if I knew anything about the Battle of Thermopylae that took place in Greece in 480 BC," Jesse had said, not looking as Rosie to put her on the spot. "She also asked me about the Siege of Alcázar which took place in Spain at the time of the Spanish Civil War in 1936, which was also the year the Special Correspondent wrote about the terrible plight of the coal miners in Wales."

The class waited.

"I'm not saying this very well," Jesse had said, and Margaret had quickly said, "You're doing fine."

"The point is I couldn't figure out why Rosie was interested in an ancient battle in Greece or a siege in Spain during the Civil War, when she was researching the lives of coal miners in Wales." Jesse had looked embarrassed. "I thought she was joking around," he'd paused, "or something."

The class had laughed and Rosie had shaken her head.

"But yesterday I got it," Jesse had said. "At the Battle of Thermopylae seven thousand men blocked a pass and stopped the Persian army of a million men, although historians now think it was more likely to have been one hundred thousand men."

"During the Siege of Alcázar a small group of the Guardia Civil and their families, including six hundred and fifty women and children, participated in an uprising against the Republican forces." For a moment Jesse hesitated. "I don't pretend to know much about it, but I do know that the Guardia Civil defended Alcázar to protect the women and children, and the Siege of Alcázar has become a symbol of moral courage. "

"The Battle of Thermopylae too," Margaret had said, letting Jesse know she was on the same page. "Moral courage can have serious consequences."

"When you stand-up against tyranny as they did in Blaina and the other coalmining villages in Wales, chances are you'll end up in jail, or lying bloodied in the road." Jesse had said, looking at Margaret and then at Rosie. "Or be forced to leave your homeland because powerful men who have made immense profits from working you half-to-death have taken away all your rights and made it so God-awful for you to stay in the village where you were born you have no alternative except to get on a bus or a boat," Jesse took a breath, and continued quietly, "while these same men, who are thought to be so noble, legalize their violations against your family and your people by putting in place a Policy of Transference."

Instantly Rachel had been on her feet, fist clenched, arm raised, and without a moment's hesitation Margaret had stood up at the back of the room in solidarity with Rachel and Jesse. She stood, as beautiful as Maya Angelou and as majestic as Toni Morrison, and she'd raised her arm and clenched her fist as a matter of conscience.

The room had been still.

Slowly, as if weighted down by the grief of generations of the tragedy that had happened in Wales, Rosie had quietly pushed back her chair and stood up, fist clenched, she raised her arm as the rest of her class pushed back their chairs and fists clenched they raised their arms in solidarity. Then Rachel had lowered her arm and Margaret had sat down, and sitting, everyone had focused their gaze on Jesse.

Jesse had looked out the window for a few seconds, and then he'd turned and faced the class as the last chair was pulled in.

"Some stories you never tell," Jesse had said, looking around the class to make sure everyone understood. "But I should tell you," he'd continued, with a grin on his face, "that Daisy Blake used to be my baby sitter and I know her Great Uncle, so I stopped by to see him after school yesterday, and I asked if I could take a look at that book of 1936 *Times* newspapers."

"I wondered how you managed to pronounce Thermopylae so flawlessly," Margaret had said, and several students laughed.

"Daisy was there with William who was into everything," Jesse had said. "She had just brought back the book of old newspapers, so after she took William home, I sat with her Uncle and we read the articles."

In the fiery moment of solidarity Jesse's face had been almost as red as his hair, but now his color had drained.

"I wanted to know how the English Government got five hundred thousand people to leave their homes and their country," he'd said. "And so that's what I talked about with Daisy's Uncle."

Jesse had stopped for a second.

"Go on," a student had shouted out, "tell us."

"The families lived together," Jesse had said, "sons went down the mines when they were twelve and had been digging coal underground for two years by the time they were fourteen, the same age as me. But when the mines started closing there was no work for the miners and the government stopped paying the small amount of unemployment money sons gave to their mothers for their keep. So their mothers had no money to feed them. Sometimes there were two or three grown sons living at home and daughters too, often with a Grandfather or Grandmother living with them as well, in two rooms up and two rooms down, and a toilet out the back, all half-starving to begin with, so when the pittance the sons got from the government was stopped, boys as young as me had to leave home."

"Daisy's Uncle said the families were between a rock and a hard place, mothers agonized because they did not want their sons to go down the mines, so they did not try to stop them from leaving," Jesse had said. "Daisy's Uncle said many of them thought they made their own choices, but they did not. He told me that what happened was hegemonous, which is a word I've heard you use Margaret, but I never understood what it meant until now."

"Basically, it means you tell a people they are lumpen and of no social worth, and they believe it and call themselves lumpen, even though they are courageous and the very fact they survived is a heroic deed."

Again Jesse had paused.

"So," he'd said, signaling he was moving on. "I finished my report a couple of days ago," he'd said, gesturing at the bound document that was lying on his desk. "My father had a cover put on it." He'd looked at Margaret. "I'll give it to him when you have read it."

Margaret had nodded and smiled, hoping the look was reassuring, but she had no idea what Jesse was going to say next, and she knew it would take her a long time to understand what had just happened to her class.

"And Margaret," Jesse had said, his voice rising, "I know you don't put A's or B's on our reports, or a number, or anything like that, but we all know when we've aced-it or when we've effed-up." Jesse had smiled, his voice dropping, "Sorry Margaret. But right now I've had enough of famous men who win great battles and great wars."

Jesse walked over to his desk and picked up his report and handed it to Margaret.

"My report is filled with the great men history remembers and the great battles that they fought, but you all know that." He paused. "The only part I would like you to read is about Cúchulainn. He's still my hero because he's my Dad's hero."

Jesse had looked around the class at his friends who were on the edge of their seats silently cheering him on. "So I am going to talk about something else," Jesse had begun. "I'm going to talk about potatoes and a famine and some of the great writers and poets from the land where I come from."

Jesse had talked about the Irish Potato Famine and about the great Irish poets and writers from Samuel Beckett to Seamus Heaney. He'd told them a story that he had heard from his father about the day James Joyce met Nora Barnacle who worked in Finn's Hotel and of how Joyce had arranged to meet her and she had stood him up.

"My father says Joyce wrote her an ardent letter asking for another date and that two days later they met," Jesse had said, hesitating for a moment. "My Dad says that on the day they met *Ulysses* both began and ended, and I still don't understand what he meant by that."

Almost as an aside Jesse had told the class that his father had been in Dublin between 1973 and 1975 and he spent every day reading in the National Library. Then one after another he went through Irish poets his father had read to him, and he read to the class from Seamus Heaney's poem *Digging*.

> Between my finger and my thumb
> The squat pen rests; snug as a gun.

Jesse compared Heaney to Yeats, but he said Heaney was much more a man of the people.

"Heaney talks about 'words as bearers of history and mystery,'" he'd said.

Jesse had looked at Rosie. It was the first time he had looked at her, except when she had stood up. He'd been worried that what he had to say would upset her, make it worse, and that she would unravel in class, and no one would know what to do to console her. She did not smile at him, but he could see by her eyes that she was sitting there listening to him as if every word was comforting.

Jesse had ended by talking about the new book by Seamus Deane entitled *Reading in the Dark*.

"My Dad gave me it to me. He says it's a book about loss and regret," he said, "I've read a few pages, just odd pages. It's about a family and it reminded me of Rosie and her family."

Jesse looked at Rosie and nodded.

"At the beginning of the book Seamus writes about an English teacher reading out a model essay. 'I'd never thought such stuff was worth writing about,' he writes. 'It was an ordinary life–no rebellions or love affairs or dangerous flights across the hills at night.'

Seamus writes, 'now that,' said the master, 'that's writing. That's telling the truth.'"

Jesse looked down and then at Margaret. "You keep telling us to find our own truth," he said to her. "I think Rosie did that when she shared her report with us yesterday. There were no battles, no castles. Just the hard lives of the miners and their families. Her family. Rosie talked about them in a way that I could never do. She was totally honest. She spoke her own truth. It was great," Jesse looked embarrassed. "I've tried to do that this morning but I'm still looking for my own truth." He'd laughed, "I might have to go to Ireland without my Dad if I'm going to find it. Sometimes I think he hid it someplace in the Dublin library."

"I am sure your father would love to go with you," Margaret had said, and the class laughed, including Rosie. "You'd both have a good time."

Jesse grinned at Rosie. For a moment she forgot what had happened the night before. It was a good sign. She knew that when she left school what had happened would fill her mind, but for a moment, just a moment, she felt warm inside.

Rosie thought about walking home from school. It seemed like such a long time ago that the sprinklers had come on and the young woman who had been soaked had grabbed the young man and kissed him. She wondered again if she would have had the courage to kiss Jesse like that. He deserved a kiss she thought, for helping her find her own truth. She felt a quiet satisfaction that all the pieces fit.

It was at that moment that there was a soft knock and the door opened.

"Want some pizza?" her Mom asked, showing Rosie a box from Figs with paper plates and napkins balanced on top.

"Are you going to have some?" Rosie asked.

Mary hesitated.

"Stay," Rosie said, smoothing the comforter she patted the bed inviting her mother to sit.

Mary put the box on the chair to Rosie's desk and carried the chair over to the bed.

"You okay?" Rosie asked as Mary sat down on the bed beside her.

"I'm okay," Mary said, nodding, and then with a half smile and her eyes on the ceiling, she whispered, "probably not."

"Do you want to talk?" Rosie asked.

"Not really," Mary said. "I'm shattered." She looked at Rosie, "You must be too."

"A bit," Rosie said, nodding as she opened the box. "I'm hungry! Let's eat!"

On Saturday Fenway was crowded. The Red Sox had won their last three games and the stadium was filled with the high hopes of their hotdog-eating, pretzel-munching fans. They were not disappointed. The bases were loaded when the last batter hit a home run in the bottom of the ninth inning to win the game, and Rosie and her Dad stood and shouted and clapped with everyone else, and it was at that moment Rosie realized she'd stopped counting to ten except for strikes, balls, and runs.

"I'm glad Sarah is coming home," Tom said, as they rode the T to the Arlington subway stop on their way home. He hadn't said much about what had happened to Sarah and neither had Mary, but they had taken turns at the hospital, Mary on Wednesday morning while Tom was at his deposition, and Tom in the late afternoon while Mary was teaching. It had become the routine for the rest of the week.

They were both shaken and ashen, but their quiet smiles reassured Rosie and she tried not to ask too many questions.

"I hope she stays forever," Rosie said as they crossed Boston Common.

"The thing is," Rosie's Dad said as they passed the State House and cut through on Joy Street to Pinckney, "I think I could have got Sarah's sandal." He was fumbling for the right words. "I've always thought it was my fault that Rosie died. I keep thinking –." He didn't finish the sentence.

"You called Sarah 'Rosie,'" Rosie said.

Tom looked at her, his eyes blank, not understanding.

"At the hospital, when we reached the tenth floor, you shouted "'Rosie, leave it.'"

"I don't remember."

"Like Sarah," Rosie said.

Tom shrugged his shoulders and shook his head.

Rosie was holding his hand and she gave it a squeeze. Then the lines around his eyes deepened as he smiled down at her.

"Have I told you how much I love you?" he said.

"Yes, on Thursday and Friday, and at least five times today!" Rosie said, laughing. "I have another question." The laughter stopped.

"What?" Tom looked at her intently. "It's okay. No more secrets. Remember?"

"Why did you name me Rosie?" she asked, before she had time to think. She thought it would be a painful question and she was surprised when her father smiled.

"Your mother wanted to call you Zoë," Tom said. "Or Sophie."

"Zoë might have been okay," Rosie said, "but Sophie?"

"Zoë Llywelyn?" Tom raised his eyebrows and grinned. "Maybe. I liked Kathryn or Margaret." Tom looked at her. "Katie Llywelyn? What do you think?"

"Mm Katie Llywelyn," Rosie said, trying the name on for size. "Sounds good to me. Margaret would have been okay too. So how did I get my name?"

"You were just a few hours old and we were trying to decide, and Sarah came in to see you. She had been working that night so she had been in and out, but this was the first time she had held you." Tom stopped. Rosie looked at him but did not speak. "I said, 'Mary likes Zoë and I like Kathryn. What name do you like?'"

"'Rosie', she said. 'What about Rosie?'"

"We didn't know if she had suddenly remembered." Tom's eyes filled with tears. "Your mother was very tired and it was such an emotional moment."

"'Rosie,' Sarah said, again. She was smiling and crying at the same time. There was a moment when we were not sure what was going to happen next and then she said, 'Let's call her Rosie Llywelyn.' Somehow it seemed the right thing to do."

"Sarah gave you back to your mother and Mary, who has always protected Sarah, looked at you and said, 'Rosie. Yes, let's call her Rosie.'"

They were at the front door. "Come on. I'm hungry."

"Welsh cakes?" Rosie said laughing."Bara brith? There are still some in the fridge from last week!"

"Afterwards, maybe." Tom said, bending over and kissing Rosie's forehead. "I want a very large, very serious, very rare hamburger and a very cold beer."

Rosie opened the fridge. There were hamburgers on a plate

ready to go on the grill. She turned and looked at her Dad. "You and Mom planned this!"

"Come on," Tom said, opening the back door. "Let's get the fire going. Your Mom will be home from the hospital in an hour or two. We have time for a burger."

The burgers were a bit burnt on the outside and a bit raw on the inside but the conversation was so intense they hardly noticed.

In years to come, Rosie would remember what her Dad said. It was a before-and-after moment, in the same way Sarah's stories had been. She would think of these moments as life-ending and life-beginning, a resetting of her clock, past, present, and future changing, because of the words that were spoken or read.

"What I find unfathomable," Rosie said, "is that Aunt Sarah has lived with us all my life without knowing that Mom was Mary Morgan."

"She didn't remember and we couldn't tell her," Tom said, with a wry smile. "She stopped talking when Rosie fell down the mine and our mother died a year later. Sarah was traumatized and had amnesia."

"And if you couldn't tell Aunt Sarah, you couldn't tell me," Rosie said. "Is that it?"

"That's it, exactly," Tom said, and then continued looking troubled. "But it was hard, especially on your mother. Mary worried all the time that Sarah would find out and that she –"

Tom didn't finish the sentence.

Rosie nodded.

"In the end it was just one of those freaky things," Rosie said, "an elevator at the hospital stopping for a minute or two between floors."

For a moment Tom and Rosie sat together not talking, both deep in thought.

"Tell me what happened in Wales," Rosie said, adding quickly when she saw the pain in her father's eyes, "to the miners and their families."

"There was no work," Tom said ready to talk about anything while eating his hamburger except the death of his sister.

Rosie told Tom about her visit to the library and meeting Daisy Blake. She told him in as matter-of-fact way as she could that Sarah had been to the library too, and that Daisy had made copies of some articles published in the London *Times* in 1936 about the King of England's visit to South Wales and of the Policy of Transference.

Tom was surprised that Sarah had been going to the library but he did not say so, and similarly Rosie was surprised at how much her Dad knew about what happened to the miners.

"We went back to Wales every summer when I was a kid," he said. "It was magical. The miners and their families' lives were filled with hardship and suffering, but they supported one another and families had a lot of fun when they got together. I remember the joy and the laughter and the sense of belonging. Everyone on the Garn took care of us."

"Sarah wrote that she only remembers the sun shining before –" Rosie stopped, and Tom nodded.

"It's true," Tom said. "I used to spend all year waiting to go to Wales." He smiled. "On rainy days we would go to Gwenny Morgan's. Gwenny's mother was always worn out so we would take care of the younger kids. But we went home to eat. They didn't have enough food for themselves and didn't need extra mouths to feed. They often ate lard sprinkled with salt on white bread."

"Mary was always sick and Gwenny would carry her around," Tom said, looking troubled. "She had a fever the day we –"

Tom stopped and Rosie quickly turned the conversation by asking her Dad what he knew about the Policy of Transference.

"It was a crime," Tom said, looking at Rosie. "They were bitter years and it was a long fight, but the miners did not lose their honor or their dignity. I used to go to the Whistle Inn with your Grandfather and sit with the old men. Sometimes he took Sarah and –" Tom hesitated, looking away he continued, "and Rosie."

"What did the old men talk about?" Rosie asked, not wanting the conversation to end.

"I remember their gentleness and how melancholy they were sitting on the wooden benches against the walls in the tap room. Their eyes twinkled when they looked at us but the conversation was sparse. Often the talk was of miners who had black lung or some other mine related ailment. Sickness. Death. Sons leaving. Australia. Canada. From what I remember they knew there was no hope of reopening the mines that were closing. "

Rosie sat quietly and waited.

"I think the miners understood that to the government they had become expendable," Tom said, putting into words what he had never said before. "With their picks and shovels they had fueled the industrial revolution. For a hundred years the miners had given their lives to the mines and their families had suffered and struggled to survive. They lived by a code of common decency and they expected the mine owners and the politicians to be as honorable as they were. But they were not, and the miners were vilified."

"It was incredible to read what the social worker had written in the report your friend sent," Rosie said. "I've forgotten his name."

"Peter Cornwell," Tom said. "The account of miners' lives in Blaina."

"I never thanked you," Rosie said and her Dad nodded.

"Thank Peter," Tom said. "I'll give you his email."

"I'll attach my report," Rosie said, smiling.

"He'll read it," Tom said. "Peter took some sociology courses when we were at university together before I left for the States. I remember he hunted through old newspapers for the depiction of coalminers for a paper he was writing on the mine closures. He found loads of cartoons depicting miners as sub-human. I remember there was one of a miner tied up like a dog on all fours being whipped. The man holding the whip was saying 'Back to your kennel you dog! You'll get only what I give you'. On the ground was a bone with 'New Terms' written on it, and on the label tied to the bone is 'From the Coal Owners'."

"The miners became an inconvenience," Rosie said, surprising Tom. "Their humanness was questioned so it would make it easier for the government to get rid of them."

"They became superfluous as human beings," Tom said nodding. "They were expendable and their families were considered a financial burden on the state."

"The English Government acted without conscience," Rosie said.

"Yes," Tom said, "but what they did was lawful because of the Policy of Transference."

"But they wrote the policy!" Rosie said. "They gave themselves the legitimate power to act!"

"Rich men write the laws," Tom said. "Poor men must obey them."

"And poor women," Rosie added.

"The rule of law protects the rich," Tom said, nodding. "Many of them believed it was their God-given right. They acted without conscience because of their belief that the suffering of the miners was caused by their low birth. They were inferior beings. They were supposed to be passive and obedient."

"And so they had to be subdued," Rosie said. "They were misled."

"It's no different today," Tom said, impressed by Rosie's grasp of the problem and her ability to articulate it.

"It's lumpen," Rosie said, smiling, knowing she was coining a new meaning of a despicable word. "It's hegemonic. Why have you never said any of this to me before?"

"You're fourteen!" Tom said sounding surprised. "I still think of you as a child, though I've learned that's not the case. Sometimes you are wiser than your parents."

"Most of the time," Rosie said, still looking serious. "Rachel's Great Aunt and Great Uncle think that the terrible times at the beginning of the twentieth century will come again and we have to resist oppression."

"In the coal mining valleys of South Wales the severe harm caused by the moral collapse of the government created a slow moving catastrophe that lasted for many years, and families are still suffering." Tom smiled at Rosie. "We're still suffering"

"Rachel's family too," Rosie said, missing for a moment that her Dad was trying to tell her something, then realizing, she looked at him and waited.

"I'm taking the summer off," he said. "Doctor's orders. Heart. I've known for some time and ignored it, but in these last few weeks you've taught me life is too precious to waste."

Rosie got up and put her arms around her Dad.

"I'll be okay Rosie," Tom said, hugging her. "It's going to be all right."

"Do I get a hug?" Mary said as she came out the back door. "Did we win?"

"We did!" Rosie said, as Mary put her arms around her too.

"Great game!" Tom said enjoying the moment.

"How's Sarah?" Rosie asked, looking intensely at her Mom as they all sat down.

"Ready to come home!" Mary said, smiling at Rosie, and then looking at Tom, "The doctor said Sarah could come home on Monday after you sign the papers."

Tom nodded.

"Max!" Rosie shouted running inside the house. "Max! Where are you? She's coming home! Aunt Sarah's coming home!"

On Sunday, a faded old photograph of Rosie Llywelyn appeared beside the pictures of Rosie on the table in her parents' room, and one of Sarah with Gwenny and Mary Morgan. Then Tom and Mary hung other pictures in the hall. There was one of three miners, two of Rosie's Great, Great Uncles with her Great, Great Grandfather when he was very young, and another of a woman in a long black dress. Rosie couldn't take her eyes off her.

"That's your Great, Great Aunt Lizzy," Tom said.

"She could talk to the dead," Rosie said, peering closely at the picture.

"Did Sarah tell you that?" Tom asked. He smiled. "The women in our family seem to be very good at that."

"Stop teasing me," Rosie said, rolling her eyes. She looked pensive. One thing still puzzled her. "Do you think we can share thoughts with people who are close to us?"

"What do you mean?"

Rosie told her Dad about the little girl in the coffin.

"There has to be a logical explanation," he said. "Someone must have told you about Grethel."

"You know who she was?"

"Sure," he said with a faraway look. "I remember Grethel. She had lots of brothers and sisters. We were on the Garn when she died. Rosie and I were in Grethel's Sunday school class. We all went to her house when she died."

"Did Sarah go?"

"I can't remember," Tom said. "She sometimes came with us. It was just our Sunday school class. Sarah couldn't have been more than four or five years old when Grethel died."

"Then how come I had a dream about Grethel?" Rosie asked, remembering the email conversation she'd had with Sarah.

"I really don't know," her Dad said, then he laughed. "Morphic-resonance, I suppose."

"What's that?"

"The sharing of ideas over great distance and through time."

"You're not serious?"

"Not really." He shrugged. "Maybe."

"In my dream there was a woman in black watching over the little girl in the coffin." Rosie said.

"That would have been your Great, Great Aunt Lizzy," her Dad said.

"I think people can share memories," Rosie said, as she looked at the ancient picture of her Aunt Lizzy.

"I think you might have overheard Sarah talking to herself, and when she started writing to you some of the things you'd heard suddenly made sense, not consciously, perhaps, but our minds are complex. I think it is possible for us to have memories without consciously knowing much about them. Sarah did."

"You're probably right," Rosie said. "Who knows?"

"Another photo!" Mary said coming downstairs from a study. "I have the same one for Rachel," she said. "You could give it to her when you go to the Cape."

She handed Rosie a tissue wrapped picture frame and when Rosie removed the tissue she laughed, "Iced Raisin and Ruby Shimmer!" she said, looking at the photograph of Rachel and herself wearing way too much eye shadow and mascara and gave Mary a hug.

"Some things I will never understand," Tom had said laughing.

On Monday, Rosie gave her research report on the Welsh coal-mining families to Margaret, but before she left for school she put a copy of the report in a folder and placed it on her Dad's desk. With the report she included copies of Sarah's stories and some of their email conversations. Then she went downstairs and gave a copy of the report to Mary, who was sitting at the kitchen table drinking a cup of coffee.

"My report on Wales," she said. "I've printed copies of Sarah's stories and some of her emails for you. I know she wants you to have them."

"Thank you," Mary said, smiling. She looked down at her blue kimono. "I'm home this morning so I'll sit here and read them. She opened the folder and found the note that Rosie had written to her.

"I love you Mom. No more secrets."

Mary's eyes filled with tears. "No more secrets," she said. Rosie put her arms around her Mom and gave her a hug.

"When you were a kid, you were hungry, that's all," Rosie said. "There wasn't enough food and with all those brothers and sisters you just didn't get enough to eat."

"I know," Mary said, "but it still hurts that the authorities took me away from my family."

Upstairs Tom picked up the folder Rosie had left on his desk along with some folders filled with notes for an upcoming deposition that he would give to Jesse's father, who was taking over the case so Tom could rest. He put them in his briefcase before running down the stairs and rushing into the kitchen to say goodbye to Mary and Rosie. He hurried out of the house with Mary's buttered toast in his hand telling them he was late for a meeting.

"Slow down!" Mary shouted after him.

"Last one," Tom shouted back. "Signing off, then going to the hospital to get Sarah."

When he reached his office Tom sat down with a cup coffee with the intention of reviewing his notes ready for the deposition, which was to be his last before he handed over the case to Jesse's father. Instead he found himself reading the letter Rosie had attached to the first page of the story "Rosie's Umbrella."

Dear Dad:

Just before I started my report on Wales Margaret was talking to us about Isaac Bashevis Singer. She wrote a quote on the board and I copied it into my notebook. I thought you'd like to read it.

Isaac Singer said, "The present is only a moment and the past is one long story. Those who don't tell stories and don't hear stories live only for the moment, and that isn't enough."

I think that's what Sarah was trying to tell us. Rosie Lly-welyn died a terrible death but we have to remember that she lived. I am so glad Sarah is coming home. I can't wait to see her.

Love Rosie

Tom told his secretary to hold his calls and to let everyone know he would be a few minutes late for the meeting, and while Rosie was walking to school, he sat in his office reading her report and Sarah's emails and stories.

In school Margaret thanked everyone in Rosie's class for handing in their reports on time and she said she was looking forward to reading them. She told them how much she had enjoyed their presentations.

"When you shared your stories about your families we imagined them," Margaret said, talking to them as if they were studying for doctorates. "You made it possible for us to meet your Grandparents and your Great Grandparents. We got to know them. We laughed with them and we cried with them. When we imagined their lives we empathized and it helped us imagine the future and the unexpected things that might happen before we are done."

"Jesse helped us put into words the ways in which we experienced empathy for Rosie and her family in Wales," Margaret continued. "I've shared with you similar stories about my family and my Great Grandmother who was born into slavery."

Margaret looked intently at Rosie.

"I know you were worried when you made those connections, but it was okay. You helped us imagine the struggles of people, in different places, at different times. You helped us empathize. In my own life I have found that without imagination there is no empathy, and without empathy there is no truth."

Margaret felt the emotion well up inside her as she looked around at the students in her class. She'd known some of them since they were in kindergarten and her eighth grade class at that time had taken books into their classroom to read to them. Some of her students came from affluent families, but most had parents who scrimped and saved to send them to the school, and a few were on full scholarships. What they had in common she thought were the human tragedies, even atrocities that had occurred in the countries their families came from, or *came to*. They also had in common their families' great desire for their children to have a different experience, to grow up compassionate and caring, as well as ready for scholarly pursuits.

"Each of you helped us realize that when we use our *imagination* to *empathize* we can also imagine life as it might be otherwise," Margaret said, standing tall in front of her class, stressing the words she wanted them to remember and never forget. "Through *your stories* each of you *encouraged* us to *be strong* and to *struggle on*. Even when the past is filled with tragedy and we do not know what the future will bring, when we *empathize* with others it not only *helps them*, it *helps us* imagine the *possibilities* of our own lives."

When Rosie arrived home from school and opened the door she saw Sarah's suitcase in the hall and she quickly ran upstairs to find her Dad standing in the doorway to Sarah's room and Sarah lying on her bed.

"We just arrived," Tom said, smiling at Rosie. "Everyone had to sign off so the paperwork took up most of the day."

He put his arm around Rosie's shoulders and together they watched as Mary helped Sarah sit up so she could have a cup of tea. Sarah was very sleepy from her medication, but she too smiled when Rosie came into the room. An hour later when she woke up Rosie was still sitting in a chair by her bed holding her hand.

"Hello Luvy," Sarah said.

"Hiya," Rosie said.

Sarah squeezed her hand and immediately started talking, in nothing more than a lilting whisper, about the way in which Rosie's

Dad had grabbed her and held on to her when she almost fell down the elevator shaft at the hospital.

"He grabbed me, Luvy," she said, as her eyes closed. "But you saved my life. If it wasn't for you he wouldn't have been there." Sarah reached out with her other hand so that both her hands held Rosie's. "You saved my life, my darling girl," she said again, as her voice faded and she drifted back into a deep sleep.

In the weeks that followed Sarah helped them remember Rosie Llywelyn and Mary told Sarah that she was Mary Morgan, Gwenny's little sister, and they laughed and cried together.

"Well I never!" Sarah said, followed by, "fancy that!" Over and over.

Mary wrote a letter to Gwenny and Tom telephoned his Dad in England and asked him if he would like to come and visit.

Rosie watched *Braveheart* at Jesse's house and she kissed him, her tongue in his mouth before he could pucker-up, and he pulled her towards him and surprised her by the way he kissed her back.

Rachel came over and they painted their toenails silver before going to the library to see Daisy, whose toenails were painted a very deep shade of purple.

Rosie asked Daisy to show Rachel her tattoos and Daisy shared with Rachel the meaning of her Runes.

"To the revolution!" Rachel whispered a shout, fist in the air.

"The revolution!" Rosie and Daisy whispered too, fists clenched, arms up. And Rachel had added, "to the gifts and talents of lumpen people everywhere!"

School ended and the whole class said goodbye to Margaret for the summer. Knowing that she would teach their philosophy class in ninth grade, they all said, they couldn't wait to be back in her class next year.

Rosie packed her suitcase ready to stay for a week with Rachel and her family at the Cape. Tom spent a lot of time exercising, walking first, then running, and lifting weights.

Life went on for all of them, except for Sarah. She still spent most of her time in her room and Rosie often sat with her.

"Where's Rosie's umbrella?" Sarah still asked, in vacant moments, even though she now had lucid memories of her childhood visits to her Grandparents in Wales.

Tom often spent hours in the evenings talking with her. Mary did the same, mostly in the mornings. She tried to encourage Sarah to come downstairs and eat her meals with them, but Sarah said she had no appetite and she stayed upstairs in her room looking forward to their visits.

"Rosie's been to the store and bought some more self-raising flour and we've got plenty of sultanas," Mary said, a few days before Rosie was going to stay with Rachel at the Cape. "Come and help us make some Welsh cakes and bara brith," she said, trying to coax Sarah down.

"Not now. I'd rather stay here," Sarah said with a weary smile. "I'm sorry to be a bother."

"You're not a bother," Mary said. Down stairs in the kitchen she talked with Rosie. "Sarah needs something new to think about," she said. "It's as if now she remembers, her life stopped when Rosie Llywelyn died. I think she's still a little girl inside."

The day before Rosie left for the Cape to stay with Rachel, Rosie went up to Sarah's room and gave her a present wrapped in pink paper tied up with yellow ribbon. Sarah pulled the ribbon and undid the bow. She carefully unwrapped the paper and inside she found a book, and she laughed at Rosie as she looked at the picture on the cover of the old fashioned cars and the baby ducks following their mother across the road.

"It was my favorite story when I was a little girl." Rosie told Sarah. Even though it was her Aunt who had read it to her, Rosie was not sure she would remember.

"It takes place right here on Beacon Hill. Let's sit on the bed and we can read together." They climbed on the bed and sat as they used to with their backs against a stack of pillows.

"I thought when we've read it we could go for a walk and see the statues of the ducklings in the Gardens," Rosie said.

She showed Sarah the picture of Mr. and Mrs. Mallard flying over the Public Gardens, and Sarah read, "There was a nice pond in the Public Garden, with a little island on it. 'The very place to spend the night,' quacked Mr. Mallard. So down they flapped." They stopped and looked at the picture of the swan boat.

"I remember," Sarah said, her eyes shining.

"The Paget family has run the swan boats since 1877," Rosie told her Aunt.

"Never!" said Sarah.

"There's the State House and Louisburg Square."

"There's lovely."

Sarah laughed at the picture of Michael, the policeman, and Rosie explained that she thought the ducks went *up* and not *down* Mount Vernon Street.

"Fancy that," Sarah said.

"Come on!" Rosie said, laughing, "we're going to have a homecoming festival!"

It was still sunny in the late afternoon when Rosie and Sarah walked down Pinckney together. They crossed Louisburg Square where the Safe and Neat Chimney Sweep was cleaning someone's chimney. They went down Mount Vernon, left on Charles and past DeLuca's grocery store, where a large black Newfoundland dog was tied to a lamp post, waiting patiently for his owner to come out of the store. They crossed Beacon and went through the stone pillars at the entrance of the Public Gardens.

"Smile," a grandmother said, as she took a photograph of a little girl on the second bronze duckling.

"Smile, Brian, Smile," a mother said, trying to get her son's attention. "Brian! Brian! Brian!"

"Tyler and Alan look at Mommy!"

"Say 'Ducks!' Haley."

"Tyler, you need to look at me and smile."

A father put a small boy on the mother duck.

"Hold on tight," his mother said. "Let me get another one. Look at Daddy and smile!"

"See," Rosie said, "They're Robert McCloskey's ducks, not geese."

"You must think me very silly, Luvy," Sarah said, in a rare moment of clarity. "I wish our Rosie could read that story."

"I wanna feed the ducks," a small boy said to his mother.

"Let's feed them when we ride on a swan boat," his mother told him.

An old woman was rummaging in a garbage can with a stick. She put in a gloved hand and brought out an empty soda can, which she put in a big green sack.

"Come on," Rosie said, holding her Aunt's hand and pulling her along the path around the edge of the pond. "We're going for a ride." They went under the bridge as a swan boat floated by. Rosie and Sarah got in line. There were strollers and bicycles left behind some ropes while families took a boat ride.

"Let's get our buggy Matt," a father said. "You've gotta wait for everybody pal." He put a slightly older boy in the back of a buggy for two. Then he called as he began to walk along. "Matt we're waiting for you."

Sarah whispered to Rosie, "I remember when you were two! You were so much fun. I loved taking care of you."

Rosie squeezed Sarah's hand and as she squeezed she felt in her heart a flutter as if it was dancing. Later she remembered it as the moment when she embraced her own past, the moment of truth when her family's history became her own.

"I am myself," she thought, "but Rosie Llywelyn will always

be part of me."

A little boy went under the rope and stood in front of Sarah.

"All right Drew," his father said, "we have to go to the back of the line," and then to Sarah he said, "I think he'd rather come with you."

Rosie looked at Sarah and they both laughed as Drew joined the line at the back with his Dad.

"Dad said when I was born you said, 'Let's call her Rosie,'" Rosie said, rushing on worrying that she should not have said it, "I'm glad you did."

"I knew you were going to be very special," Sarah said, with her eyes sparkling as she remembered Rosie's birth.

A young man in a green shirt shouted, "Right this way folks. I'll take your tickets." A woman much older than Sarah took Rosie's money, ninety-five cents for Rosie and a dollar-fifty for her Aunt.

"Where do we stand in line?" a woman asked. She had red lipstick and big gold hoop earrings and Rosie recognized her.

"How long's the queue?" the man with her asked.

"Line," the woman said, correcting him. "Over 'ere it's 'line.'"

The man laughed. He was wearing the same blue check shorts that he'd had on when he'd asked Rosie if she was all right, on the day she'd walked through the Public Gardens after the night at the hospital.

"Just a minute. Just a minute," the woman said, looking at the man and then at Rosie. "We've met you before luv. When we were throwing peanuts to the swans."

"I remember!" the man said. "Is this your Grandma?"

"My Aunt Sarah," Rosie said, smiling.

"You must be very proud of her," the woman said to Sarah.

Denny Taylor

"I am," Sarah said, speaking quietly. "She saved my life." But much to Rosie's relief the woman did not hear her.

"Maybe you don't want stand in –," the man said to the woman, pausing before he said, "line."

The woman laughed.

"D'you wanna sit down here and I'll holler to you?" the man asked, pointing at a bench and giving the woman a look of great affection.

"No, no," the woman said, eyebrows raised looking at Rosie and Sarah, "not that old yet!" Then before she followed the man to the back of the line she whispered, "We're on our honeymoon. We've both got grandchildren and we just got married!"

She looked at Rosie. "We'd just arrived when we met you. We fly back tomorrow! Been all over America! Funny meeting you like this. It will bring us all good luck I expect!"

The line moved up

Rosie and Sarah sat in the front seats of the next boat. They watched as the boat filled up and a man got in the swan at the back of the boat and began to pedal.

"Imagine that!" Sarah said, "They've been peddling around this little pond since 1877! Well I never!"

Another man in a green T-shirt hit a bell as the swan boat moved away from the dock and floated gracefully away on its short journey around the pond in the Public Gardens.

"Do you remember when Dad used to bring me when I was a little girl?" Rosie asked Sarah.

"I do remember," Sarah said. "He always looked so serious."

"Let's ask him to come with us when I get back from Cape Cod," Rosie said.

"And your mother," Sarah said. "Let's all go together."

Rosie had a bag of peanuts and she gave some to Sarah who threw them into the water for the ducks swimming along side the boat. Rosie took a handful and scattered them on the water.

"I had a dream about the swan boats," Rosie told her Aunt. "We were fishing in Big Pond on the Garn and one of the swan boats sailed by and the people threw peanuts at us."

Sarah put her hand in the bag and got some more nuts.

"I keep thinking it was my fault that Rosie died," Sarah said, tears running down her cheeks as she threw the peanuts into the water. "If I hadn't cried because I hurt my foot our Tommy wouldn't have been juggling with my sandals."

"You were a little girl," Rosie said. "It wasn't your fault. It wasn't anybody's fault. It was Rosie Llywelyn who decided to try and get your sandal. *She's* the one that died and *she* doesn't blame you."

"I know, I know," Sarah said, smiling at Rosie. "At least we've got her stories." Even though she was still wearing her thrift shop clothes Sarah looked at peace with herself.

"And we've got each other," Rosie said, throwing the last of the peanuts in the water.

"We do my Luvy," Sarah said, "And you'll always be my Rosie." Then, just in case it rained, Sarah put up Rosie's red umbrella.

Reflections on Rosie's Umbrella

Denny Taylor's *Rosie's Umbrella* is a girl's quest and an explora-
tion of the power of stories and memories. The novel is set in the
prosaic world of contemporary Boston, in a family of professionals
and academics. But Rosie's parents and aunt share a painful family
secret, which drives the aunt to a nervous breakdown and sends
Rosie on a search for her family's history.

Taylor cleverly and necessarily entangles the family's story with
the social history of Wales, where they are from. Rosie is assigned
a school project on family history, which leads her to research the
conditions of Welsh minors. As a descendant of miners myself,
both of whose grandfathers died because of the mines (one from
a cave-in while my father was still a boy, the other from silicosis
or 'black lung' later in life, struggling to draw every breath), the
account of the Welsh mines rings very true to me.

Digging into her genealogy (if you will pardon the pun) makes
Rosie aware of the power of the past —and also its malleability. It is
more than clear that her disturbed aunt, in the analysis of Freud, is
suffering from reminiscences, and in her school report the preco-
cious Rosie states, following Bakhtin, "There is neither a first nor

last word.... Even the past meanings, that is, those born in the dialogue of past centuries, can never be stable, finalized, ended once
and for all. They will always change, be renewed, in the process of
subsequent future development of dialogue" (p. 164).

But what happens when dialogue turns to silence, as it does
for Rosie's kin, keeping a painful secret yet letting it out in indirect
ways (like naming Rosie after a dead ancestor)? Silence and secrets
can harm or kill, and they are obviously plaguing the aunt, Sarah.
The only way to allow the past to live, to give it voice, is through
stories, and Sarah gradually gives voice to the stories by typing
them in emails to Rosie from the hospital. But it is not only guilt
ridden individuals who hide the truth: Rosie's research unveils how
"governments do everything they can to take them away and make
us forget" (p. 256). I am reminded here of a film about the disloca-
tion of hill folk in the 1930s from what would become Shenandoah
National Park, Richard Knox Robinson's *Rothstein's First Assignment: A Story about Documentary Truth*. Like the Welsh miners, the
mountain people were labeled as inferior, almost subhuman, and
in some cases mentally feeble and were exiled from their homes. I
also think of a PBS documentary some time ago about the English
navy's confrontation with the Spanish Armada and how, rather
than pay the sailors for their noble and historic service, England
left its ships anchored offshore until the sailors either surrendered
or sickened.

"It's about remembering our stories" (p. 256), Rosie discovers,
and honestly, whether one remembers them consciously or not, like
Freudian traumas—as the novel attests—the stories impact us. Near
the end, Taylor writes, "Looking back now Rosie understood how
the past could become the present, how stories could take place over

and over" (p. 288). The family secret that is finally aired is rather predictable, but again that is not meant as a criticism.

What Taylor would have us know is that there are no really new stories, that we live in a world of conventions and paradigms and that those words and acts live in and through us. But then part of the point, I assume, is that there is never only one way to tell the human story; humanity is inexhaustible, and both dreams and waking life, both altered and ordinary consciousness, are ingredient to human reality. As different as they are, the two novels are two perspectives on many of the same emotional, cognitive, and cultural processes.

Jack David Eller
University of Northern Colorado

There are stories so distinctive and so interwoven that the knitted fabric created by the author is sufficient to envelop the reader and both protect her as well as prevent her from escape. Those are great novels that deserve to be read and reread, for the stories they tell and the truths they reveal. There is yet another level of story that comes along very rarely where the reader begins to experience his own truth as the primary characters of the novel live their own. *Rosie's Umbrella* has done that for me. Rosie's story is powerful on its own terms, but what the book does for me is point me in the direction of my own truth.

Rosie Llywelyn is in 8th grade in a class taught by Margaret, an enlightened teacher who all refer to by her first name. Margaret has assigned a class project for each student to explore her family roots. Rosie discovers her own history in Wales, piecing together a story that surprises her and shocks her. Her story makes me wonder about my story.

Halfway through the book, the narrator describes an interaction in class about the interrelationship of life's stories. We are in that class. Margaret is speaking to us as much as she is speaking to Rosie's class when she says "Your stories had many chapters way before you were born." From *Rosie's Umbrella* (p. 160):

> At school Margaret had told her class that Martin Luther King said all life is interrelated and that whatever affects one directly affects all indirectly, and Rosie remembered because she had quoted Martin Luther King in her report on Nelson Mandela.
>
> "No one's story," Margaret had said, "can stand alone. Every story is part of another." She'd talked with them about a Russian scholar called Michel Bakhtin. She'd told them that Bakhtin had written that their lives were like novels, that their stories were their own, but that all of their stories were interconnected.
>
> "Living," Margaret had told them, "is like turning the pages of a book, but there is neither a first nor last word – no beginnings, and no endings."
>
> "Your stories," she'd said, "had many chapters way before you were born."
>
> Everyone in Rosie's class was used to the way Margaret

talked to them. They'd learned to take the ideas she shared with them and puzzle over them for future conversations – which they knew would take place at some unexpected moment – possibly in the middle of a science experiment or when they were painting a mural or in comedy hour when they wrote jokes and skits and were expected to perform them. They wanted to be ready. It was a mind game they played with Margaret, and with each other. They wanted to outsmart her, and score points – imaginary ones – against each other.

"This is my page," Rosie had said on one such occasion. "There might be others on this page, but it's not the same for them as it is for me."

"And why do you think that is so?" Margaret had asked, smiling at Rosie.

"Because each person on my page will see it differently to me," Rosie had said, without a moment's hesitation. She'd thought about it and spoke as if she was sure of what she'd said.

Will *Rosie's Umbrella* grab you as tightly as it grabbed me? Perhaps. The bigger question is – how will *Rosie's Umbrella* prompt you to start reviewing your own chapters?"

Richard C. Owen
Founder and CEO, Richard C. Owen Publishers

Epilogue

Writing Rosie's Umbrella

Geoff Ward writes, "*Rosie's Umbrella* is a moving meditation as well as a novel, one that crosses continents and time in order to explore the ways in which the ghost of things past, dramatic and disturbing, can go on affecting lives into the future. It is also a mystery – and a real page-turner. Finally and in these difficult times we are living through, with political storm-clouds getting ever closer, it is a tender and affirmative story that reminds the reader of what great consequences our small actions of remembering and affection can have, and how much we can accomplish if we just stick together – across countries, and across the generations. I read it in a single sweep, and recommend you do the same."

Reading Geoff's words two years after Rosie was published my eyes fill with tears not for the past but for the future. Whatever has happened to me and my family, which is so much part of this

336

meditative novel, does not remotely compare to what will happen to our children in the coming years if we do not act quickly to change the future now. But that is not to suggest rash acts. Instead it is a plea that we become more contemplative. Read *The Power of the Powerless*. Develop a sensitive ear to the language that is used to persuade and coopt. Read The Captive Mind. Learn from the past. Read *The Origins of Totalitarianism*. Think ahead. *Read Split Second Solution* – you will find the future we do not want in *Split*, which is eerily accurate in its prediction of what is coming to pass. Remember it is your children who will be most affected by what it happening now.

It took me 23 years to write *Rosie's Umbrella*, much longer if you include the short stories that I wove into the novel. When I began writing Rosie was always on the page, but the other characters were like cardboard cutouts, one dimensional and uninteresting. I didn't like Mary Llywelyn, Rosie's mother, very much. She was so withdrawn it took me years to find a way to reach her, and Tom Llywelyn, Rosie's father, had no time for anyone. He was distant. Strange. It was as if he did not want to be on the page. His affect was totally flat.

So every summer for 23 years I would rewrite the novel, focusing on one of the characters standing beside Sarah, Mary, Tom, Rachel, Jesse, Margaret, or Daisy, doing everything I could "to live" their part in the story. I actually didn't know the characters very well so I would rehearse their parts, visualizing the scene as if I was making a movie. In the beginning they were all strangers, except for Rosie, whom I think I have always known. She has been an imaginary member of my family for so many years it is as if we share our DNA. Nevertheless, it would be foolish for any author to presume to know their characters before they write the story. Just putting words on the page changes them. It might seem odd but I am quite sure that characters teach and the author learns from them.

Here's an example. One of the most complex scenes takes place near the beginning of the book, when Sarah falls apart in the hallway at the bottom of the stairs in the Llywelyn home on Beacon Hill in Boston. Lost in grief, over and over again, Sarah keeps asking, "Where's our Rosie's umbrella?" But when Rosie gets her red umbrella out of the hall closet and tries to give it to her, Sarah starts shouting, "that's not our Rosie's umbrella", and she pushes Rosie against the wall, knocking the wind out of her.

"That's not our Rosie's umbrella," Sarah screams and Mary Llywelyn comes running from the kitchen. But instead of comforting Rosie or calming Sarah, Mary just stands there staring at Sarah as if she has had a terrible shock. And Rosie is shaken by her mother's response and yells, "*Tell me what to do!*" as Sarah keeps screaming. "*Why won't you help her?*" Rosie yells. "*What's wrong with you?*" And Mary shouts at Rosie, "*For God's sake Rosie, stop asking questions!*" There is more to the scene, but this is the gist that kept me thinking for many years.

I was still thinking about that scene when the manuscript was copy edited, and just before the galleys were produced I learned something about Mary that I had not known before. It was a shock to realize I had missed such an important aspect of Mary and Sarah's lives, even though it was on the page in front of me. I kept asking myself how I could have missed it. It's the moment when she stands "across the hall from Sarah, staring at her, through her, making noises that sounded like deep sighs or soft moans", and Sarah looks up at Mary and they stare at each other, "as if … as if what?"

The ellipses are in the book -- "as if ... as if what?" It is the 23-year question, the key to the story, although I didn't know it when I started writing.

I know from supporting many writers that sometimes it takes years to know what questions to ask, and sometimes the answer comes just as you are publishing the book. But these are precious moments for a writer. They make it possible for the author to build characters rather than leaving them flat upon the page. The "as if ... as if what?" was not only of great significance in my getting to know Mary and Sarah, but also Tom, revealing their entanglements, making it possible to untie the complicated knots that bound them – and in that untying, possibilities opened up for me to get to know them in more kind and compassionate ways. The characters changed each other, and perhaps me, as we do in real life when we interact with one another. And it was in this way that each reworking of a character resulted in the reworking of all the other characters. It was always a dynamic process, but often unsettling, because of the impact the family tragedy had on each of them.

Some readers are unsettled by the dissonance at the beginning of the novel. The novel begins with the description of a young girl falling down a mineshaft. How could it not unsettle? Rosie's whole existence is knocked off kilter by the death of this child so long ago, and at the beginning of the book it is difficult to know if Rosie is in the past or present. There seems to be no rhyme or reason to the internal conversation that she is having with herself.

It was a risky move as a writer, but I take responsibility. It was a deliberate attempt to reflect Rosie's state of mind. I wanted the reader to experience Rosie's confusion rather than just read about it, to be *in* the book rather than just *on* the page. It does not surprise me that the beginning of the book creates a sense of disequilibrium for some readers, which is the way that Rosie feels on her way home from school as she begins her journey back through the events that have happened, some so long ago, in a valiant attempt to make sense of who she is and where her family has come from.

I am often asked about Sarah. She is such a complex character. She was born in England and only spent her summers in Wales when she was a very young child. While she was staying with her grandparents she was witness to a terrible tragedy, and she was so traumatized she lost her ability to speak and was unable to communicate with anyone for more than a year.

Sarah suppressed the memory of the tragedy, suddenly remembering forty years later when she was stuck in an elevator in the hospital where she was an emergency room nurse. The jolt of the elevator freed her memories of the terrifying accident that had occurred when she was just five years old. This sudden remembering unhinges Sarah. Her ways of being in the world crumbled, leaving her vulnerable and afraid. Losing the present she returns to the past, but she is not the little girl she remembers and she is not the woman she has become. She talks as if she is a small child living with her grandmother in Wales, but she thinks with the wisdom that comes from a lifetime of experience of being a nurse.

The complexity of Sarah's character as she struggles to come to terms with the events that happened so long ago was challenging to write. Sarah shares with Rosie her memories of Wales, but she is also remembering her family, as they were when she was a little girl in the 1950's. And so Sarah's stories are as much my mother and grandmother's stories as they are hers, and her ways of talking reflect conversations in my own life as a child, which took place more than sixty years ago, with turns of phrase that are seldom heard in Wales today.

Except for the tragic death of Tom and Sarah's sister, these stories, which are fictionalized in *Rosie's Umbrella*, are all authentic. Both my grandfathers were Welsh coalminers and my father went down the mines when he was fourteen. And just like Tom and Sarah, I spent every summer when I was a young child in Wales living with my grandparents in the village where my mother grew up. The only difference between us is that I continued to spend every summer in Wales until I was sixteen and the mines were closing, and the 19th century life of the village where my grandparents lived was fading away.

In the novel Sarah writes three stories for Rosie as she tries to tell her about the tragedy that happened when she was a little child. I always took my Nan's umbrella when I went "out the back" just in case the geese chased me, and it was the motif of the umbrella in Sarah's first short story that became so important when I wrote the novel *Rosie's Umbrella*. The story "Granddad's Bath" recounts my own experience as a very small child of watching my granddad bathe in the old tin bath in front of the fire when he came home after the nightshift at the mine. The third story of playing on the hills behind the miners' row houses is also based on my own childhood experiences. I dropped stones down the 19th century mineshaft just as my mother did when she was a child. My mother used to say, "it's a tragedy waiting to happen", when she warned me to stay away from the shaft, but she never stopped me from going up into the hills and playing there. Fortunately no one every fell down the mineshaft, except in *Rosie's Umbrella*.

My summers in Wales when I was a child were close to idyllic, and I wrote the three short stories in my thirties when I was coming to terms myself with the way my family had been forced to leave Wales. My mother and father and most of my aunts and uncles were a part of the mass migration that occurred because the English Parliament enacted a Policy of Transference, which Rosie learns about when Daisy Blake gives her the copies of the 1936 articles in *The Times* (of London) that document the dire circumstances in which miners and their families lived their lives.

Rosie's Umbrella is not an industrial history, but behind the descriptions in the book are my own lived experiences of that time. From 1947 to 1969 when I left London for the U.S., I was immersed in the lives of mining families and their struggle. My mother and father founded a Welsh Society in Kent for Welsh families who had been part of the post-industrial diaspora from the South Wales coalmining valleys. They lived every day with the injustice of what had happened to the miners and their families, and while my childhood was idyllic in many ways, with my parents I experienced their constant sense of loss, their yearning for the valleys, and their desire to go home to Wales.

This sense of loss and yearning is picked up in the to and fro in the email exchange between Rosie and Sarah, which is based on an ongoing conversation between my mother and I as she became older and increasingly frail. As her memory faded in the last years of her life and until the day she died, I told my mother stories from her childhood the way she had once told them to me. Many of these stories are memorialized in the email exchange between Rosie and her Aunt Sarah. The stories are authentic and reflect the descriptions of life in the coalmining villages of South Wales that were documented in the Mass Observation Social History Archives, which I visited at the University of Sussex and which are now online.

My mother's last words to me when she was 91 were "I wish I'd never left Wales", and I always felt her loss. Her memories are like Sarah's, and in many ways they are Sarah's. When we were together we imagined being "down home", reliving the stories that Sarah writes in the novel. The stories remained unchanged because they were severed from the present when my mother's village was bulldozed after the mines closed, leaving only the outline of the tiny row houses etched in the ground.

There is a place in the novel where I write that Rosie "couldn't put into words how desperately she wanted to know what had happened to Sarah ... she'd suddenly realized that Sarah was not the only one who had lost her memory of what happened when she was a little girl, but hundreds of thousands of people had lost their memories of what had happened to them and their history had been expunged."

In finding her own truth, Rosie came to understand that her experiences were similar to those of Rachel, Jesse, and Margaret, all of whom came from families who had experienced, under different circumstances, similar mass migrations. It is this commonality of experience that is at the heart of the novel. Nancy Rankie Shelton, who is an educator and a scholar, expresses this for us when she writes:

> Central to the novel is the friendship between Rosie
> Llywelyn whose family were coalminers in South Wales,
> Rachel Gordon whose family emigrated from Russia to
> the U.S. and Argentina at the time of the Russian Revolu-
> tion, and Jesse O'Malley whose family arrived in the U.S.
> after the Irish Potato Famine. Their teacher, Margaret

Dorsey, is African American. Margaret creates opportunities for her students to make connections between her own family history of slavery and their family histories. We all have family history and our histories, whether known or unknown, are what shape our thinking and us.

It is this reaching out, of remembering the old as we participate in the new, which shapes our lives imaginatively and creatively. It is the perpetual re-visioning of human experience – the finding of our own truth -- that is so important as each new generation reaffirms the commitment to equality and justice, and continues the struggle to attain what often seems like an impossible dream.

Impossible as it might seem the world has changed since I wrote *Rosie's Umbrella*. Metaphorically we are all falling down the mineshaft of fascism, totalitarianism, while the planet heats up and jeopardizes the lives of all our children – which brings me back to the beginning of this Epilogue and Geoff Ward's review of *Rosie's Umbrella*.

"In these difficult times we are living through, with political storm-clouds getting ever closer," Geoff writes, "it is a tender and affirmative story that reminds the reader of what great consequences our small actions of remembering and affection can have, and how much we can accomplish if we just stick together – across countries, and across the generations."

In solidarity,

Denny Taylor

December 2, 2017

Books by Denny Taylor

Teaching Without Testing: Assessing the Complexity of Children's Literacy Learning; with Bobbie Kabuto, Senior Editor, Garn Press Women Scholars Series (2017)

Toodle-oo Rubie Blue! I had fun playing with you! (2017)

Split Second Solution (2016)

Rat-a-tat-tat! I've Lost My Cat! (2015)

Save Our Children, Save Our School, Pearson Broke The Golden Rule (2014)

Nineteen Clues: Great Transformations Can Be Achieved Through Collective Action (2014)

Beginning to Read and the Spin Doctors of Science (1998)

Many Families, Many Literacies: An International Declaration of Principles (1997)

Teaching and Advocacy (1997)

Toxic Literacies: Exposing the Injustice of Bureaucratic Texts (1996)

From The Child's Point Of View (1993)

Learning Denied: Inappropriate Educational DecisionMaking (1990)

Growing Up Literate, Learning From Inner City Families (1988)

Family Storybook Reading (1986)

Family Literacy: Young Children Learning to Read and Write (Second Edition, 1998)

Family Literacy: Young Children Learning to Read and Write (First Edition, 1983)

44701472R00202